THE PRINCESS OF SECRETS AND SHADOWS

OLIVIA M. GEIB

First edition 2024

Unofficial Map by Griffin Geib

Official Map By Zs Graphics

Edited by Sierra Campbell – Editing By Sierra

Cover Design by Matthew Picinich – Sentinel Graphics

ISBN Hardcover (978-1-7380472-9-1)

ISBN Softcover (978-1-7380472-3-9)

ISBN Ebook (978-1-7380472-4-6)

Olivia M. Geib
AUTHOR

www.oliviamgeib.com

Please note this book is written in **<u>Canadian</u>** English.

Spellings may differ from both British and American English.

If you would like a high-quality PDF download of the map of Elphyne, along with a bonus map, please go to www.oliviamgeib.com/maps.

To the girls who dream and scheme and wonder

This one's for you

ELPHYNE
THE
The Spring
Court
The Azalea
Palace
The Fae
of The Sea
The Bay of
Renewal
The Land of
The Wandering Fae
The Scarlet
Palace
The Spring
Sea
The Autumn
Court
THE UNSEELIE C

SEELIE COURT
The Ember Palace
The Summer Court
The Sunfire Isles
The Pool of Memory
The Land of the Wandering Fae
Cyrissa Lake
The Elphyne Sea
The Crystal Palace
The Winter Court
URT
N
W
E
S

Everyone is screaming. A beautiful sound. What a terrific way to postpone a wedding.

Prince Archer—my enemy and the Faerie who is supposed to be marrying my traitorous younger sister—slumps to the ground, a pile of golden fabric in a growing puddle of ruby-red blood. A crossbow arrow stands at attention in his chest as my sister drops to her knees, pressing her palms to the wound, her strawberry blonde hair falling over her shoulders. Her golden wedding gown stains as her face pales.

Fabelle stares down at her *almost*-husband, terror spreading across her face.

Her hazel-green eyes lift and find mine, and our gazes lock. I smile, just long enough for only her to see.

And like magick, my head is finally above water. My ears roar. The room comes into focus with alarming clarity as the crowd descends into pure chaos.

Knights shout orders, rushing to the front of the room and leaping onto the dais. A stampede of frightened Fae in luxurious clothing shove and climb over each other as they rush for the exits. Gowns rip, chairs topple, and sobs of horror fill the room.

But all I can think about is how much the madness sounds like sweet, sweet *vengeance.*

Maylea, my accomplice, is not only the future Queen of The Spring Court but Elphyne's best sharpshooter. And, in this moment, I am thankful for her accuracy as we required both a way to stop the wedding *and* something that doubled as a magnificent distraction. As I peer around at the stampede we've created, I'd say we succeeded.

Prince Viktoryn—my ex-lover—draws his sword, stepping in front of Archer and Fabelle in an act that is uncharacteristically heroic. I cannot help the near-silent scoff that slips my lips. He is no hero.

Raven—The Winter Prince and Viktoryn's sworn enemy—leaps to his feet at the same moment I do, throwing his body in front of mine as his head scans the room for threats. I pull my dagger from its sheath.

The space continues to clear as phase two of my plan begins. The back corner of the room ignites into flames, courtesy of someone who owed May a favor. The golden banners alight, casting the room in a vibrant, heated glow.

All eyes in the room whip towards the roaring flames, and May uses the distraction to descend from above. She sprints for us, pretending she was sitting across the room instead of being high in the rafters with a bow, playing assassin.

I watch Raven a little too closely to ensure he does not have suspicions, but his storm-cloud eyes are glued to Archer as he is dragged out of a back exit by a group of frantic Knights.

May reaches us, grabbing Raven's hand and mine, tugging us along. She aims for a side exit—the one we agreed on—and shoots me a wink. I nod almost imperceptibly.

Raven tosses bodies aside as we rush out of the throne room and into one of the gold, sandstone, and marble halls of The Ember Palace.

This is my chance.

My stomach twists, but I know what I need to do. I squeeze May's hand twice, and she trips over a fallen body, releasing her grip on me. Raven goes tumbling with her, still chained in her grip, as they nosedive into a sea of bodies, swallowed instantly by the waves of the crowd.

I do not look back as I turn, darting into a servant's hallway. Screams continue to flood the Palace as guests escape, not knowing the threat has well and truly passed.

I sheath my dagger and pull out the map May slipped me earlier, studying it as I dash down the labyrinth of halls to a lesser-used part of the Palace. I slow down, checking my surroundings. Here, everything is so calm it is hard to believe an assassination attempt occurred on a member of the royal family in this very building.

I dart around a corner, almost losing my footing. My breathing comes in hard as I push my body to put as much distance between the chaos I caused and myself as possible. Adrenaline floods me like a drug, freedom igniting my veins, and the combination is a heady rush. I am terrified by how much I like it.

I climb a tight marble staircase, slowing as I spot a tapestry of The Goddess of the Sun, Cyrissa—my maternal grandmother—sitting atop a throne of cobalt blue flames on the far wall.

Fitting.

Cyrissa's daughter—my true mother, the slain Queen Valda—is the one who started all of this. When my mother got word that the Goldyn-lockes were planning a coup to overthrow her and steal The Summer Court Throne, she went to Cyrissa and begged her for a way to save her children and court.

Cyrissa, desperate to grant her daughter's deepest wish, drained power from the lands of The Summer Court and transferred them into my body, destabilizing The Courts and the natural order of magicks. All of this in a final attempt to one day give *me*—the lost heir—the ability to overthrow the Goldynlockes.

My father then took my sister and me to the mortal lands, disappearing soon after.

I shake off my thoughts and try to focus. I untie my hidden pocket and rip out the gold medallion. Not only is it a key activated by my blood, but it muddles my scent, making it difficult for Fae to track me. It pulses in my hand in anticipation, whispering sweet words as I drag my dagger across my palm.

I lift the tapestry of my grandmother with my free hand as blood wells in the other. Just like May said, an emblem identical to the one on my medallion is etched into the stone.

"Willa!"

I flinch. My name is an anguished, echoing plea on Raven's lips. I can hear May trying—and failing—to soothe him. An unwelcome wave of guilt cuts straight to my core.

"*Willa!*"

I shut my eyes for a moment. Then I press the medallion into the carving, my blood dripping down the wall. As metal meets stone, a golden light flares, and stones begin to shift.

An opening to a passageway appears, and I hastily wipe my blood off the wall with the hem of my dress. I eye the space wearily, knowing that once I am inside, I will only have room to sit or crawl. Placing my hands on the cool stone, I heft myself up.

"Willa! Shout if you can hear me!" Raven's calls are nearer now, footsteps approaching from the bottom of the stairs.

I do not hesitate, dropping the tapestry and blotting out the light. I pull a lever that sticks out of the stone near the opening, and it closes with a rumble, sealing me inside... and Raven *out*.

I pant, pressing a hand to my chest to ease the ache in my lungs. The smell of damp stone rushes into my nose with each inhale. I try to keep quiet as I shuffle further into the passage, battling my terror of small spaces with each scooch further into the endless dark.

My heart slams into my ribcage, tearing in two as Raven lets out a frustrated shout from the other side of the wall.

"Willa!" May calls, and I bite my lip to keep from chuckling.

"I could smell her, but the trail disappears here," Raven mutters, agonized.

I wait, holding my breath to see if my new ally will play her part or throw me to the wolves.

"Willa can handle herself, Raven. We must make haste. Soon, the Goldynlockes will begin to point fingers, and you know they will land on The Winter Court first," May reasons. "We must go. If *we* cannot find her, they will not be able to either."

My eyes fall shut as I lean my head against the cool stone. For someone who cannot lie, she is effortlessly convincing.

"Oh, believe me, I am *painfully* aware of her ability to handle herself. But we cannot leave without her!"

A fist slams into the other side of the wall, and I flinch as dust rains down on me. I fight the urge to sneeze as it tickles my nose, making my eyes water.

"Everyone she has ever relied on has abandoned her, Maylea. I *refuse* to be one of them." My eyes snap open at his words, a rush of heat rising in my cheeks. The comment stings.

"We need to go, Raven. *Now!* You will not be of any assistance to her in the *dungeons*," May snaps, her tone cold. So unlike her usual sun-beam self. "The Goldynlockes have been waiting years for an excuse to throw your rule into question. Do not allow them the chance."

"I did not do this! Though, I cannot deny I find myself wishing I had. I failed her. I failed her long before she knew it. And I was selfish enough to pretend it would never matter," Raven croaks. "I should have killed Archer and Viktoryn the moment I realized they had followed me to the Caprimore sisters' home all those years ago."

I should have killed Archer and Viktoryn the moment I realized they had followed me to the Caprimore sisters' home all those years ago.

Raven led the Goldynlockes to my sister and me. Raven, whom I trusted. Raven, whom I had let see me vulnerable.

He *knew.* He did this.

He knew where we were and did not warn us or help us or protect us. He knew the truth about my family. He knew his actions had put us directly in the path of the Goldynlockes, and he left us defenseless.

Raven knew *everything.*

Maybe I have learned nothing.

I almost want to laugh as I find myself deceived again. Betrayed once more. You would think that, after all this time, it would start to hurt less. But a dagger is digging its way into my heart, and my lungs are burning as hard as my eyes.

The cracks in my soul spread, and a wicked sense of heartbreak forms. I grit my teeth so hard I fear they will shatter.

This is good, I try to convince myself. *This only makes leaving everyone behind easier. I should be thanking him.* But I am not sure the knot in my throat agrees.

Footsteps sound from somewhere in the halls, followed by armour clanking and echoing shouts.

"We are going. Now! Before we cannot go at all," May commands.

Raven, without another option, concedes. I listen as their footsteps quiet and then vanish, trying to convince all the shattered pieces of my heart to go with them.

Guards rush after them, a cacophony of noise, but my muscles relax as the halls begin to quiet. I let out a sigh. May played her part perfectly, leading Raven off my trail.

The start of our plan was successful.

Abundantly so.

And yet...

I thought I would feel something *more.*

Something *victorious.*

But all I feel is heavy—*tired.*

Finally, I have landed a point against the Goldynlockes. Finally, I have freed myself from both Faerie Princes, no longer the toy they bat around like alley cats.

I have infiltrated the walls of The Summer Court.

I will avenge my family.

I did the right thing.

The smart thing.

The *hard* thing.

And yet...

I ignore the incessant, useless thoughts that buzz around my head like flies. *Never again,* I vow. *Never again will I be the fool.*

I reach into my dress pocket, removing a small faelight no bigger than my palm. I shake it hard, smacking it into my palm thrice to activate it. An eerie blue glow emits from the orb as it pulses to life. It is surprisingly bright, and I squint my eyes as they adjust.

I study the rough, gray stone walls around me. Shifting onto my hands and knees, I crawl further into the cramped passageway, using my faelight as a guide. I pause, holding it up to my small, crinkled parchment map, double-checking my route when the passageway splits into two.

After a few minutes, the passage widens, and the crawl space comes to an abrupt drop five feet in the air. I leap down, stretching my sore limbs as tension bleeds from my chest. My panic lessens its hold on me, retracting its claws while I stand in the more open space.

When we decided on this plan, I knew my claustrophobia would be a hindrance. So, I started training daily at lunch, finding small dark spaces to shove my body into and holding out for increasingly longer periods. It helped, but it did not completely alleviate the fear.

Raven caught me sitting in his wardrobe one day, taking deep breaths and asked what in the Goddesses' name I was doing.

I told him I was working on overcoming my fear of confined spaces. Not *precisely* a lie. He had given me a small mocking smile, and then his ice-blue eyes lit with mischief. He slammed the door shut, chuckling when I pounded against it, screaming.

He opened it seconds later, and we both burst into laughter as I spilled out onto his floor, tangled in his clothes. They smelled of him—pine and cranberry and everlasting wint–

I wrench myself out of thoughts of him and follow the route until I reach the end of the passage. I quickly locate the lever to open the door, but I do not pull it.

May and I decided it would be best if I waited a few hours for the Palace to come down off high alert before I made the journey to our meeting spot.

Sinking down cross-legged in the cold, dimly lit passageway, I wonder how my life came to this moment. I set the faelight down beside me, and it rolls over the stones with a soft rumble, settling in a crack.

My head falls into my hands, fingers sliding into my hair with a punishing grip. I blow out a breath and let myself hope that I can pull this off.

And then, I wait.

Six passageways, two close calls with the guards, one semi-traumatized maid, and six hours later, I stumble through a doorway that, to the outside world, looks like a worn-down bookshelf. It leads me into a small bedchamber in a part of the Palace that has long-since been abandoned after experiencing a fire.

The room is made of crumbling sandstone walls, and smells of lingering smoke, dust, and forgotten memories. A single mattress sits unceremoniously on the floor, pushed against the far wall, feathers spilling from rips in the fabric. The main door has been spelled from the outside to look like a continuation of the brick wall. A little genius on May's part.

I turn in a small circle, taking in what will be my home for as long as it takes to bring down the Goldynlockes. I am surprised to find myself content. Numb, but content. I have never really had a room that was *mine*.

In Cressa, the house was my mother's, and she always reminded me of that. In The Ember Palace, I had a room that doubled as a gilded cell.

And for my stay at The Crystal Palace, I shared Raven's room. So, even if it is not the height of luxury... it might as well be. Because for now, it is safe. It is *mine*.

I snatch some dried meat from the small stock of provisions on the bookshelf and plop down onto my mattress with a sigh. A plume of dust greets me as I lay back on the lumpy pillow, chewing and closing my eyes.

When planning to overthrow a Kingdom, I did not factor in how much time I would spend *waiting*. I wish I had thought to stock some novels.

In the silence, I fail to keep my mind from wandering. I try not to think of Raven or his panicked voice and his easy deception. How his lips felt on my neck, his hands on my body. How sweet and terrifying it felt to *almost* trust him.

I try not to think of how Viktoryn will tear The Ember Palace and the rest of Elphyne to shreds trying to find me. Or how horrified my sister looked with her hands coated in Prince Archer's blood.

How it was me who put that look on her face.

I try not to think at all. And eventually, with nothing else to occupy my thoughts, sleep finds me.

I wake with a start in a pitch-black, unfamiliar room to the sound of a door creaking open. My mouth is dry, and my heart is a battering ram in my chest. My dagger is in my hand as I leap up to meet the intruder.

"You should see your face right now," May says, giggling brightly.

"You scared me!" I hiss, pressing a hand to my chest.

"Sorry, sleeping beauty," May teases, shutting the door tight behind her with a click.

"Please do not remind me of Faerietales right now," I groan, pulling my stained pillow over my face and regretting it when my nose fills with dust. I cough.

May chuckles. "Oh, you will live."

I toss a pillow in her direction and it lands on the ground with a huff. May falls silent. Even though I can see very little, I can sense her moving further into the room. I do not know if she is aware of this fact as her Faeries eyes cut through the night like a scythe of light.

I swallow my embarrassment, my pride, my inferiority, and ask, "Should we light a candle, or is it too risky? I avoided light as I did not want to draw attention to this room." I point to the small window.

"Oh. Yes. Right. I forgot you cannot simply... *see*." She pauses. "Waiting was wise. I can block the window with some leaves and vines?" May suggests. "Allow you to light a candle without fear."

I chuckle a little at the confusion in her voice. "I can *see*! I just cannot see in our current conditions. Now, can I have my pillow back?"

"Of course not, you fiend! Who would trust you with such a deadly weapon?!"

I roll my eyes, plopping back on the bed, pillowless.

She moves to the window, the light of the moon shining through the small pane of glass, allowing me to make out her features. I watch, transfixed, as she raises her hands and vines begin to snake up the wall. They twist themselves into braided knots, using the uneven bricks like handholds as they smother the light of the moon, casting the room in total darkness.

I shake my head in a combination of disbelief and awe. *I wonder, if I end up surviving The Calling, what types of magicks I will be able to wield.* The idea of wielding magicks at all still feels like a fantasy. Most of Elphyne still feels like a fantasy.

I still, after all these weeks, find myself feeling as though I have woken up in a world of pretend. That I am a child with invisible friends in a grand world of make-believe. I have tripped into a portal and landed on the pages of a Faerietale, now trapped inside this closed-cover prison of daydreams and nightmares.

No matter how long I am here, Elphyne exists in a haze of surrealism. Colours too bright, air too sharp. Leaving me to believe that any moment I will wake in my bed in Mayfair, rise, and say, "*What a peculiar dream,*" or more likely, "*What a dreadful nightmare.*"

I light a crooked wax candle—gashed in a way that looks like someone attempted to behead it from our stock of supplies—and May joins me on the mattress. We sit shoulder-to-shoulder, leaning against the wall. She tilts her head to rest against mine and lets out a content sigh.

"We did it."

"I never doubted us." May beams, smiling brightly. She turns her head to look at me.

I peer at her and am struck again by her beauty. She is radiant. Prime and polished. Her bright blue eyes sparkle in the candlelight. Her blonde hair a perfect curtain down her back. It is almost painful to gaze at her, to look upon a being so perfectly sculpted.

I find myself wondering if I will ever grow accustomed to the violent beauty that encapsulates the Fae. Worse yet, I find myself wondering if I will ever adapt to all of the other ways in which I am lesser than them.

I force myself out of the storm clouds brewing in my mind and into the present. The plan. The things I can control instead of all my inherent mortal shortcomings.

"Who knows you can shoot like that? How soon shall it be before The Folk start speculating who has the talent to make such a shot?" I question.

"Only Raven's Inner Circle knows I can shoot at all," she replies with a conspiratorial grin.

"Truly?" I gawk at her. "Your talent is unparalleled, that angle..." I shake my head. "I am good, but you are great. How do the King and Queen of Spring not know? How do you hide such mastery?"

May's smile falters, and she looks away. "It is but a long story. One best left unwritten."

"Maylea... you can trust me," I assure her. "We practically declared war today. We are bound together. For better or for worse." My mind crawls into the past, to my sister, words once said before our trust was broken. "If you asked my sister, she would tell you that no story should go unwritten. No story is unworthy of a tale. I may not agree with most of what she has said or done, but in this, we are agreed."

"I–" May shifts beside me, staring off into the distance, lost in a memory from another time. "They do not know because if they did, I would be punished, and punished greatly. They do not wish me to be trained. They do not wish for me to do a great deal of things. I have learned now to wish for nothing and take everything."

"Why?" I ask. "You will be Queen. You should not have to wish for anything. Can you not just order what you want? Will you not require such training to rule?"

May searches my face—she has never looked so lost. "There is quite a bit you do not know about me. About my family." She bites down on her bottom lip so fiercely I fear she will break skin.

"There is a lot I do not know about everything," I say, but it comes out too harshly. I shut my eyes, drawing a breath. "We just committed *treason* together. I will not be spilling your secrets if you will not be spilling mine. I just... I want to know. I *need* to know. I am so tired of being kept in the dark, May." I open my eyes and hold hers.

"There is so much I do not know and do not understand. But I wish to. Why did you help me? Why risk Raven's wrath? Why betray Amira? I do not understand, and I do not want to be the reason you lose them. Lose *her*. If we are to be in this together, truly, *wholly*, I need to know the why's, I need to know what we are up against. Your story is worth telling, May."

She watches me, uncertain, as her eyes flick across my face. But they soon soften—whatever she sees in mine must be enough because she nods slowly.

"If we do not succeed in our efforts, Willa, I will lose Amira anyway."

I have never seen her cry. My chest tightens. May has always been bright, shining, *flamboyant.* Ever the optimist. Watching a tear track down her face feels like watching the blazing sun disappear behind storm clouds.

"May... I still do not understand."

"Viktoryn, Raven, and I..." May lets out a long breath, her fists falling open in her lap. In one of her palms, a yellow snapdragon blooms—the action seems to steady her. She does it again before she continues, "We have been keeping something from you. At first, I did not tell you because it seems everyone is keeping something from you and I did not want you to distrust me. And it did not yet seem relevant. But now..."

Raven's words hit me like a slap.

I should have killed Archer and Viktoryn the moment I realized they had followed me to the Caprimore sisters' home all those years ago.

I swallow down the emotions that attempt to crawl up my throat.

"It seems to be everyone's favorite pastime," I jest but cannot seem to keep the hint of bitterness that cracks my tone from escaping. May places a snapdragon behind my ear, an offering, an *apology*. "Nevertheless, what is done is done. Just tell me."

She sighs. "My mother and father do not wish me to be Queen, Willa. They have been grooming me my entire life to be Viktoryn's *wife*."

"His *what*?"

Her nose wrinkles. "Wife. We are betrothed."

Shock is not a strong enough word for the emotion that shreds through me. So many things, so many moments, seem to suddenly and aggressively make sense. Her disdain of him, the way she flinched away from him after the Nixies' attack. His distrusting stare when he realized she had rescued me.

But it all makes sense now.

She needed me. She knew I was the key to her salvation, her *freedom*. I cannot help feeling used—even if it was for good reason. Even if I would have agreed to help her anyway. The hidden agendas of the Fae are never kind.

"Oh," is all I manage, and she takes this as a sign to continue.

"They want my brother, Aviv, to be King." A sour smile graces her lips as she huffs out a breath that almost sounds like a laugh. "All they have done, all they did not do, is in service of this goal. Preventing me from learning how to defend myself is one of the many ways they have attempted to control me. *Diminish* me. They wish me to be submissive, eager, *pliable*." She cringes. "They wish me to be a shapeshifter, able to contort myself into the wife of Viktoryn's wanting. Though it seems you may have stolen my place in that play."

It is my turn to laugh. "It seems I may have, and there is not a day that does not haunt me."

"Who knew? All he wanted was someone he was not supposed to want." May shakes her head, a smirk on her lips. "I am helping you because I am more than clay to be moulded into a wife. I am helping you because if you take the crown, I am *free*. I can become Queen, and we can change the laws—change the *world*. I can marry the female I love. And perhaps finally, pay off my debt to your mother. That is why I am helping you," May states. "Well, that and you are my first true friend."

Her past words meet me in the present. "*I owe your mother a lifetime of favours. Fae do not like leaving things owed.*"

"You may be mine as well... but you are bold and bright and brilliant. Exactly the way you are. Why would they do this? You would make a great Queen," I say, brows knit.

May gnaws on her bottom lip, considering. "It is an old way of thinking to prefer a male heir, but it seems my kin wish to cling to past ideals. A twisted one at that, as our Goddesses were female. However, male rulers can produce a vast number of heirs compared to females. Especially as they can breed mortal women and still birth Fae children," May mutters, almost apologetically.

Rage flares inside of me, a red haze descends on my vision. If it is the last thing I do, I will free the mortals tricked and trapped into service of the Fae. I force my rage to cool, trying to focus on May's words.

"But in truth, the reasons matter not. If things continue... if the Goldynlockes continue... I will never be allowed to freely be who I am.

My father and mother would never approve of my relationship with Amira. She is Unseelie, for one, and she is also a *she*." May winces. "They are not aware of my... preferences. Our marriage would not be legal in The Spring Court. The issue of heirs has prompted past royals to outlaw such unions. And with my betrothal to Viktoryn..." She shakes her head, another snapdragon springing to life in her hands.

"It is not a bad plan *if* I was willing. I mean, to marry me to Viktoryn. I see the reason—they would have their hands not only in The Spring Court but in The Summer Court. They would have rulers on both halves of The Seelie Kingdom. I am almost envious of how wise it is. But I will not forsake myself for my parents' thirst for power."

I nod. "I am so sorry, Maylea. That this has been your tale. I am glad you have entrusted me to be at your side while we wrestle your story back into your hands..." Something occurs to me. "How do you manage to be away from The Spring Court so often? Do they not wonder where you are? If they care so much to control you, to leash you, how are you free to wander where you wish?"

"The King and Queen of Spring believe that my absence will slowly erase me from the minds of Spring Folk. I am to become merely a forgotten figurehead. Yet, despite them, I am still beloved by my Folk. But I was becoming a disruption to their plans. Now, I am not permitted to attend court, and they push Aviv to the forefront of Spring dealings. The only time my presence is required anywhere is during my occasional forced evening dinners with Viktoryn here in Summer. I no longer have a home in Spring. I no longer have a home. I have a *room* here. And

Viktoryn cares not for where I am as long as I appear when called upon like a dog." May scoffs, plucking a petal off the snapdragon in her palm.

She flicks it to the ground, her eyes tracking its fall. "I hope when you dethrone him, you make it hurt."

I smile. "It will be my pleasure."

May smirks at me but my gut twists. What a lonely life. I never imagined the life of a royal to be so restricting. When I thought of royalty, I thought of endless jewels and constant attention and everyone bending to your every whim and wish. For May, her life has been anything but.

In truth, her motivations are not all that different from my mother's. The want to marry who you love without restrictions, without fear of persecution or violence. It makes me all the more motivated to ensure she gets her happily ever after. That she and Amira rule side by side—an unstoppable force.

"Now, enough about my hallowed past," she remarks, her easy grin returning.

"Alright," I concede. "Did you have any problems planting evidence? Or ditching Raven?"

May smirks as her eyes alight with mischief. "None at all."

I slit my palm, activating the medallion and pressing it into the matching sun carving on the bookshelf in my bedchamber. A click and hiss sound, and the shelf swings open to reveal a passageway. I toss the chain back over my neck, tucking the medallion into my tunic.

"How brilliant," May squeals, jumping up and down on the spot, a grin on her lips. "I must say, your mother was always scheming. It seems to have paid off."

"Did you ever try to use the key? How did you know about it anyway?" I question, looking over my shoulder at her as I slip into the darkness of the passage, May's pink faelight illuminates the pathway.

"Queen Valda left it with me, along with instructions to give you when you returned. I did try it once..." she shrugs a little guiltily, "but it only works with Caprimore blood." She pouts, jutting out her bottom lip. "After that, I studied the maps that came with it. Memorizing the routes. I may be the only one alive now who even knows of their existence." May glances at me and corrects, "Other than you, of course."

I nod. Valda must have trusted May implicitly, and that reassures me of my choice of ally. But it also makes me wonder what kind of bargain could ensure such unwavering loyalty, even in death. Fabelle's journal had noted that most Fae deals were revoked if one party perished.

"Ready to go spy on the chaos we caused?" I ask, smirking.

May nods so eagerly that I worry her head will bob free of her neck.

We follow the map through the passageways until we find the one that ends right inside Prince Archer's room. A small slit in the stone wall casts a sliver of light across the passage, and through it, voices can be heard.

I beckon May closer, and we stand shoulder to shoulder, peering through the thin slit. From where we hide, we have a side view of the bed and his bedchamber door.

I squint, my breath catching as it lands on Prince Archer, who lounges causally upon a *ginormous* four-poster bed, carved from sandstone and inlaid with precious gems and shells—alive.

May explained previously that there are two effective ways to kill a Faerie of a royal line—blood loss and beheading. But we did not wish Archer dead—not yet, anyway.

His bare chest reveals a red, jagged scar—ugly and angry—directly covering his heart. Dried blood covers his hands and chest. His breathing is laboured, but he tries to mask it.

Beside him, lightly rubbing his shoulder, is my sister. The sight sends my blood boiling as she fusses over his blankets and fixes a lock of his blonde hair that has slipped in front of his golden eyes. I swallow the bile that rushes to my throat.

The door to Archer's room tears open, slamming into the wall as two Knights drag a fuming Prince Viktoryn into the space. His face is the picture of pure outrage as he curses at the guards, threatening them. I share a look with May, and she grins darkly.

"What is the meaning of this *dear* brother?" Viktoryn hisses as he fights the guards' grip. They struggle to contain him. "Unhand me, you moronic fools! You report to *me*."

Archer rolls his eyes. "The meaning of this, *dear brother*," he coos mockingly, "is that evidence has surfaced that *you* planned the attack on my life. Is that not illuminating? Care to explain? Or, if you wish to be efficient, skip the excuses and fall to your knees to beg for your life? I find I am rather tired. Who knew an arrow to the heart could be so taxing?"

"What evidence?" Viktoryn demands.

"I will tell you, but we have much to discuss first."

"No! This is preposterous! I did no such thing. That accusation is fictitious and insulting," Viktoryn growls.

"That is what I told Mother and Father. But alas," Archer shrugs, "we must approach these allegations with the utmost care. You are the head of The Royal Army. The future King. And the assassination attempt happened on your watch, under your guidance. So tell me, how did this happen, Viktoryn? How will our Folk rest knowing criminals run amuck in these *walls*?" I slap a hand over my mouth to keep from laughing. "This incident does not inspire great faith in your ability to protect this Court. The Folk are beginning to question your competency. And fear I am, too."

Viktoryn looks ready to burst, muscles rippling. "You would do well to rem–"

Archer begins to laugh—a laugh that ends in a cough. He clutches his chest, wincing. Fabelle leaps from the bed to acquire him a glass of water.

After he takes a few sips, he speaks, "What has happened to you?" Archer drags his eyes up and down his brother, a look of disappointment and disgust. "You are an immortal creature, and you have been bested by a child who is still but a babe. It would be humorous if it was not so tragic."

"Your heart has softened in the soil of the mortal world. Your mind gentled by her hands. How are you not disgusted with yourself? With your *weakness*? The dust-destined creature has slipped your hands not once, not twice, but *thrice*!" Archer's humor fades, his face suddenly grave, voice lowered. "You must be wise enough to see how this appears to The Court."

Viktoryn laughs, and it is cruel, angry. "A thing to which you have never needed to worry. Your words are so precious, little brother. You know not of what it takes to be an heir. You have been babied, treated with the softness of a spare child. You are nothing but a poor imitation of I."

Archer's eyes narrow on Viktoryn. "I would be fearful of how you speak. Your fate is reliant on my mercy. How does it feel to be reduced to begging for mercy from the spare?"

"Oh, plea–"

"Enough! I am tired. I did not bring you here to spit jabs. I will tell you what has surfaced against you. But first, you will tell me what I want to know. Am I clear?"

Viktoryn swallows, biting back a retort, and he nods.

"What of the girl? Do you have any leads on where she has slipped away to?" Archer pauses, waiting for a response.

Viktoryn's lips thin as he shakes his head.

May shoots me a conspiratorial grin, and I return it with one of my own.

My skin hums with victory—the high of trickery. I cannot help but bathe in the glory of Viktoryn's humiliation. Especially when it comes by my hand. And by the hand of the female forced to be his bride.

Archer clucks his tongue. "Shame. I fear Mother is correct. You are not what you once were. I am beginning to agree with her assessment of your deteriorating competency. With The Courts."

"*My* competency?" he hisses, fists balled tightly at his side. "Who are *you* to question my competency? You drink and fuck and flaunt your little plaything of a wife. You know not the work or wisdom it takes to rule anything but the bottom of a wine glass. You would be wise to remember your place, *child*."

Archer's jaw ticks, eyes narrowed, but his voice is even when he speaks. "I care not what you think of my abilities, brother. Perhaps if you had even an ounce of my charm, your mortal pet would be panting at your arm as well," Archer coos, and Fabelle attempts to hide her wince. "You must have *something* to report. Or is all you are given, legions and riches and spies, a waste? Someone has managed to frame you and you know nothing? Should I report such to Mother?" Archer presses again, and I watch my sister perk up.

Viktoryn draws in a deep breath, two before he speaks, "Our Winter Court spies have reported that she did not return with the Bird Prince." Viktoryn's lips twitch up in amusement for a flash. "I am under the assumption that she has likely fled and found somewhere to hide out. Nearby. She does not have the wits or allies to survive long in the forest. She is likely shivering like a sniveling rat in some hovel or hole. She cannot survive here alone for long. She will show herself."

"Unacceptable. You must bring that mutt to heel, Viktoryn. The future of this Kingdom relies on her. Your inability to contain her is nothing short of shameful. How do you expect to possess the skill to control a Kingdom when one little girl has caused you so much trouble? My Caprimore is *perfectly* tamed. Are you not dear?" Archer drawls, running his hand down my sister's cheek.

If I did not know her as well as I do, I would believe her when she nods meekly. But a small flame of defiance flickers in Elle's eyes as he refers to her as a simple-minded, trained *pet*.

Archer is too distracted knocking his brother down multiple pegs to see how she tenses, how her hands fist in the sheets. His gaze moves to his brother, and Fabelle covers the slip quickly, unballing her fists and smoothing the covers while leaning into Archer's side. I wonder for a moment too long what it means. *If* it means anything at all.

I am drawn back to reality when Viktoryn laughs—a wild, wicked, fiery cold thing that goes a beat too long to be natural. When he finishes, a cruel, too-wide grin graces his lips. He glares down at Fabelle and Archer with cool condescension.

"Please, Archer. You had the easy of the pair. The one made of sugar and sweets and youth and stories. To be proud of such a catch is fruitless, foolish. You opened the trap door, and she pranced right in," Viktoryn drawls, pointing at my sister. She cowers back from his finger. "I was cursed with the sister of spite and scorn and flames and secrets. What an utter *jewel* she will be caged. For what is the worth of a pet caged, if it does not wish to be *free*? What is a bird with wings if it does not long to fly? To tame her," he nods dismissively at Fabelle, "was no challenge, for she was already tame. Willa is as wild as the wind. An ever-burning fire that will take multitudes to contain. Tricking her into a cage will be a marvelous feat." His eyes glitter as he pictures it, and rage churns in my stomach.

"Do not brag about the pathetic mutt you wish to call a wife." He chuckles darkly, and Archer growls. "You know not the skill it takes to break a woman *wild*. And I will thoroughly enjoy breaking her—for even broken, she will *burn*."

My nails dig into my palms until blood is drawn as Viktoryn speaks so casually about caging me and breaking my spirit as if I am some kind of coveted wild horse.

Despite this, in place of my anger, an idea forms—impulsive and wild. It would be dangerous, a gamble of the ages, but as long as I can slam the trap door down faster than he can...

I will ruin him before he ruins me.

What better way to break an enemy... what a delicious and devious scheme. Using what he longs for the most as the lure to his own damnation.

If he wanted to tame me, let him try.

If he wanted to play with fire, let him *burn*.

"Speak not of my betrothed that way, brother," Archer seethes, stepping off the bed and swaying to stand nose-to-nose with Viktoryn. Well, almost nose-to-nose, as Archer is a solid half a foot shorter. Nose to forehead, maybe.

"For she may be many things, but she is still *mine*. You will not speak poorly of my possessions. It would do you well to remember that the next time you misstep, I may not be feeling so kind. Now, back to the issue at hand," he mutters, sinking back down to the bed as if rising to chastise Viktoryn had drained him. "What do you have to report on the rebels?"

"You threaten me, then demand I report to you once more?" Viktoryn snarls.

Archer sighs. "I am nearly through with you. Tell me what I wish to know, and we shall come to an agreement on your treason. What of the rebels?"

May and I exchange a confused glance at the mention of *rebels*. Viktoryn gawks at him in disbelief but then swallows.

"Someone has leaked the identities of the Caprimores. The rebel numbers have grown since the rumor that a true child of the Goddess Cyrissa has returned."

Thank you, Alice.

We had asked her to begin leaking select information to the gentry to further the unrest in The Court. It seems she has been successful.

"It has been said that the child will lead us from a reign of darkness. It does not help us to persuade The Folk otherwise when the weather has continued to become increasingly unstable. The initial balancing of the land that came with Willa's return has ended. The land is angry—it wishes to reclaim what rightfully belongs to it. A plague has swept a small village by Cyrissa Lake, unlike anything we have ever seen. Those it touches disintegrate into ash within days. A storm off The Elphyne Sea met the coast, and a wave like the hand of a Goddess reached the cliffside and pulled half of Goldlink Village into the ocean. Hundreds have been injured, and the death count is nearing the fifties."

My chest seizes. *My fault. This is my fault.* The land wants the power that lives in me.

Archer looks both pleased and terrified. "I see. What else?"

"The Court has steadily divided, shows of support for the Caprimore girls are popping up in villages across The Summer Court, some found even in Spring. Valda's royal crest, a blazing sun half eclipsed in shadows, has been found painted on chapels, but it is believed the rebels' numbers are still small. Nothing to concern ourselves with. No direct shows of support have appeared within the Palace, and any outright displays will be considered treason without trial, punishable by death," Viktoryn finishes.

I glance at Fabelle, but her expression is carefully blank as she continues to stroke Archer's arm. It does not seem as if she is even listening. The scene fills me with a sudden surge of fury.

"Very well. I see it is even more imperative we capture the girl and return her powers to the land when she enters The Calling..."

The mention of The Calling makes me squirm. My birthday is only months away—December 11. Once The Calling starts, I will either meet my demise or be granted the power to reclaim my mother's throne.

"Now that you have answered my questions, I can address the reason I have requested you to be detained. Royal correspondence with your seal was found on our captured suspect. Some Unseelie Troll, I cannot recall the creature's name. Randy? Rocky? Oh, no matter, it will be dead soon." May smirks as Archer waves off the thought. "The contents of which leads one to believe that *you* orchestrated the attack on my life," Prince Archer explains, shrugging off my sister as she tries to soothe him—her face cracking with hurt a second before she schools herself.

Not the happily ever after she was looking for after all. I am unsurprised, but a sense of helplessness descends as I watch her be treated with disinterested disrespect.

This is what she chose over her family.

"This is why you had these imbeciles restrain me? My *seal*?" Viktoryn seethes as the weight of the accusations settles. "You believe some common criminal over your own flesh and blood? I am innocent! You know this! The fact that you dare use this as a way to demand information from me is a gross misuse of power!" He breaks free of the guards, shoving them to the floor. They scramble to right themselves.

Archer looks unmoved by the speech, and desperation floods Viktoryn's face.

He moves forward to kneel beside Archer's bed, taking his hand, voice pleading. "I had nothing to do with this. I swear it. You said yourself I was framed."

"Were you?"

The guards rush Viktoryn, but Archer holds up a hand, and they halt.

"Archer," Viktoryn snaps. "You must believe me. My lips cannot spill a lie."

"I believe you. Yet, what I believe does not matter. Someone must be held accountable for the breach of our security. And while I believe you had nothing to do with the planning of the attack, you had everything to do with the security of this palace. Thus, Mother, Father, Princess Daviana, and I have decided that, from this moment forward, you are relieved of your duty as commander. The Folk have lost faith in your ability to keep them safe. *I* have lost faith in your ability to keep *me* safe," Archer says firmly and a little too eagerly.

"No. Absolutely not," Viktoryn hisses, pushing to his feet to pace the room. He shoves his hands through his blonde hair and turns back to his brother with fury in his golden eyes.

"How *dare* you decide this without me present? I am the *heir* to the throne!" Viktoryn shouts.

"Right now, you are not. Right now, you are a suspec–"

Viktoryn whirls on his brother. "That army is my creation! It was nothing before me—*nothing*! I have worked tirelessly for years to earn the respect of our Folk," his voice cracks, "and I have led them with pride. It was I who doubled our numbers. What will The Folk say? If they have not lost faith in me yet, certainly they will if I am stripped of my titles."

"It is done," Archer responds. "Mother and Father will make the announcement stating you need more time to fulfill other royal duties, and Daviana will take over your position as commander. Your focus is to be solely on apprehending your failed experiment."

Viktoryn shakes his head. He meets Archer's eyes and smiles wickedly.

"I wish you luck with the rebels. They will see right through an inexperienced leader. They will rally behind this instability. If I was still commander," Viktroyn sneers through gritted teeth, "I could get on this at once, but it seems Daviana will have to get comfortable with letting heads roll. Is there a reason they chose her over you? Our pacifistic sister? Or do they simply see what the rest of us do?"

"And what is that, Viktoryn?"

"Your overwhelming inadequacy."

"Oh, how your words bite." Archer lets out a melodramatic sigh, but his features grow tight. "You are hereby dismissed as commander and from my presence. Leave me. I need to rest, no thanks to you."

Viktoryn's anger fades into a desperate sort of resignation so thick it sticks to his skin, coating the walls. "This will ruin me."

Viktoryn exits the room, the guards following.

"Does this help our plan?" Fabelle asks quietly once they are alone, moving back to lean her head on her betrothed's chest.

My stomach turns.

"Yes, dear girl." Archer pats her head like a dog. "I only wish I thought of it myself. The sooner he is out of our way, the sooner I can make you my Queen."

Back in our hideout, I slam the passage shut, chest heaving. May and I stare at each other in disbelief. She conjures a black-eyed susan flower in her hand and then fiddles with it—a nervous tick. I want to celebrate the point we have won over Viktoryn, but my mind is too busy spinning.

"Why does Fabelle believe she will be *Queen?* Why does Archer think he can be King?" I run my hands through my hair. "Elle mentioned that Archer was going to make her Queen when we fought in her room before the wedding, but I believed she misspoke." My eyes find the ceiling. "If she meant it... They must have some grand plan to overthrow Viktoryn. It seems we are not the only ones scheming to steal the crown."

May nods, chewing on her bottom lip as she thinks, eyes sharp and clever.

"They must have a plan to kill him or ruin his reputation beyond salvation. If he is exiled, dead, or imprisoned, he loses his claim. The Folk must turn against him, or The Elemental Courts must rule him unfit. It is not easy to unseat an heir in The Summer Court. Or any court for that matter."

She would know. She is living it.

"Do you think Viktoryn suspects?"

"I would think not. Prince Archer has never shown any interest in the throne. He has always appeared to lack ambition. But he is a wildcard. A lover of stories and revelry and wine. A true spare, never taken seriously, never wishing to be—or so we all thought."

"It is clever. He has not shown his cards. Nor his desires. Well, to anyone but Elle," I mutter, bitterness spreading through my veins.

May nods. "Everyone assumes that the line of succession will stand." Her eyes find mine churning with mischief and pride. "Viktoryn believes the only threat to his throne is *you*, mighty mortal," she teases. "How wrong he is."

"I am not certain how we proceed with such knowledge. I am struggling to see a downside in Viktoryn battling off attacks from all sides."

May hums in agreement.

"I say we allow Archer and Elle to take Viktoryn down for us. Or, at the very least, try. Archer is the easier of the pair to dispatch," I reason.

"True. He is younger, inexperienced, arrogant. He lacks the training Viktoryn has received."

"And if Archer is so focused on Viktoryn, he will never see us coming. And if Viktoryn is distracted by Archer and Fabelle..."

"He will be easier to manipulate," she agrees, bouncing on her toes. "I say we go ahead with what we planned. Let the spare do as he pleases."

"But do we... I mean, if we get information of a planned assassination attempt... do we warn Viktoryn? Do we want them *all* dead?"

May blinks repeatedly. "They took *everything* from you. Do you not wish for their demise?" she asks, looking at me as if I am some type of strange bug.

I force a smile. Too wide. "Of course I do," I lie.

Or I think I lie. So much has changed, and sometimes it is difficult to know my own mind.

If I become as wicked as them, what does that make me? When did murder become something I contemplated as a solution to my problems? Who am I to decide if someone lives or dies?

Elphyne has changed me imperceptibly. Slowly shifting the boundaries in my mind like the sand changes with the ocean tides, creating a new landscape. One made from cruelty and schemes and ruthlessness. Jagged cliffs and murderous what-ifs.

But I have never had any desire to play God... though each taste of power that slips between my lips makes the statement ring less true.

Still, I have never, even in my darkest moments, considered myself bloodthirsty. A fighter, yes. A survivor? Of course. A warrior with a gift for violence, maybe. But a cold-blooded, premeditated murderer? I am not certain. Though the idea does not cause me as much distress as it once did, it is one thing to ruin someone's life. It is another entirely to take it.

The lives I have already taken, even in self-defence, left a mark. But they do not haunt me as they once did. Maybe it bothers me more that

I do not feel as hesitant to take a life as I once did... Maybe I am afraid to consider what that makes me.

May watches me with pitying fascination. She shakes her head as if scolding a child and sighs.

"Your humanity seeps through your skin like sweat. I hope you soon find your claws and teeth. For this battle will not be won with anything less than bloodlust, brutality, and betrayal. The Goldynlockes will not hesitate to stick you through the minute you have lost your use. You might think to do the same if you wish to survive," she states.

"You speak as though the choice is simple. As if taking the life of another is a small feat," I remark, exasperated, crossing my arms.

May laughs, her head falling back. "You have not yet known the rush of standing before your enemy and knowing it is your life or theirs." She smiles wide. "Watch how simple the answer appears then. It would do you well to remember that though we look part human, we are not. We do not struggle to free our minds from the cage of humanity in which you stand. You must. Do not trust anyone, even me. Do not think me selfless, or you may find yourself drowning in disappointment."

I spend the night sleepless. Dawn hours off, I stare at the ceiling with restlessness growing in my bones. As much as I try to bury my thoughts in darkness, they spark to light.

I wonder what Raven is doing right now. If he is still worried about me. If he has figured out I betrayed him. I wonder if he hates me. I think of his lips on my neck, his hands on my skin, and curse myself for it. I think of his lips on my lips and curse myself harder.

I am filled with anger and dread that Raven knew who I was and did nothing to warn me. In that way, he is no better than Viktoryn. He knew who I was in the wine cellar. He knew where I was in Mayfair, and yet he left me to be fed to the wolves. He *betrayed* me. But I guess I betrayed him plenty in return.

I think of Maylea's words on taking the life of another. Her warning that I need to let go of my humanity and find some teeth and claws. I wonder if killing truly becomes simple when you find yourself with no option—slay or be slain? I wonder about her motives. Her many secrets.

Why is she really helping me? I do not believe she has offered me the full story.

I wonder why Archer wishes to overthrow his brother and what role my sister plays. Mostly, I wonder if my sister is happy. If she truly has gotten all she's ever wanted—if that does not include me at all?

I wonder if I made it all too easy to walk away from me as if I was nothing to her. If my father felt the same. The thought is agony. I wonder if she's worried that I have disappeared. It hurts to think she does not. It also hurts to think she does. I wish I could simply dig a knife into my flesh and remove the pieces of me that will always want to protect her—this would all be endlessly easier.

I think of Viktoryn and his rage when he found out he lost his role as army commander. I wish he knew it was because of me. I want him to know that everything he loses will be something I gain. I will savor every minute of his misery—like he savored mine.

I toss and turn until I cannot any longer, my thoughts driving my body out of bed. I huff a breath of frustration and grab my dagger and some supplies, putting on a maid's uniform that I stole yesterday from the servant's quarters. I braid my wild red hair back and pin it tightly to my skull, concealing it by securing a scarf over my head.

Then I take off into the passageways on a whim—with some nerve and a terrible plan.

It takes three passageways and two sets of servants' stairways until I am spit out of the endless tunnels on Viktoryn's floor. The halls are quiet, but I keep to the shadows nonetheless. Even when I remember that the Fae can see in the dark. The shadows seem to encompass me in the illusion of safety. Moonlight seeps through the giant stained-glass windows, providing me with enough light to move by.

I peer down the hallway to his bedchamber door and see two guards standing stoically outside. I smirk and activate another passageway, following it down. I click open the hidden door to find myself *inside* Viktoryn's adjoining bathing chamber.

I creep into his bedchamber, and there in the center of the room lies Viktoryn, face twisted in discomfort as he sleeps fitfully. I grin, all teeth.

I hope his nightmares are filled with images of *me*. I hope I have become the monster he fears is hiding under his bed, around every corner, waiting in every shadow.

I study him, blond hair tousled on his pillows, his too-perfect body shirtless, blood-red sheets pooled around his waist.

I sneak further into the room, watching as his chest rises and falls. Rises and falls. Rises and falls, and I think, if I wanted to, I could end his life. Right now. How easy it would be to thrust my dagger into his chest—how easy it would be to separate his skull from his shoulders. My hands shake at the notion, my heart racing.

But he does not deserve such a swift and merciful end. He deserves to suffer the way he has caused others to suffer.

Quietly, I pull three dozen marigold flowers out of my bag and begin to place them around his room. *Our* flower. The once-beloved smell makes my stomach turn. The flower is an exact replica of the kind he used to steal from The Palace Gardens in Mayfair for me. Oh how things change. That feels like eternities ago now. Like those memories happened to a different girl.

I set three on his bedside table, ten around him on the bed, and a few on his bookshelves. I fill the room with fresh flowers courtesy of May's magicks, leaving them behind as a calling card—a taunt, a promise of what's to come. A return of the threat he once left me with.

I want him to know I was here while he slept. That he cannot find me even though I am breathing down his neck. I want him to know not even his bedchamber is safe, that his guards cannot protect him. I want him to know he is *vulnerable.*

Once I am done placing the flowers, I watch him for a few moments. A small ache grows in my chest and for a traitorous second, I wish I was in his arms. Safe and comforted. I wish I was the girl in my memories. I wish I could turn back time and return to the life where he was my future, where he was *mine.*

I cut those thoughts off at the root, tugging them out of the soil of my mind.

I turn to leave, but a shadow stirs in the corner of my vision. Reaching for my dagger, I try to make out the shapes in the darkness. Nothing moves—nothing changes. Only the sound of my own breath fills my ears.

I begin to turn once more, believing my mind is playing tricks on me, when the shadow flickers in my peripheral. I whip around to face it.

From the corner of the room, out steps a tall figure cloaked in darkness and danger. Watching me, considering me—unmoving and menacing.

My heart slams into my ribcage as I try to think my way out of this. I peer at Viktoryn's bed, where he continues to sleep soundly. Unaware of the two wraiths with wicked intentions dancing around in the dark.

I take one step backwards, and the figure mirrors me, taking one step forward. Panic floods my veins, and my breath catches in my throat.

Are they here to kill Viktoryn? Or me? Did they follow me here? How did they get past the guards?

I cannot risk a fight, not when Viktoryn could wake at any moment, and his guards could be upon us in seconds. If the figure kills him, good riddance. Better him than me. I take another step back, but the figure follows, and I curse under my breath.

Here for me, not Viktoryn. *Wonderful.*

I do not believe it makes you a coward to run. Strategically, sometimes, running is your best option. So I do just that. I turn, diving into the passageway, my body colliding with stone. I force myself to stay quiet as pain rises with the impact. I kick the lever that activates the doorway and it begins to slowly swing shut. *Too* slowly. I watch in horror as the figure nears.

No longer worried about being quiet, I brace both feet on the door and slam it shut with a groan. The figure reaches seconds too late. I hear their fingers on the wall, pressing into the stone, trying to figure out how to open the door. The sound of fingernails digging into the grooves of the brick makes my stomach tighten.

Viktoryn's guards shout, and I hold my breath. But the figure does not flee, nails continuing to drag over stone. I press my body into the cool stone of the door, waiting for it to fly open and deliver me to the hunter on a silver platter, an apple stuffed in my mouth. A dish ready to be devoured.

But it remains firmly shut, unable to open without the key. For the first time, I thank my dead Fae mother a thousand times over for creating these passages with me in mind. She did a lot wrong, but this was one thing she did right.

"Your majesty? Are you alright? We heard an intruder," someone—I assume a guard—says. "What–"

"Yes, of course. I am well. It seems they meant me no harm. It was just trickery," Viktoryn replies but his voice is uncertain. I can imagine the surprise on his face when he awoke surrounded by our flower.

"Prince, are you certain? Why is your room scattered with flowers? What kind of trickery do you speak of?"

"It is not of concern to you," he snaps. "I said it was fine. I said it was trickery. I am unharmed. Leave me!"

"But, Your Majesty, this is a serious matter. Are the flowers a message? A threat? This does not seem to be a jest."

"That was an order. Leave me. *Now*!" Viktoryn shouts.

They seem to hesitate, but soon, they exit. Moments after the door shuts, I hear glass shattering and objects crashing.

"That little witch," he seethes, and I grin.

Crash!

"How did she enter my room? How dare she defy me! Disrespect me!"

Bang!

He continues to rage until he tires. I wait, counting the minutes until the room goes silent.

When enough time has passed, I crawl down the passage and back to the main hallway, where I need to switch passageways to return to my room. I wait a few minutes by the threshold, letting my heart slow while hoping the cloaked being lost me. I have no desire to find out what they wanted.

Dagger in hand, I open the passageway, peering down the hall from behind a hung tapestry. I check for guards, but find no one. Only darkness and solitary shadows await me.

The silence in the halls feels charged, not comforting. As if the walls have hushed in anticipation of a show. The moon a spotlight to a grande event, whispering bets and predictions to the watching stars. The hair on the back of my neck rises, but no one—or thing—approaches. The shadows remain as still as night.

Stepping out into the main hall, I begin the short trek to the next passageway, keeping my head down. Relief floods me as I pass the halfway point without incident.

But relief arrives too early. It is chased away by panic when a lurking shadow appears, looming over me from behind. I quicken my steps, peering back, but I see nothing. An empty hall. My eyebrows furrow, and I shake my head to clear it, forcing my feet to move faster.

The passage nears, only a few feet separating safety and myself, when a warm breath ghosts my neck. I am pushed firmly into the stone wall. I stumble, hands out before me to protect my body from the collision. A hand slams over my mouth as a cloaked figure drenched in black towers over me.

I do not waste a second, looping my leg around the inside of theirs and sweeping the soft spot behind their knee. They groan, and their leg buckles. I thrust my elbow into their chin with a sickening crack. They take a single staggering step back, giving me room to duck around them and take off into a sprint. I bite into my thumb until blood wells.

I cannot hear any footsteps behind me, but I keep running, not risking losing any speed by looking back. Flipping up the tapestry that covers the passageway, I smear my bloodied thumb on the key, activate the door, and rush inside. I go to pull the door shut, but a boot slides into the threshold.

I swallow a sound of surprise, kicking frantically at the boot, but the figure wrenches the door open as if it weighs nothing and stalks after me. My heart flies into my throat, pounding so hard I struggle to breathe around it.

Pivoting, I attempt to run. However, as soon as the door closes, they are on me again. My stomach is pressed into the cool wall as they lean their body weight into me. Wrenching my arms behind my back, immobilizing me. We stand in complete darkness.

For several moments, the only sound is our combined breathing. And my frantic heartbeat.

Inhale, exhale.

Inhale, exhale.

Inhale, exhale.

This is how I die, I think.

After everything.

How pathetic.

"What did I say about flying away without saying goodbye, firebird?"

"*Raven.*"

"What are you doing here? How did you find me?" I hiss, pressing into him, trying to free myself, but he does not yield an inch.

I cannot help but feel a modicum of relief in knowing that it is only Raven. But my relief is swallowed up by the knowledge of what we have both done. What *I* have done.

"Why marigolds?" he asks, and I blink, surprised by the question.

"If you are not going to answer my questions, I will not be answering yours."

"Always such a stubborn creature."

My breath catches in my throat as he trails fingertips down my neck, settling over my pulse. I try to leash my battering heart, but his proximity is as intoxicating as it is terrifying. An amused hum leaves his lip.

"How did you find me?" I demand, breathless. And then again, angrily, as I curse myself for being affected by his nearness. "How did you find me, Raven?"

Raven chuckles darkly, and he turns me, pressing my back into the wall with his hips. His lips brush the shell of my ear as he growls, "Do you have any idea how worried I was that you had gone off and gotten yourself killed?"

I try to reply, but all of the air has been sucked from my lungs. He moves quickly, securing my hands above my head with one of his. His free hand begins to move, fingers tracing lines across my neck, settling on the chain of the necklace he gave me. Shame smears across my cheeks—I cannot bring myself to take it off.

"You kept it," he whispers as his lips ghost my neck.

"Raven," I warn, not sure if I want him to stop or keep going. "Answer my question."

"Why, pray tell, would I do such a thing? So you can flee from me once more?" He *tsks.* "You have been a very, *very* bad little creature." His voice turns cruel. "I do not take kindly to those who break my trust, Willa." It feels odd to hear him speak my name with such coldness.

"As if you have never broken mine?" I scoff. "I am doing what I need to do. And I will not apologize for that. Not to you. Not to anyone."

Raven *laughs*—a dark, hollow, dangerous thing. A warning.

"That, firebird," he purrs, "is where you are so alike the Fae you claim to hate. You take what you want. Do as you wish. And *never* apologize. It is almost admirable... *almost.*" His fingers stroke a gentle line across my stomach, dipping under my tunic.

"And what if I do? Hate the Fae?" His fingers still on my bare skin. "Hate how you have all taken and taken from me until I am nothing? What if I hate *you*?"

"I am not *him*," Raven hisses, startling me with the direction of his thoughts as he tears his hand away from my skin.

"No. You are your own kind of *poison*. You trick and cheat and steal and kill. You may not be *him*, but you commit the same sins and find ways to justify them. I know what you did, Raven. I know that you led Viktoryn to Fabelle and me. I know you are not who you pretend to be."

Raven says nothing, and with every passing second, the fire inside me rages hotter.

"You have nothing to say? Truly? Will you not defend yourself? Will you not deny it?" I growl, waiting. But still, he says nothing. Furious tears begin to trail down my cheeks. "Tell me, is it hard to look the worst parts of yourself in the eye? Is it hard to look at him and know all of the ways in which you are similar? Is it hard to pretend that what you hate about him, what you hate about how he treats me, is no better than how you treat me? Tell me, *hypocrite*? Is it?"

He does not deny it. Defend himself. He is a frozen fortress, and I have been denied entry. And I hate him for it. I hate him for making me trust him. For making me open up to him, only to lock me out, to shatter me like Viktoryn did. My heart was already bleeding, and still, he twisted the knife—I cannot help but twist it back.

"I know who you are, Raven. I know you are not him. You are *you*. And somehow, that is so much *worse*."

He recoils in the darkness as if burned, body weight melting away from mine, even as he keeps a firm hold on my wrists. I wait to feel victorious, satisfied even, for hurting him, but all I feel is *raw*.

When he finally speaks, his voice is as sharp as a knife. "All that fire and nothing to *burn*. Think of what you could accomplish if only you could master your anger instead of *it* mastering *you*. It is not I that you should be angry with." His tone is bitter. "My sins pale in comparison to his. You know nothing of me. Nothing of my motiv–"

"You have ensured that," I snap.

"Perhaps I did. But that is not why you hate me. You hate me because I *see* you, Willa. Every furious, fiery, festering bit of you. I see you, and it *terrifies* you."

I try to think of something cutting and clever to say, but I cannot hear my thoughts over the pounding of my heart. I hate this. I hate how I feel so out of control around Raven. Viktoryn was a much simpler opponent—stick him at the right angle with the right pin, and he would slowly, or very quickly, devolve into anger.

Raven is a different story entirely. It seems I can stick him until he resembles a pincushion—but he never explodes. His rage is quiet, calculated. It is unsettling, foreign, *terrifying*.

He reads my hesitation like only he can and pushes his advantage. "I do wonder if Viktoryn bought it."

"Bought what?"

"This act. I am certain he got a good taste of your poisonous tongue, but did he ever see the calculating darkness in that vicious mind of yours?" He releases my hands, and I know I should attack or run, but I cannot. "Did you fear it would scare him? Intimidate him? If he saw all you could be—all you are."

I blink at a sudden assault of light. An ice-blue faelight begins to illuminate the passage. I swallow hard as Raven's face comes into view. Harsh and beautiful and cold. His furious eyes filled with storm clouds I could get lost in.

"I do not know what you are talking about. There is no act. You speak nonsense. Someone, some*thing* like Viktoryn, would never fear someone like me. I am a blip of nothingness in his eternal life."

"How wrong you are. How small you think." He shakes his head. "I do not know how you fail to see that under all that fear and rage, you are something sharp, ruthless, and cunning." He gently cups my cheeks in his hands, like even now, I am something rare, something precious. "Somehow, you have convinced yourself that being half of who you are is safer than risking the wildfire I see blazing in your eyes."

His thumb brushes across my cheekbone, goosebumps rising across my body. "But you were not created to be safe or quiet or contained. You were born to burn. Once you embrace all you are—the darkness, the light—you, my love, will be a *reckoning*."

You, my love, will be a reckoning.

For a moment, I let myself imagine what I could be if I was un-leashed—if I stopped holding myself back.

Fear blooms in my chest.

But among that fear is also a trickle of excitement.

Power.

Longing.

Fire.

Some buried part of my soul perks to attention at his words, craving the freedom to burn, to *be*.

And maybe...

Maybe Raven is right. Maybe in shoving down all of the unsavory pieces of myself for fear of what they could do—what *I* could do—I limited myself. Maybe all the years I was told I was nothing branded my mind with layers of white-hot doubt and insecurity.

Maybe it is time I stop tripping on my own leash. Maybe it is time to burn those words—that uncertainty—to ashes.

In Mayfair, I knew that to survive the world I was living in, I had to be small and quiet. Obedient and underestimated. I was punished for existing too loudly, too boldly, or even at all. But I am not living that life anymore. I am not that *girl* anymore. And while I crumbled myself down into manageable pieces to become invisible and digestible, maybe I had made myself less.

Maybe I am ready to be more—to be *everything*.

I think of the addicting head rush I felt while fleeing the wedding. How everyone around me has been vicious and calculated.

And suddenly, the world I used to live in no longer exists. Because Elphyne is not Mayfair. Faeries are not human. And if I keep fighting to maintain a desperate grip on my humanity, a desperate grip on who I once was, I fear I will never best them.

The Fae have made no accommodations for my human weaknesses. And they will not start now.

"What if I do not want to be dangerous? Destructive? What if I do not want to burn?" I question.

"You say this as if you did not burn me without hesitation," Raven states bitterly—any remaining warmth bleeding from his face.

"Then why are you here, Raven? Why did you come? I am certain you did not follow me to lecture me?"

"I am here to get answers. You left my court in *ruins*. The Summer Court is looking for a way to pin Archer's attack on my court. You were missing. Maylea abandoned me to return here as if nothing had happened at all. And I think it all leads back to *you*."

"So, what? This is an interrogation? You stalked me through the night to fling accusations?"

"I have questions, Willa. Questions that must be answered. So I am here to give you one chance to tell the truth. After which, each lie that falls from your lips, I shall punish." I roll my eyes at him, and he tilts his head, watching me like a predator circling its prey. "Who helped you escape the wedding, Willa?"

"I am not doing this with you." I laugh bitterly. "Who do you think you are? You lied to me. You lied about *everything*. You have no moral high ground to punish *my* lies—not when you wear yours as a coat of armor." I turn to stalk off, but Raven grips the back of my cloak, hauling me backwards.

"Wrong answer, Willa. Who helped you escape the wedding?"

"I acted alone," I snap, narrowing my eyes on him over my shoulder.

His eyes flood with amusement, and he smiles coldly. "You lie almost as effortlessly as you breathe. It is brilliant and *terrible*. I have watched you lie to me before but never so boldly, so *outright*. How fascinating to bear witness to a being who can speak without being caged to the truth. Do it again, will you, my love? Just once for me."

I press my lips together, shaking my head. "You can trap me here, but you cannot force me to answer your questions."

"That is where you are wrong, Princess. I can. You decide how this goes. How far *I* go to get my answers. But you *will* answer me," he threatens. "Who helped you?"

"No. One. Helped. Me."

Raven *tsks*. "Liar, liar. I take no enjoyment from this, Willa, but I must protect my court. I am bound to my duty. My oaths. One day, you will understand."

I am about to question what he means when he turns me, pushing me into the wall and forcing my arms above my head. Before I can react, ice spreads from his palms, securing my wrists to the stone. A hiss escapes my lips at the sudden assault of cold.

"Raven," I warn.

But he just studies me, smirking. Fear rises in me, but I force my body into inaction, neutrality, falling into that place of numbness that allowed me to survive years of abuse.

Raven watches the shift in me, tension spreading across his face. For a second, he looks almost regretful, stepping forward to run a hand down my cheekbone, expression softening.

"Tell me, sweet girl. I know you want to tell me," he leans in, my breath catching, "I know you want to show me how clever you have been. How you outwitted me. Just tell me... who helped you?" he mutters, gently brushing his thumb across my bottom lip.

Part of me wants to, the part of me that has always wanted to melt into his touch—into him. But he is betting on that. I shake my head, not trusting my lips. It is not just me at stake here, it is May. I must protect her.

He drops his hand, eyes growing distant as the ice cuffs sprout a thousand needle-claws, digging into my sensitive flesh until blood runs down my arms. I bite back a scream. My eyes flood with unshed tears, but I do not let them fall.

"I do not have endless patience, Willa. Just tell me—tell me, and I will let you go. Tell me, and I will make you feel good. Who helped you escape the wedding?"

"I acted alone," I snark through gritted teeth.

The pain increases as the ice needles burrow deeper into my flesh, and this time, I cannot hold back the yelp that is ripped from my lungs.

"Who. Helped. You," Raven demands.

"I..." I pant, solidifying walls in my mind to block out the pain, "acted *alone.*" I glare at him with all the fury in my heart, hoping he can see that no amount of pain will force the answer to part my lips. "Are you dimwitted? Do you need the definition of the word, Prince?"

Raven sighs, eyes drifting up to the ceiling—as if torturing information out of me is terribly inconvenient.

"I do not wish to cross this line, as I know how you feel about compulsion." My muscles lock up in terror. "But it seems you are far too willing to endure pain to conceal your allies' identities," Raven reasons, more to himself than me. "I do not want this, Willa."

I smile, feral and wild, and his eyes narrow. "Such a hypocrite," I taunt, even as I am swallowed by fear as he so casually threatens to steal my free will. Like it is a pouch of coins that he wishes to snatch. A thief once more.

I will not beg. I will not break.

"Do you remember lying in your bed with me? Condemning Viktoryn for using compulsion, preaching about free will? We both know this is not about my allies," I hum, and his jaw tightens. "Or is it *precisely* about my allies? About how you are no longer one of them? Jealous, are we?"

The ice cuffs retract their claws, the bite lessening. And I think for a moment I have won. I have convinced him. He does not want to be this. He is not a monster.

"It is futile to deflect and distract. I came here with a singular purpose. I will not leave until I succeed. I do not struggle with mortal moral dilemmas," Raven says.

True, primal terror grips my spine with iron fists. I straighten, tilting my chin high, trying to appear unafraid, formidable. But I am terrified. I am trembling.

"You would never."

"Why do you behave as if I should show you mercy? Is it because I *kissed* you?" My cheeks flame, embarrassment twisting through my guts. "Because I am attracted to you? You endangered those who I would die to protect. *This*," he hisses, gesturing to us, "is not my doing. You acted first. You shattered our alliance. If you are not my ally, you are my enemy, Willa."

He leans over me, nothing like the Raven I know. He is utterly petrifying. A force of nature. A storm unleashed.

"I do not show my enemies mercy," he says.

"We do not have to be enemies. But if you do this, Raven, I will never forgive you," I vow. "Do this and prove me right. Prove to me that Fae are monsters. Prove to me that everything you were, everything you are, all the kindness and whispers and *kisses*," I spit back at him, "were lies. Do this, Raven, and we *will* be enemies."

My words seem to have no effect on him at all. I feel as though I am staring at a stranger. A monster. A being of sharp teeth and razor claws waiting to pounce.

"Why would I desire the forgiveness of my enemy?"

My panic loosens my tongue. "Raven, I need you to trust me when I say I pose no threat to your court. If that is what you fear—if that is why you think you must do this... I cannot betray the trust of those who have handed me theirs. Do not ask me to do this," I plead, the words coming out too quickly.

Raven laughs, the temperature of the room dropping as he loses a bit of the hold he has on his power. Pain flashes in his eyes.

"But you could so easily betray *my* trust, I see." His lips twist into a bitter smile. "Do you consider me foolish? Naive? To trust the word of a girl who lies as easily as she breathes? Your word means *nothing* to me."

I hesitate, fear crawling over my skin. I look away. What can I say? How can I convince him I will speak the truth when I am not bound to it? When I have told him lie after lie? *Nothing.* Nothing I say will fix this.

"I see. Well, let me be perfectly clear—I am not foolish. I am not naive. I know of only one person, other than the girl who stands before me, who could have made that shot. How odd that once it was made and we were forced to flee, a Faerie known for her surefootedness would trip and pull only *me* down with her." His accusatory eyes spear me. "I do not need your confirmation to know that what I fear to be true must be." He shakes his head. "Bold. Bold almost to the level of stupidity, to use a member of my own Inner Circle. You outwitted me once—fair play. But I promise you, this will never happen again."

"Rave–"

"After all I did to help you…" He looks away from me as if he cannot bear to look at me. "A *mistake* I will not make again."

I flinch at the word.

"What I cannot figure out is why. Why she would help you. What you could possibly offer her that I could not. I only know she did. I wish you were brave enough to claim your ruthlessness to my face," Raven states.

I fight a wince. I wish he did not ask me to claim what I have done. Daring me to own the worst parts of my nature. Daring me to admit the darkness he sees within me.

I should not be surprised that he has guessed correctly. Raven, who is always scheming. Raven, who is cunning and clever and excruciatingly observant. Raven, who always knows. But now he knows too much. And as much as I want to ask what he will do to her, that will only confirm what he believes to be true.

"You are right. I can offer her and you nothing. So let me go, Raven. Stop following me. If we are enemies, let us be enemies. I do not need an overbearing shadow," I snap.

Violence brews in Raven's eyes, hate glazing over any type of tentative respect we had built. He nods once to himself. And I wish for a traitorous, fleeting moment I could take the words back. My breath begins to cloud as the walls are painted in a thin layer of living frost. It grows, slithering across the stones in a thick sheet of sparking white hoarfrost.

He looks at me like I am the worst kind of poison. And I know I should not care. Not when there is so much I still do not know about how he orchestrated my wicked fate.

But I do.

I do care.

And it is the most painful feeling I have ever had the misfortune of experiencing.

I watch the place I held in his heart freeze over, wither, and die, and something inside me *cracks*. So thoroughly, I worry it will sound through the Kingdom, a thunder so violent it will shake even the clouds and coasts of the mortal world.

He steps forward, towering over me. In a deadly whisper, he says, "Do not think for one second that I am following you around this palace because I have fallen for you like some love-sick puppy. I have real responsibilities. I have a court without a King and a Queen without a want to rule. And yet, I am *here*, being insulted by a foolish child who is the only hope for the Kingdom." At that, he laughs bitterly, like the universe has told a particularly good joke.

"When I look at you," his eyes are searing, "I see only reasons I should hate you—*ruin* you. I see everything I have lost and continue to lose to keep a dying Fae's last wish. Do not mistake my actions for fondness. I am chained to you. Do you think I want to be here? Do you think I want to *want* you? And yet, here I stand, as to not forsake the dead."

He looks broken. *So broken*. And for the first time, so very young. A boy, not yet a man, who has lost too much. Who is desperate to hold onto something—the expression is a mirror I wish to turn from.

"So please swear you do not want my help—*say it*. Set me free from the madness of your company." His tone turns pleading—eyes searching mine for what, I do not know. "And do what you do best and *run*. Run before I do something that cannot be undone." His eyes fall to my lips for a second before they fall closed.

"If I were smarter," he mutters, leaning in so his lips brush my ear, "I would have let you run that night in the passageway, let you doom your own fate. You would be so much less work *dead*."

The words are cruel. I feel them in every part of my body. They shred my soul, shatter my glass heart—they *ruin* me. More than any of the other cruelties thrown at me because they come from his lips.

"I hate you," I whisper.

He studies me, pride gleaming in his eyes as he runs his hands down my arms, trailing gentle fingers across my wrists. My body betrays me, and my skin heats. It takes all of my self-control not to arch into his touch. Not to wrench my arms free and wrap them around him or shove him away.

I do not realize what he is doing until it is far too late.

His fingers close around my invisible ronan berry charmed bracelet, and my heart stops. Time slows. And he tears it from my wrist, ripping with it the last of my trust in him, my best intentions, my shattered heart.

One final, *killing* blow.

"No," I breathe, but it is too late.

"*Who helped you escape the wedding?*" Raven's voice is thick with the sweetest venomous-honey-thick compulsion and the deepest, heart-wrenching betrayal.

I try to resist as the compulsion digs its ecstasy-dipped claws into my mind, ripping down my walls, wishes, and will. And though only one word escapes my traitorous lips, so much of me is torn with it.

"May," I choke.

Raven's smirk is cruel, wicked, *mean*. As painful as a slap. As loud as bridges burning and collapsing. As final as a cold body in the ground that will never rise again.

And all I feel is *stupid*. Naive.

I learned a long time ago that the people you trust the most will always hurt you. And more than anything, in this moment, I wish Raven had proven me wrong. Proven, I had not needed to be protected—not from him.

A senseless wish.

I want to be furious but instead I am broken. We both know he did not need my confirmation. We both know he already knew the answer. And yet, he chose to cross a line so final, so brutal, simply because he *could*. Because he wanted to hurt me. Hurt me as I hurt him.

And he did.

I hope he feels successful. Victorious.

I hope it is everything he wanted it to be.

He says nothing as he rips the gold medallion from my pocket, running it through the trail of blood still dripping down my neck. I want to tell him he does not need it to open the tunnels from the inside, but my throat has closed, lodged itself shut with my hemorrhaging heart. He scoops up his faelight, activates the door to the passageway, and tosses the medallion down at my feet as he exits.

He leaves me pinned to the wall by his ice, the only thing still keeping me standing, alone in the dark.

He does not look back.

The cuffs take hours to melt. Stuck down here, unable to track the rising of the sun that I am certain has passed, all I can do is ruminate on what I have done—what he has done. How undoable and final what happened here is.

I wish I could leave it all behind, hidden in this passageway, a secret to exist only within the confines of these walls. I wish I could erase his words, his actions.

Mostly, I wish I could be in the arms of my sister. Crying while I tell her all about a boy and my broken heart. While she consoles me and runs her fingers through my hair. Planning devious pranks to get revenge on him until I am laughing. Until I am feeling human again.

But I refuse to acknowledge how badly I miss her. How alone I am. How a great deal of the reason I am alone is my fault.

Another part of me wants to lie down in this tunnel and never get up. But I will. I always do. Even when I want nothing more than to falter, I will push myself to my feet and fight. It is the only thing I am still certain of.

I will survive this as I have survived all that has come before.

Eventually, my hands free. I rub my aching wrists and curse at the pain throbbing down my arms. As I rip a piece of my skirt into two strips, tying them around my bloody wrists, one question nags me. *How did Raven find me?* I think of how he reacted when I demanded he tell me. How his fingers trailed my neck... and a sinking feeling fills my stomach.

I need to find May.

It takes me almost an hour to find the key on the floor of the passageway in the blackness without a faelight, but I eventually make it back to our hideout.

And that is where I wait. Hoping that May comes before she is caught by Raven. Or worse—Amira.

While waiting for May, I stumble onto my mattress, tumbling into a fitful sleep. When I eventually wake, the room is dark, and my stomach is hosting a riot. I must have forgotten to eat with the chaos of yesterday. I wonder if it's not the first time... My cheeks are hollower than they were months ago—I am hollower.

I look at myself in the mirror and find I do not like the girl I see staring back.

I quickly wash the cuts on my wrists, the water stinging. I examine the countless puncture wounds before wrapping them tightly with clean fabric.

I feel everything and nothing as I move out of the bathing chamber, scooping up some rations and filling my stomach with dried meat and cheese. I would kill for some real, warm food. Perhaps I can steal some from the kitchens later.

May arrives soon after, huffing. I startle as she rushes into the room, slamming the door shut before pressing her back against it, grinning like mad. I stare for a moment before setting my food aside and jumping up to pull her into a tight hug.

A surprised laugh tumbles from her lips. "I know I am wonderful, but you are never this happy to see me," she teases, squeezing me back.

"I am so glad you are alright," I breathe, lost in a labyrinth of her blonde hair. It falls in front of her eyes in a golden curtain, and she blows it out of her face.

I take a step back, searching her flushed features for any sign of how she is going to take what I say next. I swallow three times and force the words out.

"Raven knows."

May smirks. *Smirks.* I blink.

"About time," she says, planting her hands on her hips as she rolls her eyes. "I was beginning to believe he had lost his touch. Perhaps you are a more delectable distraction than I first believed," she says with a smile, but it falters, her arms wrapping around her middle as she sways. "Amira is going to be *so* angry."

The drop in her demeanor does not last, though, her lips twisting into a scheming smile.

"Though I am certain I can find a way to encourage her prompt forgiveness. I can be very convincing," May declares. "Raven, however, will be much harder to break. He is as stubborn and unmoving as his ice palace, I swear it."

"May! So not the time," I hiss, swatting her. "How can you be so nonchalant? You have angered the most powerful Prince in Elphyne."

"I can assure you, with Amira, it is always the time." She winks, and I flush, wrinkling my nose.

"May. I beg you to be serious for a moment. Raven is furious. Are you not concerned?"

"Why? Because he is '*the most powerful Prince*,'" she mocks. "That title is not impressive. I am the most powerful *Princess* in Elphyne." She looks me up and down. "Well, I was until you... but no one seems to take stock of such before angering me. It would not be the first time, nor will it be the last, I find myself on the receiving end of a powerful ruler's fury. You, too, mighty mortal, have angered many."

"You are all too correct. I fear we excel at it." I chuckle.

"It is a talent, is it not?"

"I do not know if I would call it such. I seem to do it so effortlessly."

"Is that not the definition of talent?" May grins a little wildly. "With an eternity to practice, we shall be able to ignite a war with a single spoken word."

I shake my head at her, smirking. "I do not know how you managed to convince anyone that you are a delicate little flower Princess."

"I told you, I can be very convincing." May flutters her eyelashes, the picture of false innocence as she presses her hands together in front of her.

I choke on my laugh, rolling my eyes at her little act. "You look ridiculous."

"Ridiculously *delicate*. It is disgusting." She shudders. "I am far too good at it."

My good sense returns. "May, this means you cannot walk freely. They will not have you in The Winter Court... or in Spring. Even here, you must behave with an abundance of caution. Raven will be looking for you. Amira likely already is."

"You forget yourself. I am capable of handling myself."

"I know. I know. Just... Raven is... I am not certain *mad* is the correct word," I sigh, running a hand through my curls. "I swear I did not tell him anything... willingly."

May's face pales, her bright pink cheeks draining of colour. "He did not!"

I prickle, renewed shame settling in my gut. "He did... and oh, how I wish he did not." I throw my hands over my face. "He used compulsion and then said he wished I was dead."

"I should kill him for this," May responds fiercely.

I drop my hands, seeing her murderous expression. I worry I may need to restrain her so she does not go and hunt down Raven. But she looks at me, and something in my expression causes her to pause.

"It is alright, Willa. I am forever grateful that you chose to protect my name regardless. I am sorry he said that—and did that. Give him time. He did not mean it," May assures, taking my hands in her own with a reassuring squeeze. "He... there is so much more to him. To his story. So much you do not know... He did not mean it."

"Faeries cannot lie, May. He would not have been able to *say* it if he did not *mean* it," I mutter, shutting my eyes tight when they burn.

If you are not my ally, you are my enemy, Willa.

You would be so much less work dead.

Why would I desire the forgiveness of my enemy?

My eyes open just in time to see May's flare with anger as she examines my wrists, unbinding them.

"I will make him hurt for this. For hurting you," she whispers under her breath.

"It is not as if I did not deserve it," I mutter.

"What happened? You need to tell me *everything*," May demands.

I hesitate but May narrows her eyes, and I can tell she is not going to let this go. So, I tell her—I explain what Raven did. She listens with rapt attention, glancing sadly at my wrists before moving to heal them with her healing magicks. It flares over the cuts, metallic magick filling the air.

"Enough about that particular crisis. It seems we have another. Actually, we have quite a few..." I sigh. "If you did not already know all of this already, why do you look as if you ran across the Kingdom with a swarm of angry bees on your tail?"

May laughs, the sound bright and grounding. "Well, I knew someone was trailing me. It took a great deal to lose them. I am not certain if it was one of Raven's spies or Viktoryn's or even my parents." Her face scrunches. "But someone knows I was where I ought not to be."

"What a long list of enemies we have gathered. Are you certain you lost them?" I ask, eyeing the door wearily.

"Incredibly certain. I have spent most of my life hiding and sneaking. I am nothing if not the master of a double life." She winks. "Where do you think I learned all I know if not in secret?"

I shake my head, envious of her ability to be constantly positive—to smack into a brick wall of bad news and bounce off unscathed. She seems to exist in an endless well of sunshine, only ever eclipsed in darkness for a breath. I wish I was more like her in that regard.

"Fair point." I twist my hands together, gathering courage. "So... Raven said something... the day of the wedding."

I should have killed Archer and Viktoryn the moment I realized they had followed me to the Caprimore sisters' home all those years ago.

"Oh." May stiffens, shifting on her feet and conjuring a flower. "You heard that?"

I nod. "What did he mean?"

"It is not my place to share. But I will tell you what I can, in good conscience. What is common knowledge in Elphyne. Raven's family was close to your own. Queen Valda met your father, William, through Raven's father. He was his most trusted guard. When your father had to flee with you and your sister, The Winter King, Edur, went with you to ensure your safe passage to the mortal world."

She pauses, watching me for a reaction. When I do not give her one, she continues, "Queen Valda distracted the Goldynlockes to give you time to escape, forfeiting her own life... But so did King Eldur. Raven caught wind of this plan and followed in the shadows. He watched his father die at the hands of the Goldynlockes to protect your family, and he held him in his final moments as you escaped. I am assuming the promise he is speaking of was to his father. But I know not of what the promise was," May says, a pained expression on her face. "I wish he did not blame you. We have all lost at the hands of the Goldynlockes."

I nod as a bead of guilt grows in my heart. I wish he never had to watch as his father died, binding him to a promise he did not wish to keep. A promise that has caged him to me in some way.

But I did not ask for his help until he forced it upon me. I never wished for a Prince to come and save me. I do not need a Knight in shining armour—I *am* one. And I will not feel responsible for the actions of a monster when I was but a child.

I am done letting people—Folk or mortal—make me feel less than. I empathize with his loss, but May is right. We have *all* lost something at the hands of the Goldynlockes. I, too, lost my father at their hands.

I will not carry the weight of those lives when I did not take them. When I was too young to understand the politics of power surrounding me. And if he needs someone to blame, if he needs me to be his villain, *fine,* but I will not carry the weight of that title with shame. I will not be a monster simply because he believes me one. But I also will not roll over and hand my birthright to the Goldynlockes.

For if Raven and I agree on anything—whether we are allies, enemies, or nothing at all to each other—it is that the Goldynlockes need to pay for what they have done.

With trepidation in my stomach, I lead May to the tunnel from the evening prior. Following only the hunch formed in my stomach that night.

I think Raven unknowingly showed his hand. I need now only to prove myself right.

I lean down to scoop up the necklace Raven gifted me, the one I purposefully left behind. I hold it up to May. Her faelight reflects the red and orange gemstones in the sun and moon design, sending spirals of gleaming light dancing across the stones.

"Could a necklace or a gem be spelled to be a tracker of sorts? I asked Raven how he found me, and he refused to answer, yet he toyed with this necklace. A necklace he gifted me only hours prior to the wedding. I think he knew I was up to something," I mutter, staring at the necklace as if it has grown teeth. "I fear he always seems to know when I am up to something."

"Well, that is not difficult. You are always up to something," May says as she takes the necklace, rolling the gems between the pads of her fingers.

"Not always," I reply, and she gives me a look. "Alright, almost always."

May grins, but my eyes fall back to the necklace in her hands, and I try not to think about the confusing feelings I have about it. When Raven had gifted it to me... it had been the nicest thing anyone had ever given me. One of the *only* things anyone had ever given me. If it had all been a lie, a tri–

"It has been spelled," May confirms.

My stomach sinks.

"I can feel traces of magicks," she continues, "but I cannot say for certain the spell... it does, in hindsight, seem likely it was a tracking spell. Personal objects can be spelled to show one's location... I would question why he did not use it sooner, but I warded our hideout against tracking magicks. The spell would have been disabled by the wards I placed to keep the room hidden. It makes sense that he was able to follow you to Viktoryn's room once you were outside the wards, though," May explains, shaking her head with amusement. "That sly, *sneaky* little Prince. It is smart, I will give him that."

Anger swells inside me as I squeeze my hands into fists. "Unbelievable," I snarl but cannot help but be a little impressed—at his nerve, at my own deduction.

Well played.

"What do you wish to do with it?" May questions, still fiddling with the gems.

I smile viciously.

May smiles back, eyes brightening as she takes in the look of pure trouble on my face.

If Raven wants to play, game on.

16

After changing into a fresh stolen maid's uniform and leaving May in the hideout, I sneak into a busier part of the Palace. I keep my head down and my eyes lowered, but no one seems to pay much attention to the mortal servants.

The other servants I pass have an odd glaze to their eyes. When I bump into one, they hardly react. As if floating through the halls like wraiths, stuck in a haze of emptiness.

A few more pass me before I cannot help myself. I pull aside a young mortal woman with short brown hair and too-wide brown eyes, pressing her into a darkened alcove. The young woman does not resist, staring lifelessly at the ground.

"I am to report to the kitchens to help prepare for supper," she mumbles under her breath. "I am to report to the kitchens to help prepare for supper."

Horror rises in me as I recognize her. *Jenny.* One of the girls who went missing from Mayfair. From Fabelle's school. Only days before Fabelle herself went missing. No older than fourteen.

I feel sick.

"Jenny? Are you alright?" I whisper, shaking her shoulders slightly until she meets my eyes.

"I am to report to the kitchens to help prepare for supper," she repeats, her voice quiet and frail. An empty shell encased in human flesh.

"Alright, alright," I soothe, rubbing her upper arm calmingly. "You can do that in a moment. Do you know where you are? How you got here? Do you recognize me? You were in classes with my sister, Fabelle. I am Willa, we have met before," I mutter, searching her eyes for any sign of recognition, but they remain glazed and distant.

"I am to report to the kitchens to help prepare for supper. I am in the hallway. You are like me. We are not to use our true names. True names cause pain. Excuse me," she murmurs distractedly, moving around me and out into the hall.

And then she is off.

I consider following her. Finding a way to sneak her out of this place. Return the light stolen from her eyes. But I do not know how she has been spelled or how to remove the magicks. And I have nowhere to take her. We cannot return to Mayfair without fear of time catching up to us. Even if I knew *how* to return to Mayfair. And if I am caught...

I stand in the shadows of the alcove while a slimy feeling imbeds itself in my bones. I did not know Jenny well, but we had spoken on occasion. She *should* have recognized me.

I begin to wonder if all the mortal servants with lesser duties are spelled, drugged, or compelled in some way to keep them compliant—mindless.

I think back to Alice and Beatrice, the servants I was given when I was locked here in The Ember Palace. They showed no signs of being spelled or corrupted in any way. But I wonder now if that was on *purpose*. That it was decided that I should not see how the Fae truly treat the vast majority of mortals they keep as servants.

They needed my cooperation, and Viktoryn would have known that if I had knowledge of mortals being kept here and mistreated, I would have fought even harder.

I wish I could break every single mortal free from this place. The thought is wild, reckless.

Yet... if I did, *hypothetically*, take the throne... I could fix this. Stop the Fae from taking humans from the mortal lands as brides or servants. Stop the corruption that grows from the ground like rotting moss, covering everything and everyone.

I am shaken from my thoughts by the chatter of guards down the hall. I gather my focus, chiding myself for standing outside the wards with the tracker in hand. *Foolish.* I force myself forward.

After getting turned around three times, I find the messenger's office blissfully empty. Stacks of paper stand in endless rows like a miniature village of crooked houses. I wonder how they manage to keep track of it as I scan the ten or more tables in the tight rectangular room.

I slip an envelope onto one of the many tables of what I assume is outgoing mail. I smirk to myself as I turn to head back to my room. But I halt as I hear Viktoryn's and another male's voices.

I spin, looking for somewhere to hide as my heart rages against my chest, palms slick with sweat. I spot a desk in the far corner and break into a silent sprint. Ducking down, I slip myself underneath the desk. Wedging myself under the wood, I squeeze my eyes shut, focusing on slowing my breathing and heart rate, a hand pressed over my mouth. Quietly, I activate the key so that it will muddle my scent.

"Greetings, Your Highness. I did not expect you until later. I assume you have come to collect your seal—the ring, yes?" He must nod. "Very well. It showed up here last evening."

"What a senseless act to try and frame a Prince! I cannot comprehend how they even managed to take such a thing. The ring never leaves my hand. I allow no one close enough to rid me of it. And stranger yet, I cannot find the sense in mailing it back. Why steal it if not to keep it?" Viktoryn says.

I do not fight the smile that slips onto my lips. May slipped it off his hand at one of their forced dinners. A bit of good coming from her parents' unshakable insistence that she get to know her future *husband.*

"It is odd, Your Highness. Alas, I do not claim to know the minds of criminals."

Boots scuffle on the floor, and my smile falters. Who I assume is the messenger rounds the table near inches from me, digging through piles of paper on the desk.

I sink into myself, holding my breath, as a letter slips off the table, plummeting from the ground an inch from my foot.

I lean forward, reaching for the envelope, attempting to push it closer to the messenger, when a longer-fingered hand appears, patting the ground.

I snatch my arms away and wrap them around my knees to make myself smaller. His hand explores the stone, searching, but he misses.

And continues to miss.

If this is how I get caught...

He bends lower, one arm braced on the table. The weight of his body causes the table to creak viciously above me. My heartbeat hammers in my ears. I resist a flinch, squeezing my eyes shut as his hand brushes my boot.

Once, twice.

"What is–"

"Whatever is taking you so long? I have places to be," Viktoryn snaps, murmuring something about incompetence under his breath.

The messenger rises to mutter his apologies and then bends down *again*.

I want to kick him.

He continues to pat everywhere but the letter. Cursing, he bends even lower. *An inch more, and I will be discovered.*

I slowly snatch my dagger out from the hidden slit in my skirts, preparing to strike and run.

But his hand *finally* closes on the envelope, and he lets out a sigh, straightening. I do not dare to breathe until he begins his trek back towards Viktoryn.

"Here it is, Your Highness. The envelope was plain. No address. Somehow sealed with your own ring... I am afraid I was unable to track its origin," the messenger relays.

Viktoryn sighs dramatically as the messenger scuffles away. "Useless, the lot of you. I am beginning to fear I am the only being in this entire Kingdom that possesses a shred of competency."

A few beats of tense silence follows.

"Indeed, Your Highness. We are under your guidance. Now, I must get back to work if there is nothing else I can do to assist you," the messenger says, tone tight.

Viktoryn does not seem to notice.

"Yes, yes. Do whatever it is you do," Viktoryn drawls dismissively. "I must attend to a prisoner in the dungeons... Perhaps torturing the wretched Troll will lessen the foul mood I have found myself in."

The messenger says his farewells as he stuffs his bag full of letters and rushes from the room, leaving me alone with Viktoryn.

Viktoryn immediately starts grumbling to himself under his breath, followed by the sound of a fist striking a wall.

"First, that stupid mortal mutt escapes me *again*, then my royal seal is stolen, then those marigolds..."

I smile, a fist pressed to my lips to suppress my laugh.

I shall have to congratulate May on her brilliance. She *may* have mentioned to Fredrick, the mortal-hating head of guards in Raven's Inner Circle, that his orders may have changed. And that he should most definitely stand in the perfect spot to be captured with a bow and set of arrows identical to the ones used in the attempt on Prince Archer's life.

May had her own reasons for wanting revenge on the Troll. But I was happy to frame him simply for suggesting that my and my sister's lives were worth nothing more than dust.

Better yet, Amira mentioned to May that she believed Fredrick was the one to allow Viktoryn into The Crystal Palace the night he strangled me. Which, as Fredrick *was* the head of guards for The Crystal Palace, makes an awful lot of sense. I swore I would make those who crossed me suffer. And I will make good on that claim.

One scheme at a time.

Dawn is a few hours off but the moon shines brightly, casting the garden in an eerie but dazzling silver glow. Placed periodically around the main path stands poles that are tipped in yellow glowing faelights.

"You truly think we can sneak out of the Palace without being noticed?" I ask May quietly as we peer out of one of the tunnels that lead to the exterior of the Palace.

May eyes me with exasperation. "I am insulted," is all she offers as reassurance before she turns back to study the gardens. "Guards round in two. Once they pass that bush–" She points to a bush shaped like a life-sized Prince Viktoryn, gaudy crown and all.

I roll my eyes. "I pity the poor soul that has to shape and maintain that perversion of nature," I interrupt her, wrinkling my nose. "Someone should do all of us a favor and burn that down."

May chuckles quietly. "We shall add it to the list. Now, focus. Once they pass the bush, we will be hidden from view for ninety seconds. Understand? Ninety, no more."

I nod.

"Brilliant. Then, all we must do is cross the garden, scale the wall, and slip into the trees on the other side without being noticed. It is simple. Child's play," May says with a smile, hands planted confidently on her hips.

When she sees my face, she laughs.

"Child's play," I repeat uncertainly.

She shoves me back into the shadows of the tunnel as the guards round the corner. I stumble into the wall, scraping my elbow with a soft curse. I shoot her a glare as my heart begins to beat with anticipation, and adrenaline rushes through my veins.

The guards dip out of view, and we are off, sprinting into the gardens. We pass the bush, which I glare at as we take a sharp left turn that has me scrambling to stay on my feet. The night air is cool but clings to my skin, humid from the nearby sea.

We reach the outward stone wall that sprawls several feet in the air, and May begins to scale it with practiced grace. Her long blonde hair reflects the moonlight down her back as she uses the indents in the stone to ascend.

I am all too aware of the clock ticking down as I force my hands into the indents and attempt to follow her path. She is up and over the wall before I even reach the halfway point.

"Make haste!" she hisses from the other side as if it will magickally make me climb faster.

It does not.

Huffing, I reach for an indent but fail to find purchase, feeling around blindly, my hands scrape across the rough stone. I find a hold and heft myself up again and again. I reach for another indent, my hand closing around the rock, but the stone begins to crumble beneath my palm.

I lose my grip, slipping, my weight baring down on my shoulder. I swallow a yelp of pain as I hang from the wall by one arm.

Ignoring the scream in my shoulder, I force my hand into a new hold and place my feet back on the wall. My heart batters against my chest and rushes in my ears. I grit my teeth, finally finding another hold.

Right as footsteps sound around the corner, I slip again, my hands ripping open on the jagged rock, flesh tearing. I bite my lip hard, swallowing a cry as blood spills from my palms, leaving them slick.

"Did you hear the rumors? About the lost heir?" a deep-voiced male guard chatters, only a moment from rounding the corner.

"Do not speak of such. The Prince has declared such nonsense treason," another chirpy voice adds.

"No! Not treason!" Another sputters.

My arms tremble, but the top of the wall is within my sight. I will strength into my muscles, flipping as I toss my body over the side. I land with an undignified grunt.

"Did you hear that?" a guard asks as May half-drags me into the cover of the dark forest before my feet even fully find the ground.

"Sir Merrick warned that some of the forest beasts have been..." The voices fade as we reach the treeline.

Out of view, May stops, and I fall to my knees, huffing hard. I wipe my bleeding hands on my breeches. I blow stray hair out of my face as I peer up at May, who appears as if the sprint and climb were a mere leisurely walk. She lazily leans against a tree, twirling her hair with her fingers, eyes gleaming with amusement. A taunting grin is plastered on her lips.

"Cutting it awfully close there, mighty mortal," May teases, pushing off the tree to help me back to my feet.

I grit my teeth as my wrecked palm meets hers, but healing magicks flare instantly, and the sting cools.

Still, I narrow my eyes on her. "First off, I am taller than you."

"Barel–"

I hold up my finger to halt her. "Second," she smirks, "I do not regularly break out of palaces and scale walls for fun. Third, I am not blessed with fancy immortal Fae agility and strength," I snark. "*And* I still cannot see in the dark!"

"Sore loser. You look like a tree creature," May chuckles, moving to pull rogue twigs from my hair.

"Oh goody," I huff, then peer around at the dark forest surrounding us. "What now?"

"You shall see."

Without another word, she takes off briskly into the darkness, not checking to see if I am following. I huff out an annoyed breath and follow.

Every shadow has me on edge as I recall all of the nightmare creatures Raven warned me lurk in these woods, hunting mortals and Fae alike.

I shiver as my mind pictures all sorts of dreadful creatures of claws and teeth and rot.

Tall trees sway in the gentle summer winds, casting moonlit shadows across the mossy forest floor. Glowing-winged pixies the size of large butterflies zip through the air, weaving between trees as they play, giggling quietly. They leave a mist of glimmering sparkles in their wake.

I feel a tug on my hair, and I squeal. I bat the little beast away, and it slips me a serpentine smile, tittering as it disappears into the foliage.

We reach a clearing where two large saddled horses as dark and mighty as the night itself stand. Their manes look like woven silver starlight dancing on an invisible breeze. Fascination floods me.

May turns around, hands on her hips, smiling smugly. "Never should have doubted me."

"Not bad," I drawl, impressed.

"Not bad? I am brilliant," she declares. "I stashed them here last night. Once you told me your plan."

"Where did you find such impressive beasts?" I question. "They are magnificent." I move to pat them both on the nose, and one huffs, nudging its nose into my palm.

"Stole them."

I halt, blinking at her. "From whom?"

"Raven."

I choke out a laugh. "You did not."

"Did too." May shrugs, grinning. "It is the very least he deserves for what he did to you. Plus, they are his favorites. Night Stalker and Death Curse." She rolls her eyes. "He was a young boy when he named them. Who sees a beast this radiant and thinks, 'Ah, yes, I shall call you *Death Curse*'?"

"Boys," we chime in unison, sending us both into a fit of giggles.

I study the horses, grinning. "Very impressive... You are a good friend, May."

May's eyes soften, a gentle vulnerability under the surface as she beams like I have handed her the sun.

"I am not as good as you wish. However, I am delighted to help." May worries her bottom lip.

Her voice is quieter when she continues, "It can be exhausting to have to hide pieces of who I am. It is invigorating to be able to fully embrace my skills with someone other than Raven's Inner Circle. To prove I am worth more than my hand in marriage," May states, her eyes meeting mine again. "To have someone choose me to be their ally, simply because of who I am and what I can do..."

"I work for Raven because of Amira. He never would have asked me to join if it was not for her. They all have this," she motions her hands in the air, creating a circle, "special bond. I am forever glad they have found it, found each other. But I will always be an outsider. I will never be *one* of them. I was not forged in the same flames. I did not grow beside them as they did each other... And that is alright. But now..." May studies me for a second. "This feels close, this feels like real friendship. With you, I can be me—all of me."

I pull her into a hug, my throat burning. "Me either," I confess. "You are worth endlessly more than your hand. I would have never been able to pull any of this off without you—your knowledge and resourcefulness. More than that, more than what you can offer, I am proud to call you my friend. You have nothing to prove to me, May. I see your strength. From the moment you stared down The Siren Princess with unwavering command. I saw you. Admired you."

May holds me tighter and I feel in that embrace how much she needed to hear those words. Even as my skin crawls a bit with the vulnerability, I am glad they mean something to her. That *I* mean something to her.

"Always allies, forever friends," she whispers like a vow, and I smile brightly.

"Always allies, forever friends," I echo her words, hoping beyond hope they remain true.

Horse hooves clomp over the intricate arched wooden bridge as we cross over a raging river into The Spring Court. May leads the way, and I urge Death Curse to follow.

"Where are we going?" I ask.

"It matters not. Just remember these rules, and you will be fine. The trees will reach for you; do not allow them to grab you. They will scream, wail, and sing. If you hear something calling your name, no, you do not. Do not look. Do not flinch. Keep your head down and your feet forward."

"What happens if I break one of those rules?"

"Let us not find out," May says darkly.

The landscape begins to change, gnarled roots obscuring our path as the ground turns from plush moss to a substance like ash.

Death Curse rears up, whinnying nervously. I pat the horse's neck, trying to steady the animal even though I do not feel steady in the least.

May navigates the treacherous ground with ease, and I do my best to imitate her path.

"Here we are," May mutters. "Welcome to The Wailing Woods."

The shift in the air is instant, ominous. Gray, oppressive fog descends on us, creeping towards May and me through the trees. The land buzzes with a presence that can be felt in each step—something haunting and ancient.

These lands do not belong to us.

As the fog reaches me, it wraps around my limbs with an almost-sentient awareness, my skin tingling. The scent of rot and decay assault my senses. I raise my arm to cover my nose from the smell.

"You get used to it," May remarks, watching me with a playful smirk.

She barrels forward without fear, even when the trees quickly shift from tall and thin to thousands of huge, near-touching willows. Their long, claw-like branches are carpeted in leaves that brush the ground. Some are so dense their trunks are obscured from view. They vary in colour, from midnight black to petrified gray to bone white. The leaves are a void black that swallows light, shifting with the shadows.

Goosebumps explode on my skin as the wind whistles a final warning before the forest is blanketed in silence.

The branches begin to reach out, brushing against the horse's legs, causing them to whinny and rear up. I pat my hand on Death Curse's neck and whisper soothing words, but the branches begin to weave up my arms.

"May."

"It is alright. Do not stop moving," she warns from ahead.

The hair on the back of my neck rises. And I suddenly feel as if I am being watched by millions of eyes. The trees soon become too thick to wade through on horse, and we dismount.

May finds a relatively open place to tie them off before whispering to me that they may be dead when we return, a notion she shrugs off. Like it is not a horrifying idea but a very likely inevitability. I open my mouth to protest, but she is already stalking away.

The path disappears into an endless wall of thick, menacing willow trees. Nothing but a labyrinth of branches hangs before me. A sharp knot forms in my throat, and I swallow as my fear becomes a noose around my neck.

"This way," May beckons as she slips her arm into the branches to part them. They coil eagerly around her limbs, and she curses softly.

I pull out my dagger to slice her free.

A mistake.

The *wailing* starts.

Shrieking and sobbing surround us—a keening chorus of a thousand voices, young and old, feminine and masculine. From everywhere and nowhere. Worse yet, the chorus contains *children*.

I press my hands to my ears as the sound rips into my skull. May looks at me with an apologetic smile, shrugging a little guiltily. She waves for me to follow. I blink at her as if she has lost her mind, wishing for nothing more than to flee back to our horses as terror grips me so tightly that I worry my spine will burst from my body.

I continue to cut a path through the trees as they attempt to restrain me. One even ambitiously wrapping around my torso. Rough and sharp, they snag my body, waiting for me to make a mistake so they can pull me away to become a part of their haunting chorus.

It takes everything in me not to yelp as a branch hungrily loops itself around my neck. Suddenly, I am being yanked back. My palms hit the ground, slamming into the soot-like substance. I claw my fingers into the soil, trying to find purchase as I fight to maintain my grip on my dagger. But it is no use—I am dragged towards the trunk. The very truck that meets my eyes with eyes of its own.

In the center, made entirely of bark, is a mortal. Or what was once a mortal. It screams, bark cracking as teeth and lips of midnight black part. I scream back.

Branches snake greedily towards me as the one around my neck tightens. I slice through the branch at my neck. It falls lifelessly to the ground, shriveling.

I leap to my feet, pivoting just in time to slice the branches headed for my ankles. I dive back out onto the path and cling to the back of May's body as the cries turn to anguished screams that rattle my very bones.

"May... there is someone in that tree..."

I hold onto the back of her tunic like she is a boat in this angry ocean of branches. She glances over her shoulder.

"I know," she answers.

"You *know*."

"Of course."

I consider tossing her into the trees and trying my luck alone. But another branch lurches for me, dodging my blade, and she cuts it away. And I decide she can stay. For *now*.

We continue to force our way forward. Just as I begin to adjust to the noise, the horror—the forest quiets. The trees sharing a single held breath.

"*Willa*! Help me! Please!" I hear Fabelle scream—as if her body is being eviscerated, her sobs echo around me. "Willa! *Help*!"

I am moving towards my sister before I can think. I rush through the trees, slicing in wide, panicked arcs as they reach for me with renewed aggression. It is as if they can sense my dread and desperation, drinking it down in greedy gulps, impatiently wanting to consume it whole.

I dash around a bend in the path, and branches cut slashes into my skin. Each burn as if filled with poison.

"Willa! Help me, please!"

I sprint down a small opening between the trees, closer and closer towards her voice. My muscles scream from exertion as I force my legs to pump harder, leaping over a branch that shoots for my feet. I hit the ground hard, slipping in the sooty substance, but I keep my body upright with pure adrenaline.

"Please, Willa! Help me! Stop, please! You are hurting me!" Fabelle's voice is nearer. *"It hurts!"*

I reach toward the tree I think she is hiding in, parting the branches—her voice is so close. She must be right here.

"I am coming, Fabelle! Grab my han–"

I am yanked backwards, right before I can leap towards the trunk, towards my sister. I scream and fight, but a hand closes over my mouth.

"What did I say?" May hisses, blade to my throat. I swallow. "Do you want to make it out of here alive? That is not your sister! *Think*, Willa! You were moments away from having your soul consumed!"

I still as the frenzied panic and adrenaline begins to dissipate. May's warnings come back to me in a rush.

The trees will reach for you; do not allow them to grab you. They will scream, wail, and sing. If you hear something calling your name, no, you do not. Do not look. Do not flinch. Keep your head down and your feet forward.

I blink as if escaping a heavy fog and begin to relax in her arms. I nod once to show I understand.

Slowly, May pulls her hand away from my mouth as the sound of my sister fades. I suck in painful, gasping breaths as a rogue tear falls from my eye.

"I-I am so–"

"Do not apologize," she snaps as the trees return to their original chorus. Her arms remain wrapped around me as she whispers, "Can I release you?"

I nod again, trembling as my sister's screams still echo in my head.

"It is always hardest the first few times," she says more gently. "We were almost there, but now we are a bit off course. Let me lead you. Do not let go of my hand," she commands, threading her fingers through mine with a grip so punishing it is painful.

"Who do you hear?" I ask as she leads us back to the path.

"I do not wish to speak of it," May replies harshly.

I snap my mouth shut.

The path begins to fan out. The branches less aggressive in their touches as we reach a clearing in which a single tree stands alone.

The forest quiets.

Built in the center of a giant willow tree that is five times as wide and twice as tall as the others is a home. The branches are a pale ivory, the trunk a petrified ash gray covered in carvings of swirling shapes. Thick black moss and deep emerald ivy creep along the trunk. An intricately carved circular door inlaid with precious gems sits in the middle.

I halt as my eyes take in the decor. Hundreds of what look like *human* bones hang from the branches, clinking together like wind chimes in the breeze, creating an eerie rhythmic song. A skull dangles not two feet from the door.

"May are you cer–"

"Keeper of The Weeping Willows, Treefolk of The Forest, I wish to speak to The Wise and Just Ruler of Your Kind, The Consumer of Lost Souls," May declares.

"*The Consumer of Lost Souls?*" I hiss, eyes wide enough to fall out of my head as I bat May hard on the arm. "You failed to mention that the '*friend*' who owes you a favor is a soul consumer."

May rolls her eyes and waves me off, playing with a lock of her hair. "You scare so easily, mighty mortal. I come here with only pure intentions and a clear and free mind," May states as, to my own horror, the trees in the forest all take a full *step* towards us with a resounding *boom*.

"They are alive? They can walk?!" I hiss, dagger in hand, as I spin, waiting for the attack.

May looks judgmentally over her shoulder at me. "All trees are alive."

"Right," I mumble. "But most trees cannot walk or consume your soul or scream to you in the voice of your own sister," I snap, pointing to the branches still reaching for us from outside the clearing.

May sighs, flicking her hair over her shoulder. "Will you settle down? The Keeper and I are friends of sorts. I would not let her or The Treefolk eat you..." She considers me. "*Actually*, if you keep complaining, I might."

"Oh goody," I mock. "When I said I wanted to send Raven on a wild goose chase to somewhere unpleasant, I do not recall requesting a location of soul-consuming trees. An unpleasant bog would have done just fine."

"Your plan was fine. It simply needed a little... *flourish*. My specialty." May gestures to the trees, eyes bright.

"*Flourish*." I grit my teeth. "Alright. Sure. I respect the vision, May. You have really outdone yourself."

May bows overdramatically. "I *am* brilliant."

I shake my head as I laugh, unable to resist the smile creeping onto my lips.

The door of the hut swings open with a resounding creak, abundantly loud in the now-silent woods. I gawk as a tall, spindly being with a body of twisted black bark and glowing milky white eyes steps out.

They have an open, lipless mouth, displaying rows of blackened teeth and a singular slit for a nose. Their long hair is made of void black leaves, and it brushes the ground as they prowl forward. They are horrid and hallowed. With long, thin arms that reach far past their knees, tipped in sharp, curved claws that gleam in the moonlight.

A creature of nightmares.

"Did you bring me a snack, Princess Maylea?" the creature coos.

May just chuckles as The Keeper towers over us, casting long shadows. I fight my instinctual reaction to flee, holding my ground on trembling legs as my heart batters like a perpetual punch to the ribs.

Their eyes find me, gazing intensely like I am prey they cannot wait to devour. When they shift back to May, their expression breaks out into what I assume is a smile. A black, snake-like tongue slips between their lipless mouth.

"It has been too long, dear friend. I was left to wonder if you forgot I was here at all," The Keeper says in a raspy, deep tone. "If I am not to eat your mortal friend, do you bring with you an alternative offering?"

"I could never forget you. But I do fear this is a visit of duty, not pleasure. I have come to request a favour owed," May speaks evenly, shoulders squared, and all at once, I can see the royal blood coursing through her veins.

She steps forward to hand The Keeper a pile of animal bones. They snatch them greedily from her hands.

"Ah yes," The Keeper gestures to me without removing their gaze from May, "I did get this one's messenger."

"Do you mean my message?" I question.

The Keeper's head turns to me, milky eyes pinning me in place as a sickening smile curls over their lips.

"*No*. His soul tasted of terror and thyme." Their tongue darts out as if they can still taste it, and their eyes fall closed with a pleased hum. "You, child—your soul tastes of secrets and shadows, rare and royal indeed." The Keeper points a long, clawed hand at me, and I shrink back from it, grimacing. "I so wish to consume it." They sigh wistfully. "But a favour owed, is a favour owed, Maylea of Spring."

"Perhaps another time," I say, trying to keep the terror from my voice. "My name–"

"Yes, yes, I know your name, child," The Keeper interrupts, brimming with impatience. "I assume you have made the journey as you wish to watch the show. It is not often we get to put on a play for royalty. I shall ensure it to be our best."

The trees rustle behind me as if they are murmuring their agreement. The Keeper bows low, and May follows. I attempt to curtsy with mixed results.

"I am certain it will be delightful," May states diplomatically.

I nod my agreement.

"Very well. Come, children, you can watch from my abode. I have a spelled window." They pause. "Are you certain you want the boy alive?" The Keeper asks, clicking its claws together. "My Folk are so very hungry—not many wander into my woods these days. Certainly not ones with souls so *rich*. The Prince of Shadows' reputation precedes him. Royal blood does sipith the sweetest."

"Alive and mostly unharmed. We do have a point to prove. Aim to maim, not kill. A good scare will do," May chimes, bouncing on her feet in anticipation.

"As you wish. But then we are square, Maylea of Spring," The Keeper states as they lead us into the warmth of their home.

"Square and settled," May agrees.

I hesitate in the doorway of the hut, overcome with the feeling that if I enter, I will never leave. I imagine myself stripped of my soul, a leftover husk in a witch's cauldron, bones swinging from branches.

May rolls her eyes at me, grinning as if she can sense the direction of my thoughts, and beckons to follow. I shake off my terror and step inside, finding the space surprisingly warm, almost cozy.

The home sits inside the hollowed trunk, all dark wood and carved furniture. A welcoming orange glow radiates from a hearth built of bones directly across from the door. The space contains a small kitchen with a bubbling cauldron filled with what appears to be blood.

I move to study The Keeper's shelf, caught in the snare of my own curiosity. I run my fingers over all the small items that line the wood. I spy a small porcelain doll, a frayed yellow hair ribbon, a pair of worn leather shoes with golden buckles, a small pile of finger bones, locks of golden hair, and various necklaces and opulent rings. Hundreds, if not thousands, of these small trinkets sit in endless rows. I notice too late that some are splattered with dried blood.

"I do not only collect the souls of the lost. I am a collector of all kinds," The Keeper purrs.

I swallow and turn. "You have a lovely home."

May snorts a laugh.

I move to her side, unwilling to become one of The Keeper's trinkets or toys. The Keeper gestures to a ladder near the end of the room. May climbs first, and I follow, finding myself in a cramped loft space with a circular window the size of a dinner plate. The fog has begun to clear as the sun crests the horizon, basking the world in peachy glow.

"The window and loft are spelled to be hidden unless I bid them otherwise. I hope our performance pleases you, princesses," The Keeper calls, and I listen to their footsteps slip away.

May and I share a wicked grin, lying side by side on our stomachs. We peer through the window—it must be spelled to be more hidden as it offers a perfect view of the entire forest. It is an impossible visual from where we actually lie.

"Are you certain they will come?" I ask.

"If you are correct about the tracker? I am certain," May says. She studies me for a minute, but I turn away from her scrutiny and back to the window. "You do not see it. Do you?"

"See what?"

May simply shakes her head, biting her lip.

A half-hour later, four sets of hooves sound from the outskirts of The Wailing Woods. Not even waiting for the first blow, The Treefolk begin to wail. I peer out at the endless sea of crawling trees as excitement and nerves twist into a deadly potion in my stomach.

I note how much the trees look like a hedge maze from above. Some spots so thick they could pass for a solid wall. From a safe distance, I can admit they are wondrous and terrifying and terrific.

Four cloaked figures dismount their horses near the edge of the willows. They huddle up and, after a short conversation, begin pushing a path through the branches, weapons in hand.

It is then that I realize the trees were holding back before.

The trees wail with a renewed fever, the sound is *deafening*. They attack relentlessly, wrapping around the figures much more aggressively than they did with May and I. Working as an army to dispatch Raven and his Inner Circle.

As they fight, the Inner Circle's hoods fall back, one by one. I spot Raven's dark curls as he spins and slices in an arc to sever the branches that grip Olden, wrapping around his horns and tangling in his brown hair. Olden glowers, clutching his book bag in one hand and a sword in the other.

Amira fights at Raith's side, her swings meticulous as she forges a path through the severed branches.

Raith bellows in pain as a tree rips his sword from his grip, sending it soaring across the forest floor. The tree wraps around his throat and wrist, slicing his flesh with its razor-sharp leaves.

Raith lets out a wicked laugh as bloodlust overtakes his eyes. He whips two deadly-looking twin axes from his back and begins to hack at his restraints. Blood drips from his brow as he whirls through the trees effortlessly—a God of Battle and Bloodshed. And I know with a sudden certainty why he is Raven's Army Commander.

Amira waits, watching until Raith is free, making no move to help. Then she continues forward, unaffected.

May smiles in her betrothed's direction, staring at Amira like she is the sun, the moon, and all the stars. She feels my attention on her, turning to me, and her smile widens.

"I love watching her in action. The boys like to think they are untouchable, but in truth, Amira could fight circles around them with one hand tied behind her back."

"I can believe that."

She watches me thoughtfully. "Did Raven ever tell you what the other courts call his Inner Circle?" I shake my head. "The Unkind."

"The Unkind?" I chuckle. "What sort of name is that?"

"I know, I know," May snorts. "But a group of ravens is called an unkindness. And they have certainly been unkind at times," May explains.

I am about to ask why. How the group earned such a reputation. What cruelties and crimes left The Folk so marked by The Unkind's actions.

But my attention is pulled back to the fight by a yelp. A string of curses fall from Raven's lips as branches snake around his middle with unparalleled speed, ripping him out of sight.

The Keeper howls with laughter as I suck in a breath. I am worried their hunger has gotten the better of their patience—favour owed or not. I push up on my arms to crawl towards the ladder, but May grips me tightly, shaking her head.

'*Watch*,' she mouths.

I let myself drop, eyes glued nervously to the spot where Raven vanished. The willow branches begin to rustle, and just as I am certain Raven has managed to get his soul devoured, he leaps from the trees covered in severed frosted twigs. The feral gleam in his eyes matches the menacing grin on his lips. My gaze roams over his figure, and I find myself biting my lip. May notices and puffs out a laugh.

"Oh, shush." I bat at her, and she laughs harder.

"Raven, I did not sign up to be sliced apart by Treefolk at dawn for a girl who convinced May to betray us," Amira growls, baring her teeth like a beast as she cuts through willows, her patience apparently fading.

May stops laughing, and I wince.

"Have you yet considered that if Willa wandered here alone, she may no longer be breathing?" she snarks.

"Rude," I huff under my breath.

"Definitely still breathing," May mutters, pinching the sensitive skin under my arm and causing me to squeak. She chuckles.

"Hey!" I hiss, but my lips tip up.

"Just checking," May remarks.

"Please, Amira, have some faith. You have met Willa! She has advanced skill with a bow. And a sword. She would have put up a decent fight before she got her soul consumed," Raith calls out with a dark laugh, tone teasing.

I roll my eyes at his assessment. Glad, at the very least, it is more positive than Amira's.

"Both of you would be wise to shut your mouths, or I will find a sudden, pressing need to feed *your* souls to the trees," Raven hisses through clenched teeth as he shakes the frozen twigs from his curly black hair, sword swinging in his other hand.

Raith eyes Raven a tad wearily. Olden just sighs, his shoulders rising and falling dramatically as he cuts his horns free from the branches for the twentieth time. I cannot help but smile.

Suddenly, I hear my voice screaming for help somewhere within the deepest part of the willows. I nearly slip off the platform, jumping up so high my head collides with the roof. I rub my head while May laughs so hard that she snorts like a prized pig.

I shoot her a look. "That is *so* disturbing... How do the trees steal our voices?"

"The Treefolk are affixed to the souls of all beings who reside in Elphyne. They can connect with their prey and seek out the soul of who they would run to—who they would die for. Then they steal that voice to lead you astray," she explains.

"Creepy," I breathe.

"Brilliant," she replies.

"Willa!" Raven calls desperately. His eyes turn ravenous with rage as he sprints full speed towards the sound of my agonized voice.

"Raven, *wait*!" Amira shouts, stalking after him with a scowl. "You cannot trust what you hear in these woods!" She sighs heavily when Raven does not slow or halt or even seem to hear Amira's warning, much less heed it. "I am surrounded by imbeciles," she hisses.

Raven pushes his body harder, swinging at the attacking branches as he navigates the labyrinth of trees. He skids to a halt as my voice vanishes as quickly as it appeared.

Raven slowly turns in a circle, one ice-crusted hand raised as his eyes scan the trees around him. He looks formidable, unstoppable.

A Prince of Ice and Shadow.

He pauses, eyes meeting mine with such acute accuracy that I worry the spelled window has failed. His eyes hold mine for a moment, and then his gaze returns to the forest, sword shaking as his hand trembles. I expect to feel guilt but I do not.

I know that he only seeks me to balance The Courts. I am a means to an end. Elphyne will be doomed if I die—I am the key to the Goldyn-lockes' downfall. He is not here as my savior. He is here as my keeper. A harbinger of my forced fate.

If Raven wants to be enemies, I will show him what it looks like to be an enemy of mine.

My voice reappears across the forest, and Raven springs back into action, cutting his way across the entire forest, one slithering branch at a time. His chest rises and falls rapidly, his eyes wild and searching.

Amira stands dead still in the center, her face the picture of irritation. Raith seems to be enjoying the action. Olden... not so much.

When my voice switches directions for the fifth time, Amira races to grab Raven's arm, jerking him firmly to a halt.

"It is not her, Raven," Amira snaps. "You utter fool! She is a mortal who could not, even on her best day, move this quickly. Turn your little bird brain on and *think*. The trees are tricking you."

Raven refuses to meet her eyes, his gaze still glued on the spot where my voice is sobbing.

"I have brought her here once before," May whispers. "She would know. They would be wise to heed her words."

He shakes his head as if trying to wake himself from a bad dream. Squeezing his eyes shut, he presses his free hand into his forehead. "I cannot risk it," he confesses hoarsely. "I cannot risk even the smallest of possibilities that it is her."

Wings spring from my stomach and flutter into my lungs. I want to run from him. I want to say I am sorry. I want to get in his face and scream, "*You deserve this!*" I want him to beg for my forgiveness. I want to tell him he is terrible and all I can think about. I want to kiss him. I want to punch hi–

No. No.

I want nothing from him.

"You ignorant, lovesick fool. Get your head on straight!" Amira snarks, knocking him in the side of the head with her palm.

"*Ow!*" he cries out but his eyes clear as he glares at her. "I am your Prince! You cannot smack me aside the head!"

"I can, and I did. Do not make me do it again. I will enjoy it," she threatens. "Now focus, Prince. Let us try an actual plan instead of running about senselessly." Raven glares at her, arms raised to block her hands. "That look? That glare? Hold onto *that*. Do you have the gem? Check where it is leading you."

Raven sighs and runs his free hand through his hair, his rings glinting in the early morning sun. He studies Amira for a moment and then the forest before he calls out to the others.

They all convene in a space barely open enough to call a clearing. They whisper, Raith nodding, Amira standing with her arms crossed, and Olden turning every few seconds to cut away the approaching twiggy limbs. He looks as if he would rather be anywhere else as he protectively cups his book bag.

After a moment, they break, Amira now holding a glowing red crystal above a map, the same red of the gem in the necklace Raven gifted me.

"We were right about the tracker," I murmur, and May nods.

For some reason, I wish I was wrong. I wish that Raven did not do something so... violating. But I should not be surprised—not after what he did in the passageway.

Raven hands his weapons to Raith and shrugs off his black cloak. He leaps into the air, transforming mid-jump into a large black *bird*.

A large black *raven*.

22

"What the–" I mutter, gawking. "Did Raven just turn into a *bird*?"

May looks at me, brows pinched. "Uh... yes? A raven. Like his name-sake? You knew he could do that... right? It is a family trait. Did you not wonder why all his sisters are named after birds? Dove, Robin, Sparrow..." She lists off on her fingers. "Not particularly creative if you ask me, but his father stems from a long line of avian shapeshifters."

"*Shapeshifters?*" I rasp incredulously. "Um, no... I assumed his parents had some kind of unhealthy obsession with birds."

"You did not know? Truly?" May laughs, cupping a hand over her mouth. "It is common knowledge, I assumed..." May trails off when she sees my expression. "I can see this is a shock," she continues, gently patting my arm.

"Can he shift into anything? Could he steal my face and be me?"

May fails to hide her grin behind her hand, amusement swimming in her eyes as she clears her throat. "No. Shifters only have one form, usually an animal. I am unsure why his family is all birds. Raith, for example, can shift into a silver fox. Shapeshifting is a sacred Unseelie magick, a generational one, though it is rare. Amira cannot shift. Neither can Olden or Ricky," May explains. "But Trolls tend to hold fewer magicks in general."

I blink at her, my mouth open as my brain grapples with this new information.

"Huh," is all I manage.

This makes a lot of things about Raven make sense. If he can wield shadows and turn into a bird, it would have been easy for him to hide in the wine cellar that first day we met. No wonder I could not find the escape route he used—there was not one.

"Sometimes I forget how mortal you are." May smirks at me.

I scratch my head, trying to come up with a witty reply, but my mind remains hopelessly blank as I watch Raven—in *raven* form—scour the woods from the sky. His blue-black wings reflect the sunlight as he leads the group towards the hut.

Movement from directly below us catches my eye as The Keeper steps out into the clearing in front of the hut. My necklace glints in the light as it dangles tauntingly between their long claws. They wait for The Unkind's impending approach with a tiny scroll of paper grasped in their free palm.

Amira breaks from the trees and into the clearing first, the gem in her palm glowing brighter as she nears, Raith and Olden behind her. Amira's steps slow, her eyes landing on the necklace dangling between The Keeper's claws.

"I am to deliver a message to The Prince of Shadows," The Keeper states, unaffected, as Amira raises her sword to their chin. The Keeper eyes Amira, unimpressed. "Only The Prince of Shadows. I have no need for his pets."

Amira does not grace the insult with a reply. "Raven," she shouts. A squawk echoes back from the sky. For some reason, I almost laugh. "Tree lady? Tree person?" Amira shrugs. "Has requested your fancy royal presence."

"I am no lady, nor am I a man. I am a being of earth and dust and eternity. Crafted by the Goddesses themselves," The Keeper corrects.

"Ah, pardon me," Amira replies genuinely. "Tree Being of Earth and Dust and Eternity requests your fancy royal presence!" Amira calls, meeting The Keeper's eyes as she raises a brow. "Better?"

"Much," The Keeper says curtly.

Raven dips from the sky, landing and shifting back into his clothed Fae form with a graceful stretch of his limbs. I blink, still dazzled by the bird revelation. Raith hands Raven back his weapons and cloak.

Olden and Raith stand with their weapons aimed at The Keeper, expressions blank as they flank their Prince. Raven shutters his expression, the picture of casual arrogance.

He transforms from bird to Fae to feared ruler in seconds. I am impressed by his ability to switch masks like pairs of shoes.

"I come bearing a message for The Prince of Shadows," The Keeper repeats, dangling the necklace in front of his face, toying with him.

"Very well, kind Keeper. Do tell," Raven drawls, pushing his hands into his pockets after securing his weapons.

The Keeper reaches out their long spindly arm and passes a note to Raven, their claws brushing his skin. He does not recoil or flinch in the slightest, meeting their eyes with a lazy expression so opposing to the panicked frenzy he was filled with moments prior.

Raven reads the note, eyes tracking over the script twice. His jaw ticks as his eyes swim with irritation. There is also a minuscule amount of pride that is drowned out so quickly that I am not sure I saw it at all. The Keeper leaves them, prowling back to their hut, slamming the door in The Unkinds' faces.

Raven clears his throat, daring an uncertain glance at his companions before he speaks.

> This is my official vow freeing you from the madness of my company.
> Keep the necklace—tracking gems are not my preferred dressing style.
> – Willa ~~Capri~~ Caprimore
>
>
> P.S.: You are likely correct that I would be much less work dead. Though I would be far less entertaining.

Raith barks out a laugh, slapping his thigh and earning himself a glare that promises violence from Raven. Olden grumbles under his breath, running a hand across his face.

"What? It is a tad bit humorous. It seems you have incurred the girl's wrath," Raith mutters, shrugging.

Amira's eyes narrow at Raven's back. "What does she mean, Raven? Are you telling me the girl managed to get us all out of bed at the crack of dawn to chase a damn necklace? How did she figure out about the gem, Raven? How did she locate or even gather knowledge about The Keeper?" Amira pauses, eyes calculating. "*Maylea*. That little brat," she snaps, a tad affectionately.

May chuckles, blushing.

Raith smiles and I am again struck by how captivating his grin is. "I told you that you were underestimating her clever mind, Amira. Willa is as sly as a fox. I would know." He winks.

Amira rolls her eyes and punches him in the gut so hard he lets out a pained breath as he doubles over. A wicked grin slides over her features, but she kills it a second before Raith rights himself.

Olden sighs again. "Let me ensure that I am hearing you correctly. Willa has gained knowledge of the tracker and," he gestures to the hut, "disposed of it. She could now be anywhere, and we have no way of knowing her location?" Raven nods a little guiltily. "How did this happen, Raven?"

Raven dodges the question. "I placed a second tracker in her ronan berry charmed bracelet, but I know for a fact that it is no longer in her possession."

My hands ball into fists. I grind my teeth together in irritation as that little fact settles like hot stones in my gut. A second tracker. May and I share a look that proves she is equally unimpressed.

"How do you know for certain that she no longer wears the bracelet?" Olden inquires, rubbing his temples as if he already anticipates he will not like the answer.

"I may have used the gem to locate Willa a few days ago," Raven replies, a blush staining his cheeks. "We needed to have a conversation." At the look Amira shoots at him, he clarifies, "A *private* conversation."

"I was not made aware, as your second or your spymaster, of any missions that included a pending visit to the Caprimore girl," Amira snaps, one hand on her hip, the other on her sword.

"It was need to know," Raven shoots back.

"Oh, of course. Need to know. Alright, Raven." Amira scoffs, securing her sword at her side and crossing her arms. "Let me be *very* clear. Everything you do is need to know. It is my job to know. All of our jobs." She gestures to the others.

Raith and Olden nod in agreement. Raven's eyes narrow on them.

"Your job is what I tell you it is. Your job is to follow and respect my orders. Perhaps I have been too lax," Raven says, tipping his chin back. "This was need to know. And I say that you did not need to know it. Must I remind you that you do not give the orders here, Amira," Raven hisses, turning his full height on his second in command. "Not unless I am dead or otherwise indisposed."

Amira smiles cruelly, like she would be happy to ensure that he is soon dead or indisposed. "Is that so, *Prince*?" She does not yield to his intimidation. Instead, she takes a full step forward until they are standing nose to nose.

The tension between them is tangible, even from a distance. Amira's long black hair sways in the wind, the only movement between the two.

"Did a tree branch hit you in the head while you were flying? I am your second in command. I need to know everything. And the only time you pull rank, Your Highness," Amira states evenly, "is when you are in the wrong or hiding something. Do not try that nonsense with me, with *us*." Amira looks at the group. "It will not stand. We do not keep things from each other. That is one of *your* rules, remember?"

Tension ripples down Raven's shoulders as he continues to hold his ground. In a silent battle of wills, they stand. Raith eventually sighs, clapping Raven on the shoulder and pulling him away. Amira scoffs and stalks off.

"Get it together, boss man. We need a plan," Raith says, his easy smile gone. "Trackers gone. We need to know what happened. What happened with Willa?"

"I shall tell you. But I will not be shamed for doing what I needed to do," Raven starts.

And I laugh. I laugh so hard it hurts. I laugh and laugh and laugh. Because if I do not, I may cry as he echoes words I spoke to him and paid for nights ago.

"You lying little hypocrite," I huff as my laughter dies.

May glances nervously at me.

He clears his throat. "I did indeed follow Willa, corner her, and then... *speak* with her." Raven winces slightly. "To confirm Maylea was working alongside her."

Amira freezes and slowly turns to Raven.

"Why was I not informed?" she demands.

"Why do you think? In this, you cannot be objective," Raven challenges.

"Oh, but you can?"

Raith steps between them. "What do you mean? Spoke to her how?" Raith asks. "What did you do to Willa, Raven?"

"I... Uh..." Raven trails off, shaking his head, lips pressed into a firm line.

"You–uh–what, Raven?" Amira hisses. "Spit it out."

"I may have attempted to *gently*," he holds his hands up before him, "sort of... torture the information out of her. When she did not break, I broke her ronan bracelet and used compulsion... I may have also said something along the lines of... she would be less work dead." Raven grimaces.

Olden shakes his head. He looks so disappointed.

"Hence the note," Raith realizes, running his hands down his face. "She will never work with us agai–"

"Good. She never should have worked with us to beg–" Amira starts.

"Not here," Olden cuts in, forever the voice of reason. "We have already said more than we should. We need to go. But this is not the end of this conversation," Olden says, eyes locked on Raven.

After a tense pause, they begin the treacherous journey back through the willows.

With the tracking gem taken care of, and the horses returned safely to their stables, it is time to enact another plan. But first, I want to do something fun. Something that will free me from the endless looping thoughts of Raven.

A cowardly part of me had begun to wish I had never met him, that I could stop thinking about him all the time. I may have released him from the madness of my company, but my mind refused to release me from his. He had burrowed into my brain like an over-eager earthworm.

For now, I force all thoughts of him away.

Fun was to be had.

My steps slow as I signal to May that the hall is clear. We step into a dank servants' stairway descending to the dungeons. The smell of stale wet stone and unwashed bodies slams my nose.

Reaching the bottom step, I silently push the door open, revealing a long, underground corridor filled with rows of dark, iron-barred cells.

The sound of prisoners moaning and pleading fills the air. I wearily eye my surroundings, trying to drown out the chorus of suffering.

I count the guards as they pass and turn to hold my hand up, indicating four to May. She nods, shoots me a wicked, eager smile, and pushes through the door as if she owns the place. Her steps are effortless and arrogant.

A Queen without a throne.

A Queen who did not need one.

"Hello, pardon," May bellows, tone irritated. "I was to be escorted to the dungeons hours ago!" She saunters deeper into the hall with her chin raised, long skirts brushing the dirty floor.

Atop her head is a flower crown of deep purple lilacs and lavender, her blonde hair flowing straight down her spine and reaching her lower back. She dawns a breathtaking, floor-length lavender gown threaded with white flowers that have been enchanted to close and open, blooming over and over. A never-ending spring.

The guards' eyes widen as they recognize her, and they begin to stutter a whole host of apologies, dropping into bows so low they almost topple. May ignores them, studying her nails.

"Your Highness, our deepest apologies. We were not made aware of your pending arrival," a guard with brassy hair, a thick, crooked nose, and dewy yellow eyes mutters, head bowed in submission.

I watch through the cracked door as the four guards tremble in her presence, and it takes everything in me not to burst out laughing at their sniveling.

"I could have you dismissed for this. I should!" She plants her hands firmly on her hips, and the brassy-haired guard flinches. "I could hang your bodies from the Palace gates! Flay the skin from your bones! You are responsible for guarding those deemed most dangerous to our Kingdom, and yet you do not know of its comings and goings?" I bite my lip as a smile spreads across my face. "Prince Viktoryn would be furious to learn of this."

They all begin to grovel—one even falling to his knees to beg for her mercy. A red-haired guard begins to list all of her most marvelous qualities—a very, *very* long list.

None of them even questioning *why* she is here.

Or if she is supposed to be.

Marvelous.

"You mindless fools. Get up. Kissing the floor will not save your necks. The Prince shall hear of this, but for now, a more pressing matter is at hand." She waits until they have peeled themselves from the ground. "I am looking for a *specific* prisoner," she says slowly, as if talking to a small child. "Take me to where you keep your records this instant."

"Yes, Your Highness. Sir Clide, please remain to guard the halls," the brassy-haired guard says to the redhead, Clide.

May lets her mouth fall open in surprise, a hand pressed delicately to her chest. "Are you *mad*? Absolutely not! You must all come. I do not trust the security of this place after what I have witnessed. Any manner of bandits and hooligans could be hiding in the shadows!" May squeals, contorting her face in disgust, feigning a fearful shudder.

The guard looks as though he wants to insist otherwise, opening and closing his mouth like a trout as he looks between the cells, May, and Clide.

"Now!" May barks, stamping her foot, and they all scatter towards the offices with May in tow.

She winks at me over her shoulder, and I shoot her a wicked grin. They disappear out of sight, and I sneak into the halls, searching each cell for the prisoner *I* came to pay a little visit to. While hoping May can keep the guards occupied looking for her non-existent prisoner long enough to buy me some time to... *play.*

It takes a few minutes—and close to two dozen cells—before I stumble upon the right one.

"Hello, Fredrick," I purr. "Or do I get to call you Ricky now that we are Inner Circle rejects?" I scan the Troll's body. So similar to his twin, Olden, yet with a personality so foul, they could not seem further apart. "I was worried you would be getting lonely down here. I thought you could use some company." I cross my arms over my chest, leaning against the empty cell behind me.

Frederick looks like a cornered beast in the dim lights of the dungeon. When his eyes find mine, he growls a noise so inhuman the hairs on the back of my neck rise. But I do not flinch.

The weeks in the dungeon have done a number on his well-being. I study him lazily as if I have all the time in the world. Taking in the long, unkempt hair, the fresh beard of spiky brown hair that jets from his jaw like a tangle of weeds. The small cell is not much to look at—stone, iron bars, and straw scattered across the floor and a bucket.

"You fucking bitch! Mortal mutt!" he snarls, and I smile wider. "I know what you did! You and that little Spring whore framed me. When I get out of here, I'm go–"

"Ah ah ah," I chastise. "I would be careful about what you say next. Because maybe, just maybe, I pinched the keys from the guards when I made my way down here. And threatening me will not get you out of that cell. Will it, Ricky?"

"No," he hisses.

"So sorry it took me so long to visit. They have really upped security around here since you tried to assassinate the little spare."

"I did no–"

"I have a few questions for you, Ricky. Answer them honestly, and I will let you go. Do you understand?"

Fredrick looks like he's ready to snap my neck in two, but he hesitates as I hold up a pair of keys, dangling them in front of the bars. He huffs a breath and squeezes his eyes shut, tension ripping through his muscles like a white water river.

"Fine," he grits out, opening his eyes.

The hate in them is blinding.

I like it.

"Did you grant Viktoryn access to The Crystal Palace and show him the secret tunnels leading to Raven's room? The very same room I was staying in?"

His jaw ticks, but he refuses to say a word.

"Come on, now. *No answers, no key,*" I sing, dangling the keys through the bars.

He rushes forward to grab them, but I pull back quickly, grinning at him.

Fredrick's leash snaps, and he snarls like a rabid dog. "Yes, I did. I hoped he would kill you so I would not have to lower myself below a dust-destined mortal child. Is that *honest* enough for you?" he growls, gripping the bars only to release them immediately as the iron begins to burn, sizzling his skin.

"Just what I was looking for." I smile too innocently, turning to leave. "You have a good rest of your hopefully short and miserable life, Rick-Rick."

"Wait! You said you would let me out! Come back!" he shouts, slamming his fists into the bars, cursing as they burn him again.

Faeries really are affected by iron. I thought that was an old Pixies tale.

"Did I? My bad," I chime, pressing a hand to my chest before making a show of tossing the keys into the cell. They clatter on the ground inside his cell.

He scrambles across the floor to snatch them up, hands trembling as his arms snake around the bars. He shoves the first key into the lock and growls with frustration as it fails to free him. The iron begins to create raised, red burns on his skin but he does not halt. I watch with amusement as he tries the other two with no success.

"What is this?!" Frederick shouts, staring at the keys.

"I think I said I *may* have stolen the key. That might've been a slight exaggeration. Those are keys, but not *the* keys. I am certain they open something." I shrug. "Just not that door." I point to his cell. "I lied. One of the upsides of being a dust-destined mortal child."

I grin when he lobs the keys at my head. I catch them one handed and wink. "Very well. I will leave you to it. Have fun in this lovely little dungeon until they send you to the gallows for your crimes, Ricky."

"They will not. They cannot! They have no proof. We both know I did not do this, girl! *You* did!" he howls, and I turn back to face him.

"Oh, but they will. Whether you did it or not does not matter much, now does it? You know how this works. You are the only suspect they have. And they are not going to let a crime of this magnitude go un-punished. It would be perceived as weak if the crown could not capture the person responsible for a direct attack on a Prince's life. And if they cannot find the true culprit," I eye him, unimpressed, "you will do. I would say it was nice knowing you, but I would prefer not to lie to you twice."

Ricky is seething, anger boiling beneath his skin as his entire body goes tense. Then he shatters, beating his fists against the bars until they bleed, eyes wild.

"You little *bitch*. Raven knows what you did, does he not?"

"What nonsense are you spewing? *I*," I say with a hand pressed to my heart, "did nothing. But if you are asking if Raven is aware of your circumstances..." I gesture to the cell. "Then yes, he is."

Ricky's face falls.

"This surprises you?" I hum thoughtfully. "I cannot for the life of me understand why, if you are as innocent as you so claim," I tap my chin, "your good pal Raven has not made some epic gesture to break you out. Maybe he does not take well to traitors." I would know.

"You will not get away with this! I will tell them that Maylea made that shot and set me up and that you planned the attack," Ricky hisses, pointing at me with an accusatory finger.

I hold my hands up in innocence. "Who would believe that sweet, harmless Princess Maylea would be able to do such a thing?" I bat my eyelashes at him. "Especially when everyone knows she has no combat training? What a wild and unfounded accusation. That of a soon-dead male gone mad, perhaps?"

Ricky's eyes jet back and forth as if he's searching for someone to come and back him up. A wide smile graces my face. I feel *powerful*. The feeling is so foreign yet headily addictive. And I know for the first time why people chase this high, pushing people down, stomping on their broken bones to climb to the top of the world—just to plummet over the edge.

I worry that I should feel ashamed. But I do not. Ricky let Viktoryn hurt me—*hoped* he would kill me.

He believes mortals are worth nothing.

How I relish in proving him wrong.

"And I was sitting in the front row, just as shocked as everyone else. Do you really think they will take your word over hers? Truly? They might, however, take your word over mine, but as you likely know, no one knows where I am. I have vanished... *poof.*" I open and close my fists.

"I am nothing. No one." Ricky winces. "And I plan to keep it that way. You may have helped Viktoryn, but we both know he hates Trolls and The Unseelie."

I wait a moment, letting him process my words. His glare brands me with hate.

"Pretty good for a useless mortal, *eh*?"

"If I ever get out of here, I will kill you!" he vows, and I feel a tinge of magicks swirl through the air.

"Oh, please, get in line. You tried. And that did not work out in your favour." I pause as I turn away. "And Ricky? Remember... as your head separates from your body... that *this* is what happens to those who cross me."

"How did it go?" May asks back in our warded room.

My smile is wicked. "I feel better. I said what needed to be said. Was it hard to keep the guards busy?"

"No, they were rather dim-witted. I am glad you said what you needed. *And* I have news. I received word from Alice that the Goldynlockes plan to hold a gathering this eve for The Folk to come and speak their grievances," she informs me.

"Oh. Are they? Shall we crash the party?"

"From the walls, you mean?" May teases.

"It is not as if we can truly attend, but I would like to see what The Folk are saying. It has been over a week since Alice began spreading rumors of '*the true heir's*' return. Or whatever she has decided to call me."

"It would be a great opportunity to gauge our progress. See if any of the court has begun to doubt the holiness of the Goldynlockes' rule."

"So it is settled then. Let us go play spy."

We choose a passageway that gives us a full view of the throne room, settled in the back behind a portrait of The Goddess of the Sun in battle with The Goddess of the Moon. If any of the Fae find the eyes of the painting too lifelike, too real, they do not mention it as May and I peer through the eye holes we cut. Perhaps they are used to ghosts lurking in the walls.

The dias stands empty, save for the two magnificent gold-wrought thrones and four extra, less magnificent chairs that I assume will remain open for the heirs and possibly Fabelle.

The room begins to fill as Fae file in under the marble arches. Unlike the other events I have attended in Elphyne, they are dressed in daily wear. No excess luxury, no dripping jewels.

The air buzzes with an uneasiness, Fae shifting from foot to foot and glancing at one another with uncertainty. The space quickly becomes too crowded.

"They do not look pleased," I whisper to May in the darkness of the passage.

"No. No, they do not."

Two twin horns sound and a guard appears on the dias as he begins the long-winded task of introducing all the members of the royal family. I do not listen, too focused on scanning the crowd, attempting to read the room as Queen Florence, King Ambrose, Prince Viktoryn, Princess

Daviana, and Prince Archer make their way to the dais. If the crowd seems uncertain, the royals do not.

Behind them, delayed in a move I cannot help but wonder is purposeful, trails Fabelle. Time seems to slow, the noise of the room dulling and my heart stalling as I watch her stalk across the stage. My hands curl into fists.

The Folk bow, and if it is a shallower bow than I have seen in the past, the royals seem to pay no mind to it. I worry they should.

I steady my breathing, though I cannot tear my eyes away from my sister. May's hand closes around mine, squeezing reassuringly. I squeeze back.

"You may rise," Queen Florence commands and sits, fanning her blood-red gown out around her. Her eyes cunning and cruel as she assesses the two hundred or so Fae before her. A crown dipped in rubies sits upon her blonde hair.

The King, heirs, and Fabelle take their seats, dressed in matching red attire, a show of unity. Viktoryn, Archer, and Daviana sit expressionless and tall. Fabelle sits tall but her eyes betray her as she surveys the room as if looking for something, *someone*.

No crown sits upon her brow, unlike those perched on the heirs' heads. Murmurs break through the crowd as The Folk rise, conversations had behind cupped palms. Some point accusatory fingers at Fabelle. The Queen gives the King a look.

"Silence!" King Ambrose barks, and the room falls quiet. He beckons a servant over, whispers to her, and she scurries away. Within seconds, the female Fae returns with a cup of red wine for the King. He reclines in his seat, sipping from the crystalline glass, apparently done with his part of this meeting.

The Queen does not seem to mind. I had once suspected her of being the mastermind of the court and this only furthers my suspicions. She waits, letting the room stew in silence while her eyes cut through the gathered individuals.

Slowly, she rises once more to address the crowd, clasping her hands together in front of her.

"I have heard whispers that my dear Folk are displeased. This will not do. Our court, while weakened, must remain *unified*," the Queen declares. "Together, despite the tumultuous fates that await us, we will rise. We will concur. I asked you all here tonight as representatives from each of our villages—and anyone else who wished to come—to speak your worries. Lay them on us—let us hold your burdens and heal your weary souls. Let us lead you. Who would like to speak first?"

The crowd descends once more into murmurs as desperate hands fly high in the air, nearly a hundred. The Queen pales a tad. But then, she points to a small female Fae with green-hued skin and dragonfly wings. She tightly grips a young Fae's hand in her own. He wobbles on his feet, gripping her skirts.

"Your Majesty," she curtsies. "I am Knore Lixinton. My child and I hail from Glarindale—a small farming village. My village is starving. In recent weeks, our crops have withered and died. The sun has beat relentlessly down on us, and the clouds have dried up in the sky. I cannot feed my children... Their cheeks grow hollow. We throw ourselves on your mercy, and we beg for your assistance."

Many Folk nod along, muttering their agreements.

The Queen's voice is drowning in faux sympathy when she speaks. "I hear you, Knore Lixinton of Glarindale. I hear you, so hear my judgment. We shall send you with three baskets of fresh fruits and vegetables from our own royal gardens. And wishes that the weather soon turns in your favor." She holds her arms out as if she had made a great declaration. But she is met with unhappy murmurs, not applause.

The Fae's wings twitch nervously, and her child grips her skirts tighter in his tiny fists.

"I appreciate your judgment, my Queen, I do, b-but," Knore's voice shakes, but she wills strength into her tone. "Three baskets will be gone in days. I have children to feed, and The Folk of Glarindale have children to feed. I am here to speak for them, not only I... If I may, Your Majesty, request that you, like in the times of Queen Valda when drought found our lands, open trade between the Seelie and Unseelie border. The Autumn Court has an abundance of food, and we could trade our skills. I am a skilled painter, our community is filled with a wealth of talent, and with your help, I can feed my child. Glarindale Folk can feed their children. The Unseelie... I have heard rumors they are willing," Knore pleads. "Queen Valda was also known to send those who hold will over water to assist... I know *we* cannot call upon the elements any further, but perhaps The Sprin–"

"You turn your nose down at my offering?" the Queen's voice booms. "You dare be ungrateful when offered food from my very home? My very *table*? Do you not trust in your Queen? Do you not trust that the lands will bless us and provide? You want me to lower myself to begging Unseelie filth for substance? You wish your Kingdom to appear weak? In need of assistance from lesser kingdoms?" the Queen snarks, eyes losing their soft focus in favor of sharp slits.

The Fae look at one another, faces painted in many levels of discomfort, disdain, and worry as they watch this interaction. Some hands ball into fists, and the crowd shifts.

"N-no, of course not, Your Majesty," Knore says, voice shaking as she lowers her head in deference. "It is just that I cannot bare to watch my chil–"

"Then it is settled. I shall have your baskets arranged. You are dismissed, Knore of Glarindale. I shall hear the next now."

Rage rises in my chest, my hands trembling at my sides.

Knore curtsies shakily, scooping her now crying child into her arms before moving to leave. Fae place supportive hands on her shoulders, murmuring words to the mother as they clear a path. Some go as far as to slip coins into her apron pockets.

My eyes burn. Hands raise once more, but hesitantly, as if afraid moving too quickly will manage to catch them in the Queen's wrath.

I watch Knore make for the exit, head bowed, fighting tears, and something in me ignites. I peek at May and whisper, "I will be right back."

"Willa, wait," May whisper-shouts, reaching for me, but I am already disappearing down the passageway.

25

I am through the passageways and into the nearby kitchens in minutes. I do not have time to don my maid's uniform, so I simply steal an apron off a hook near the door and tie it around my waist. Pots and pans bangs. Steam makes the air impossibly thick. Bodies rush about, hands painted in flour and berry juice.

I search the kitchen, looking for anything to hold food in—a lot of food—knowing I do not have much time. Minutes, if that. Luckily, no one pays much mind to an extra mortal body in the chaos.

I stumble past the stoves, around the cooks and servants, murmuring my apologies as I collide with Folk and mortals alike in the cramped space. Then, my eyes land on something perfect.

I am outside and rushing after Knore's disappearing figure, three pitiful baskets held precariously in the crook of her arm, in a few moments' time.

A creaky wheelbarrow filled with bread and rice and vegetables leads the way. It is a mishmash of everything. Whatever I could grab from the cupboards and off the tables without drawing too much notice.

But it is food.

And I know firsthand that anything is helpful when you are starving.

The gates have been left open and mostly unguarded to allow for Fae to come and speak to the royals, the majority of experienced guards inside with the royal family. No one seems to care about a mortal servant *leaving* the Palace.

When I am out of the guards' eyelines, I shout her name. "Knore! Knore, wait!"

The Fae halts, slowly turning, her black amphibian eyes lined with long lashes and silver tears. She uses the back of her palm to wipe them away, forcing her shoulders square and her chin up even as she pulls her child closer to her side.

"Yes?" she questions without that shake in her voice.

I am panting as I push the wheelbarrow towards her. "Here, take this."

Knore's eyes go wide as she peers at the wheelbarrow overflowing with food and then back to me. "Has the Queen changed her judgment?"

"Not precisely."

"So you are a thief?" Knore asks, tilting her head.

I wince. "Not precisely."

"I do not understand, strange mortal creature. Your motives are milky. Your hands sticky like honey. If you are caught... they will have your head for helping me. This is an act against the crown," she whispers, leaning closer to me as her eyes scan the trees like they might be listening.

"It is not my first act against the crown. I fear that threat has lost its thunder. Would you believe me if I told you that, even if I never stole a thing, I would still one day lose my head?"

Knore's brows furrow. "I beg your pardon? Who... who are you? Why do this? Why risk your head for someone like me? I know how they treat your kind." I watch her eyes as she studies my face, my clothes. They flare, and her voice drops even lower... "You are her... the one they fear. The Divine Daughter. The child who was promised. It is true."

"True or not, does it matter? My name? My title? I am someone who knows what it is to starve," I say, my eyes burning. "I am someone who understands what helplessness does when you have someone to protect. I am someone who wants to help you—I am no one. In truth, who I am matters not. Just... take this," I finish, pushing the wheelbarrow in her direction.

"No one will know, and if you need more..." I scratch my head, trying to think. "If you need more, leave this," I hand her the green ribbon keeping one of my twin braids tied back, "tied to that tree," I point to the largest oak tree in the clearing, "in a fortnight. And I shall find a way to hide more food inside the opening in the trunk before the sun sets the next evening. If not, I... I shall send someone else." I shove the ribbon into her hand. "I must go. Take it or do not. Trust me or do not. I cannot decide for you. I just know some people are worth the risk."

I glance at the child clinging to her skirts before turning to sprint back towards the Palace.

I stumble back into the passageway, practically collapsing onto May, who hefts me up. My chest heaves from sprinting around the Palace, a thick sheen of sweat coating my forehead. The Queen still stands, addressing her subjects.

"What," *breath*, "did," *breath*, "I miss?"

"What did you do?" May hisses.

"The right thing."

May studies my face, swallows, and then nods. "Very well, mighty mortal. Let us hope your luck does not run out today."

"What did I miss?" I repeat, turning back to the gathering.

A male Fae with glistening brown skin and radiant sunrise orange eyes awaits the Queen's judgment.

"More of the same. Crop failure, another village hit with a plague, a tornado has ravaged a few villages near the coast..." May shakes her head, eyes sad. "It is bad, Willa. The Lands cannot remain unbalanced... or I fear there will be no more Summer Court... and without Summer..."

"The balance, the magicks that created these lands by splitting them evenly between all four courts, may fail. Elphyne may fall," I finish for her.

She nods. "I fear far more rests on your shoulders than we once anticipated."

"Wonderful..." I sigh. "And I cannot do anything until I reach The Calling... and even then..."

"We do not know how to transfer the power back," May finishes.

"Add it to our list?" I tease.

"It is a rather long list. We may soon have to enlist a small army," she teases back, and I chuckle.

Suddenly, a collective gasp rings through the gathered crowd. May and I whip our eyes back to the throne room in time to see the crowd parting, an aisle forming down the very center of the room to the dais. A being with glowing, bone-white hair and a matching wispy skirt that seems to rise on a phantom wind parades into the room, arms raised at her sides.

The room falls silent. I catch the side of the Fae's face before she turns to walk the aisle. Her eyes are a milky, unseeing white, her skin the same. A serene expression lines her face. There is something all-knowing and ancient in her.

"Oh my..." May mutters and I turn to find her eyes wide, face pale.

"What is it? Who is that?"

May says nothing, staring open-mouthed through the holes in the wall. I glance back to find the royals are all in similar, varying degrees of wonderstruck shock. Only Fabelle seems unsurprised. My brows furrow.

The Fae drop to their knees, bowing and muttering thanks to the Goddesses

"May," I hiss. "What is happening?"

"She... how... this is..." May shakes her head as if to clear her mind. "She is one of The Great Oracles. One of four. Creations of the Goddesses to give The Folk of early days direction and guidance. But... they have not been seen in centuries. They are unnamed. Near God-like beings." May's voice is full of reverence. "They are said to emerge in times of deep unrest, chaos, or change."

I blink... and blink again. "Oh."

The Queen's hands tighten where they are clasped in front of her, a too-wide smile plastered on her lips. "Great Oracle, to what do we owe the blessing of your rare appearance?" she asks as The Oracle settles at the bottom of the steps.

The Fae remain bowed, some so deeply their foreheads press into the stone. Some still murmuring praises, prayers.

"To what do we owe the rain? To what do we owe the sun?" The Oracle purrs in a gentle voice that seems to echo from everywhere and nowhere. "To be Fae is to owe. But it is not about the owing."

"Did you come to spit riddles? Or do you have a grievance you wish to air?" the Queen challenges.

"The answer is *everything*," I whisper to May. She rolls her eyes.

The Oracle peers over her shoulder, milky white eyes seeming to meet mine as if she heard my answer. A sneaky, secretive smile parts her lips as she dips her head in a small, knowing nod. Fabelle follows her gaze. I suck in a breath, ducking away from the holes.

"Did you see that?" I ask May as she ducks down beside me, nodding.

We wait a moment until The Oracle returns to address the Queen before rising to peer back at the scene. Fabelle's eyes are still locked on the wall where the tapestry we hide behind hangs. May shares a look with me.

"Do you think...?" she asks.

"With mortal eyes? I should hope not."

But my sister's eyes do not sway. She finally looks away when The Oracle speaks.

"False Queen, I come to speak for The Folk of Summer. I come to speak for their souls. The Folk you claim as yours are dying. The lands you wish to grasp turn to ash. And you do nothing. Your reign has brought only destruction. Greed. Your sins stain your every breath. It reeks of death. Of decay. Cyrissa has declared it time for the true golden line to return."

The Oracle pauses, raising her arms as if summoning the sky and sun itself, her body glittering with light. My body hums under the power. Like calling to like.

"The Folk's souls have spoken. If a true heir of the sun, of Cyrissa, is present, we will have them," The Oracle speaks, her voice expanding into many. Young and old. A voice of The Folk. A voice of the Fae. "To save our lands. To save our court. We will have them. Mortal or not."

My eyes swing back to Fabelle, the one who would be the true heir if not for me. But her face is expressionless. I am stuck to the spot as I remember I have missed her birthday.

Sixteen now.

An ache sprouts in my heart.

I shake the thoughts away as my eyes shift to Viktoryn, Archer, and Daviana. They all sit so still it seems as if they are not breathing. Viktoryn's hands grip the arms of his chair so tightly his knuckles blanche. But Queen Florence sneers down at The Oracle. Unimpressed and unmoved by her words.

"You would let a lesser being be your Queen?" she questions The Oracle and turns her eyes to The Folk, still bowing, her tone turning accusatory. Some raise their heads, uncertainty watering their resolve. "Your superior? You would forsake your own kind for that of dust and death? A mortal? A *nothing*?" she seethes. "We have ruled you fairly. We do not command the land. We do not control the weather."

"No. No, you do not. But that is the problem. Is it not? The land only answers to true heirs, to chosen children. Not False Queens and Kings. You have angered the Goddess. You have slain her daughter." The crowd gasps. They knew this, but to hear the accusation flung outright at a Queen is shocking.

"You are one to speak of lesser beings! Your rule has stripped The Summer Fae of power, of true immortality, of our connection to all that lives and all that is. *You* have made them lesser. *You* have made them weak. The Goddess is punishing them for your sins. And I fear you all shall not survive her wrath. If the mortal carries her blood, her bond, her connection to these Holy Lands, she is not lesser. She is far greater than any Fae who could claim that throne. She is far greater than even *you*."

"What you speak of is treason! What you speak of will be the ruination of The Summer Court," Queen Florence growls.

The Oracle turns, a sly smile on her lips as she takes in the Fae. She turns back to the Queen. "No, False Queen. It will be the rebirth."

The Queen laughs, fiery and filled with mocking disdain. "You think yourself invincible, Oracle?" she spits the word like a curse. "Untouchable because you are a creation of the Goddesses?"

"Let us not play games, you hold no reverence for Cyrissa in your heart—only greed. You think yourself as high and holy as the Goddesses themselves. You do not respect their creatures, their daughters, their heirs, and it will be your end."

"You speak nonsense. Locked away somewhere in the earth all these years. She has clearly gone mad," the Queen declares, addressing the crowd.

Some of the Fae nod in agreement, and others shout, outraged to bear witness to the Queen's blasphemy.

The Queen levels her glare on her Folk. "Do you all truly wish to be ruled by an unseen creator? Chained to a Goddess who has forsaken you? Who does not show in these times of hardship? It is not your Goddess that stands before you, offering help and judgment. It is *I*," the Queen points to herself, and some Fae begin to cheer in agreement. "Do not listen to this *thing* gone mad. I am your Queen."

It is hard not to agree with her, despite her true motives. Where is Cyrissa?

The Oracle laughs. It echoes through the very foundation of the Palace.

"When the clouds of your delusion clear and the sun breaks through once more, you will find reckoning. It will not be kind." The Oracle turns her back on the Queen, pure dismissal in her movements as she raises her arms to speak only to the Fae. "In these days comes a child who was born to burn, a child who will rise from the ashes and usher in an age of change, of rebirth. Join her or find yourself in ashes, too. Forsake your False Que–"

"Seize her! End her now! Your treason will not go unpunished, Oracle!" the Queen screams, but the guards hesitate. "End her, or I will have you end each other!"

Hesitation gone, the guards rush The Oracle, swords raised, but her expression does not shift away from supreme knowingness.

She is peace. She is light. She is endless.

The Oracle's voice rises, ringing through the space as if amplified by the air itself, "Or Forsake your creator. The choice is you–" A sword ends the sentence as it drives through the back of her skull and out of her mouth.

The Folk scream. The Oracle, as if in slow motion, closes her eyes and begins to fall forward. Before she can hit the ground, she explodes into a thousand gold-dipped bees. Fae flee as the room descends into chaos and buzzing.

But the Queen stands tall, unshakable as she announces, "No being, Great Oracle or not, shall speak against their Queen and Kingdom, and live."

May and I do not hang around. We make it back to our room, out of breath and shaken. A kind of heaviness hangs in the air between us. Grief. A feeling too familiar to me now—I almost find comfort in it.

May, however, does not. "That wretch! That evil, tricky, scheming wretch! One does not defile a being of the Goddesses... How could she? If I could end her myself, I would. I *should*!"

I am too detached from their beliefs, their Goddesses, to feel true outrage, even as a descendant of Cyrissa...

But I feel May's.

"I will not stop you if you choose to remove her from the board, but that might complicate things," I mutter as May stomps around the room, tossing daggers at the pillow we stuffed into a shirt for target practice.

"You are right, I know you to be. But... *Ugh*!" She tosses a dagger so hard the pillow explodes into a plume of feathers. They sail down on us like snow, coating everything in fluff. May blows one out from her mouth and hisses, "Some things are meant to be *sacred*. Even to someone as corrupt as High Queen Florence."

It is hard to take her particularly seriously while she is covered in fluff.

"I did not know how much the Goddesses truly ruled the Fae. They seem so..." I wince, "distant."

"They are... but they are what we are. *Who* we are. Our existence is owed to them. Has anyone bothered to tell you the story of how this all came to be? The Tale of Two Sisters?" May questions, tossing another dagger. It hits home with a thud.

"No. I think you will find no one tells me much of anything around here until it serves them."

May huffs. "Right."

I sink down onto the mattress, and after a moment, so does she. She collects herself, smoothing her hair down. It sparks with static, and her hand comes away plastered with feathers. She scowls at them. I cannot help myself. I laugh. I have never seen May scowl; it does not suit her at all. It is almost adorable.

"Whatever are you laughing about?" she asks incredulously, shaking her hand to try and free herself from her feather glove.

"I have never seen you scowl. It is like trying to place a frown on a kitten."

May scowls harder. But slowly, her lips tip into a grin. "I am no kitten. I am a feared and powerful rule–" May begins to laugh. "Oh, let me be true, I cannot say that with a straight face."

"A kitten in a crown," I tease, and she shoves me.

"A *fearful* kitten."

"Whatever makes you feel better, Your Highness."

May rolls her eyes. "Let me tell you the tale. Stop jesting me."

"Very well, Kitty Queen."

"I am choosing to ignore you now." May dramatically clears her throat. "Everything began with two sisters, twins—Esmerae and Cyrissa—birthed by the stars, mirror images of the other. One cast in darkness, the other in light. Made to balance each other—perfect equals. For years, they wandered the stars, exploring all the endlessness the sky could offer. But they grew lonely, tired, and weary. They began to wish they had somewhere to stop, a place to rest and nurture. For since the moment they came to be, they had been racing. To where they never knew. They just knew it had always been that way and always would be. Until one day, they decided to use their combined power to create a safe haven, a resting place," May says, her voice taking on a tone of wonder.

"Elphyne."

"Not exactly." She waves me off. "They found a place in the stars they agreed felt right. *Whole.* And together, they combined the power of the stars, of themselves, to create a home. And for a while, everything was wonderful. Quiet and restful. But as all immortal creatures do, they grew bored, restless."

"This sounds dreadfully familiar," I groan.

"Will you please let me finish? Be quiet!" May hisses.

"I shall try, but it is not my strong suit."

"Soon, word had spread across the cosmos of what they had done, what they had created. And other Lesser Gods swarmed their home. Eager and greedy for pieces of this new, abundant place. A place of places. A land where not all Gods must wander. These Gods demanded the sisters share what they had created, that they hand pieces of the home they had made with the very essence of themselves to these beings. Esmerae refused. Unwavering as her darkness. But Cyrissa, drawn to things that twinkled in her light, was tempted by Angelus, the Lesser God of Unrequited Love and Trickery. She had begun to consider the Lesser Gods' bid for a claim. For who could blame her?"

"Of course, she loved her sister, the other half of her soul... but for so many endless years... it had just been them, in that neverending nothing and nowhere. Cyrissa longed for more. For love and light and laughter. She had grown lonely. Bored of only her sister's company for eternity."

"Please do not tell me my familial line is one of misguided love," I moan. "This is all far too prophetic."

May glares at me. "There is more. It is never so simple. Cyrissa went to Esmerae to plead the Lesser Gods' case. And it is said that the sky turned midnight black and fell from the heavens, encasing the lands in total darkness. Esmerae felt betrayed by her sister. How could she abandon her for a Lesser God? How could her sister campaign against her wishes? Why was what they had created together not enough? When the darkness cleared, Cyrissa and Esmerae fought. An epic battle of celestial power that raged for forty-four days and forty-four nights."

"Is this why there are four courts?" I ask dryly.

May smacks my arm. "Willa! Let me tell the story. Anywho, their new place, their new home, was suffering. To fight, they had to drain the power they had injected into the land back into their cosmic beings. Fields of green withered and died, stars fell from the sky like boulders, the oceans swallowed the lands, and chaos reigned. Everything they created together was decaying into nothingness once more. Esmerae was distraught as she witnessed all they had done. So, as the land began to crumble like ash, Esmerae stopped. Instead of pushing the remains of her power into her war against her sister, she placed it back into the land," May explains.

"This story is horribly sad. And frighteningly familiar," I mutter.

May does not chastise me this time. She gives me a small, sad nod.

"Esmerae begged her to stop, but Cyrissa continued to rage until her sister offered a solution. A trade. To split the lands into three. A home for the Lesser Gods to share and people—mortals—for them to rule over. Then, a home for her and her sister to rule—lands and Folk abundant with their magicks. When the Lesser Gods argued, Esmerae countered that the magicks in the land still belonged to her. That with a thought, she could lay it all to waste, and they would have nothing left to argue over. If the Lesser Gods wanted to stay, they would have to forfeit their powers and swear to never raise a hand against its creators."

"A bargain."

"The very first. Cyrissa, weary of fighting, agreed. But Angelus and the other Lesser Gods did not want a lesser land with lesser creatures. Cyrissa pleaded with Angelus to take what Esmerae had offered. For she now knew she and her sister were perfectly matched in power, balanced. The war he had encouraged her to rage on his behalf could never be won. And she would not choose between Esmerae and Angelus. Not after learning how much Esmerae was willing to sacrifice. But still, Angelus refused the lands, refused Cyrissa, and escaped into the cosmos, leaving behind the other Lesser Gods who still wished for their share. Cyrissa's heart shattered, and the lands shook. Esmerae tried to comfort Cyrissa, but she cried for a hundred days, flooding the lands with her misery, drowning all they had created," May continues.

"But with her tears, the magicks she had drained to fight returned, and on the one hundred and first day, Esmerae—unable to deny the requests of the Lesser Gods any longer—split the lands. Separating the power from Cyrissa's tears into water and magicks, Esmerae pushed the water into what would become the mortal world. With her sister's magick, she created The Seelie Kingdom and its Folk—a gift for Cyrissa. A place full of light and gemstones and wonder. A place full of beings for her sister to pour her love and attention into. Where she would come to be known as—The Seelie God of Light and Life. For herself, she created The Unseelie Kingdom and lands, a place of rest and peace and quiet. Where she become know as—The Unseelie God of Death and Rebirth."

"And so... Elphyne was born. Eventually, Cyrissa grew to love her lands and Folk. So she decided to bless them. She leaned her lips to the land and yielded what was coined The Kiss of Creation, drowning the lands in light and warmth, flowers and thunder, creating Summer and Spring as we know them today. The Courts were born later as the lands grew and changed, dividing into quadrants."

"What about the Lesser Gods? What did they do?" I question.

"The Lesser Gods loved their creations. Blessed them with what they could. Eventually, some of the Lesser Gods grew bored of this place and its lack of magicks and abandoned the mortals to rule themselves. In time, all the Gods and Goddesses took a step back into the sky to watch the world they created. Cyrissa as the Sun, Esmerae as the Moon, and the Lesser Gods among the stars. Cyrissa found love once more, and thus, your mother was born. She also chose a favored family and injected power into them. They would become my family, rulers of Spring. Esmerae, weary of love and its inherent dangers, never did seek it. Instead, she bestowed her favorite subjects with extra power and the gift of shapeshifting. And they became the ruling families of Winter and Autumn."

May pauses before continuing, "I do agree, Willa. That your story is akin to that of our creators. Though, you are an anomaly. A child bestowed with power, born of both kingdoms, grown to maturity in the soils of the mortal realm. A new twist in this tale... Sometimes, though, I fear that, as everything began with two warring sisters," May looks at me, eyes grave, "it will end that way."

May's telling of Elphyne's origin sticks with me, wrapping around my bones and invading my thoughts. Even when she leaves for the night to attend to royal business.

I fear that, as everything began with two warring sisters, it will end that way.

I find myself wishing often that I could leap into Fabelle's mind, root around for a while, uncover her motives or find the right way to win her back to my side. But we have chosen our fates.

Though she is gone, May leaves me with a tip she received from her Summer Court allies. Viktoryn has been called to meet his mother in her chambers this eve. After the explosive meeting with The Folk earlier, both May and I are curious to see what will be said.

I ready myself and head off into the passageway that will lead to the Queen's Chambers. They are to meet shortly after dinner and I am eager to be early. Ready and in place before they arrive. I pass through halls and passageways until I arrive at what appears to be a dead end. I peer at my map, perplexed.

This *should* lead right to the Queen's room. I shove the map back into my pocket and study the bricks around me. On the far wall of the damp passage is a sun emblem. *There.*

I activate the key and press it into the emblem. The wall shudders and shifts before opening into what appears to be a large wardrobe.

I shove past extravagant gowns, drowning in taffeta and tulle. My ankle gets caught in the skirt of an especially atrocious red thing. I trip, tumbling into the wardrobe door, only to be spit out onto the floor.

My heart slams into my chest as I land in total darkness. *Wait, no.* I rip the red gown off my head and freeze.

I have fallen into the Queen's bedchamber.

I leap to my feet and scan the room. My heart slams into my chest. But thankfully, I am alone. I force the red gown back into the wardrobe and press the door shut. Wiping off my hands, I turn to study the room when the door blows back open, spitting the red gown out on the floor.

"Is this a jest?" I grumble under my breath.

Frustration builds in my chest as I swipe it off the floor and begin the task of forcing it back into the wardrobe.

I will not have my plan foiled by an unruly hunk of fabric.

I slam the doors shut as quietly as possible, listening for a click to ensure they are properly closed. Slowly, with my arms raised, I back away from the wardrobe as if the gown might leap out to tackle me. But blessedly, this time, it remains shut.

I blow out a breath and begin to make my way across the Queen's bedchamber. May's informant said that they would be meeting in the Queen's attached parlor, but only one passage led into the Queen's chamber. So now I must find the parlor on my own.

I press my ear against the double doors directly across from the bed. I listen but hear nothing. I begin to turn the handle, waiting for a guard or an indication that someone is on the other side. When nothing happens, I open the door and step through.

I find myself in an elaborate library with floor-to-ceiling books and a gold-wrought skylight. I pass shelves and shelves of books to reach the next set of doors. Again, I wait. Nothing. I push the doors open and enter a room full of plush seating and a still-steaming tray of tea.

I halt, head whipping around the room to see if the servant who brought the tea still remains, but the room is empty. There are only chairs and a small center table. This must be the parlor. I look around in hopes of finding a good hiding spot but come up empty-handed.

"Come now, son, we must speak." The sound of Queen Florence's voice on the other side of the door sends my heart pounding.

My ears ring, and my muscles lock up. I shake myself out of my stupor just before the door swings open, diving behind a golden settee at the last second.

I will myself not to move.

Not to breathe.

I try to not even think, worried my thoughts may be too loud, as Viktoryn stalks into the room after his mother. My hand presses into the medallion under my tunic as I pray that it continues to muddle my scent.

"If it is just so you might lecture me again, we do not need to speak. I am certain we could switch roles, and I could deliver this verbal lashing now, Mother," Viktoryn says under his breath.

"You will not speak to me like that," the Queen snaps, and I hear the sound of a palm meeting skin.

I flinch instinctively.

"Have you learned nothing? I raised you to be *great*. I raised you to be ruthless and competent. And you have failed me. All you do is live and breathe and *fail*. It disgusts me," the Queen hisses.

"Yes, Mother," Viktoryn answers in a voice so vulnerable I almost think it is not him.

"You know what to do."

The room goes quiet for a few moments except for the sound of clothing rustling. The Queen saunters across the room and I get a glimpse of her skirts as she frees something long and thin from a hidden compartment by the unlit hearth. I choke down a gasp when I recognize the object. A cane. She pulls on a pair of thick leather gloves and grabs three small circular metal discs, no bigger than her palm.

My brows furrow, and I startle as fabric slap over my face. I look up to find Viktoryn's tunic draped over the settee and my face.

I need to find a better hiding spot. Now.

It is nothing short of a miracle they have not spotted me yet. But they seem to be too caught up in this strange routine.

The Queen crosses the room towards Viktoryn, and silence descends. But it is broken by a teacup shattering on the ground followed by a shriek.

"*Agh*! Useless mortal maids. They have gotten my tea wrong! Again! Viktoryn, child, clothe yourself and go grab a new pot," the Queen growls, and Viktoryn's tunic vanishes from my head. "Ensure they do it correctly. I will change and meet you back here. Make haste!"

"Yes, Mother."

Doors open, and footsteps retreat. I wait a second, two, before peaking around the settee to find I am alone.

I rise, heart rattling in my chest, and begin to search the room for a better hiding spot. Part of me wants to flee—that was too close. Whatever is to be said or done here cannot be as important as getting caught... and after seeing the cane... I am not certain I want to be present for what is coming next. But the Queen has headed back into her bedchamber, so I will not be able to get to the passageway, and the front door will surely be guarded. There are doors to a veranda on one side of the room, but I am not certain I want to jump from this height.

That is when I see it.

Above the veranda doors, there is an opening where large marble statues of the Goddesses are raised on a ledge. If I can get up there, I will be hidden from sight while also having a full view of the room. I do not hesitate, shoving my hands into the slits between the bricks while I begin scaling the wall.

My hand slaps down on the ledge just as the doors to the Queen's bedchamber slam open across the room.

I pause, certain I will be spotted hanging from the wall, when the Queen exclaims, "I forgot my gloves! What a day." She turns on her heel back through the doors, leaving them wide open.

I use the chance to pull myself all the way up before hiding my frame behind the statues. My hands are shaking. That was all so close, too close. Perhaps spying is not my calling after all.

The Queen returns, and seconds later, so does Viktoryn, tea in hand. I watch as he sets the tray down and begins to move to clean the shattered glass when the Queen halts him.

"No. Tunic off. Kneel." She points to the broken glass.

I expect Viktoryn to refuse. To shout at her and storm off. Instead, his entire body tenses and he slowly nods obediently before stripping off his tunic and kneeling on the broken glass. My chest aches at the sight. I may hate him but something about seeing him like this feels wrong.

"Good. Are you ready?"

He nods. His face is so drained of fire. Of *hope*.

"Do you understand why I do this? I do this because *I. Love. You.*" She punctuates the words with the crack of her cane on his back.

Viktoryn winces but does not move to rise, red welts beginning to rise on his skin.

"Because I want you to be *better*."

Crack!

"Stronger."

Crack!

"Weak rulers find themselves at the end of enemies' swords. You have been weak. You have failed me. You still do not have the Caprimore girl. It is pathetic. *You* are pathetic," she spits as she pulls on her gloves and retrieves the small metal discs from the table.

"Yes, Mother."

"You were supposed to seduce her. *Subdue* her, Viktoryn. Archer has hit no such resistance. What is the matter with you? She is a mortal. A nothing. And yet, she has bested you!? A Prince? My disappointment is so deep I could drown. You are the heir! *My* heir! And no heir of mine will fail!"

His face is slack. His eyes resigned. His bare back is on full display as he places his hands on the small table, bracing himself. The Queen places one of the metal discs on his back, and Viktoryn barely bites back a scream as steam rises from his flesh.

Iron.

She is setting iron discs on his bare flesh.

That is why she is wearing gloves.

I swallow the bile that rises in my throat as his skin bubbles, shifting into a violent shade of red and purple under the plate.

"Tell me," she demands.

"I am pathetic. I have failed you," he grits out.

She sets another plate on his shoulder blade and Viktoryn cries out.

"Tell me!"

"I will be better." Viktoryn's body contorts with a silent sob. "Stronger."

She presses the last disc into the small of his back. Viktoryn arches to escape the pain, but she slaps the cane across his arm in a stinging blow that causes him to still.

"What is your objective? What have I offered you, unworthy as you are, if you can leash the Caprimore girl and balance the lands?" the Queen asks.

"The throne," he chokes. "No more waiting. You will step down and allow me the honor of your throne."

Your throne.

Not the King's.

Not The Summer Court's.

Her throne.

"Do you believe you deserve my throne, Viktoryn? Are you worthy?"

"No," he whispers as tears spill from his golden lashes. "No."

His skin sizzles and an impulsive part of me wants to jump out and shout. To tell her to stop. My eyes water. I loved that boy once. And that is what he looks like now. Just a boy.

"Then prove to me you can do this. Prove to me you can be this court's heir. Prove to me you are deserving," she demands, removing each of the discs from his back. "Worthy."

Viktoryn collapses to the ground into a puddle of blood and broken glass. He does not seem to flinch as it cuts his skin. I cannot look away from the three awful blistered circles on his back. I did not notice be-fore—the Goldynlocke Royal Seal is burnt into his back.

The smell of burning flesh is vile, and I press my hand over my mouth and nose to keep from retching. Viktoryn's body racks with silent sobs and the Queen grins down at her son, triumphant.

"You will make me proud, son, will you not? You will become worthy of my love, of the throne I will grant you. You will not fail me. I know you want that throne. But more than that, I know you want to make me proud. Yes? I will give you everything you want, but first, you must give me what *I* want."

"Yes," he answers so softly I almost do not hear him.

"Good, my son. You are free to go. You are not to get those healed until either girl is found or they heal on their own. Do you understand?"

He nods, and she stalks from the room, leaving her son in a bloody heap on the floor. It takes what feels like an eternity, but Viktoryn eventually drags himself from the floor and exits. The Queen leaves her chambers soon after to attend to something and that is when I make a break for it.

I understand now why he is the way he is. I even feel for him. I, too, was beaten and abused... but I did not let it turn me into a monster.

He did.

May and I sit in our hideout, sharing dried meat and hard cheese as we work on putting our outfits together for Lamasa, a festival that is about a time of change and transition.

According to May, it is a day that marks the halfway point between The Summer Solstice and The Autumn Equinox, so The Summer and Autumn Courts take turns hosting.

This year's host is The Summer Court. And they are about as excited to host a shared party with The Unseelie as they are to willingly set themselves on fire. But it is *tradition*—as are the half masks that are worn to symbolise the halfway point between seasons.

May was able to get in contact with Alice and Beatrice, who have been working tirelessly, in secret, to supply us with gowns and masks in time for the event in three days. An event where I will hatch my newest scheme.

I also put in a request for a new ronan berry-charmed bracelet since Raven destroyed mine. Something—and someone—I take great pains to avoid thinking about.

"Why in all of Elphyne would the Goldynlockes think it wise to hold a masquerade ball, outdoors, while the true attacker of Prince Archer is still running free?" I question, dumbfounded by their stupidity.

"The Goldynlockes are not known for their cunning minds." May taps her temple. "They care for power, tradition, and debauchery. The masks are a tradition. And in Elphyne, tradition is akin to law. Plus, choosing not to hold the event would be a show of weakness. Of fear. They cannot, especially now, afford to show any weakness."

"Well, for once, I am thankful for tradition." I smirk, holding my gown up against my chest, smoothing the fabric over my body.

It is whimsical. Fit for a Princess. A beautiful maroon colour with delicate, puffed sleeves that hang off my shoulders. It has a low neckline with a ribbon corset that is inlaid with golden leaves and delicate pearls that cinch around my waist. The skirt is a masterpiece of intertwining golden vines that run up and under the corset, making the dress look like the golden trees that cover the lands of The Summer Court.

"Alice is a genius with fabrics and thread," I mutter wistfully.

I set my dress down on the edge of the mattress, snatching my mask off the table and holding it up to my face. It is made of golden lace that conceals my forehead, stopping at the tip of my nose. My green eyes stand out starkly in contrast to the gold. The mask is large enough to disguise my face from anyone who does not know my features well.

"She really has done a tremendous job," May remarks as she adjusts her equally gorgeous periwinkle blue gown. Pride radiates from her every time Alice comes up. "Mortal or Fae, she is the most talented seamstress in The Seelie Kingdom."

"How do you know Alice? How did you know you could trust her, not only with this but with a secret as world-altering as the key?"

May's grin falls as she shifts, sucking her bottom lip between her teeth. She tosses her dress over a three-legged chair before turning to me, hands raised in front of her as she conjures a handful of daffodils.

"Sometimes, you just know," May replies, avoiding my eyes as she fusses with the flowers.

"Convincing. A very Faerie answer. Did you somehow compulse her to always keep your secrets or something?" I tease.

May goes preternaturally still in a way only Fae can. Then she stalks after me until I am backed into the wall, eyes callous and cold.

Her voice is a velvet-soft threat. "Never accuse me of something of that manner *ever* again."

Chills skate up my spine as I hold her cruel eyes. May seems to tower over me, a being of bloodlust and barely leashed rage, and for the first time, I fear her. The look in her eyes is so primally protective that I instinctually sink into the cool stone.

I open my mouth, but nothing comes out.

"Am I clear?" she threatens. "Never again, Willa."

Irritation gobbles up my fear, and I huff out a hollow laugh. "No. About Alice, you are never clear. It seems none of you are ever clear. You all ricochet between playfulness and threats while hiding behind a thin veil of secrets." I shove her away from me, and anger colours her cheeks red. I soften my tone. "You can trust me, May. After all this time, I'd hope you would know that."

"We both have secrets we would prefer to stay secret!"

"I did not ask to offend," I profess. "I am simply attempting to understand your relationship. You are so odd when her name appears on my lips."

"Yet, you ask. You ask, and you pry. Stop! Do not ask again. Do not ask at all. And never accuse me of using compulsion on her again, or you may find yourself without a tongue," May hisses, turning away from me to set the flowers down on what we had affectionately named *The Weapons Table* in our hideout.

Her shoulders rise and fall with a few deep breaths before she turns back, expression more sunny. "Enough of this. It is nonsense. We must focus if we wish to accomplish our goals."

I blink at her. More confused about her and Alice than ever.

"Alright," I concede, tired of this conversion. Tired of Fae and their endless secrets. "Have Alice and Beatrice begun to spread fresh rumors through the gentry?"

"Yes," May squeaks, smiling. "Alice says they are spreading like wildfire. Some of The Folk are beginning to speak of The Bright Days of Queen Valda's rule. The return of her daughter is revered as a *miracle*. It has become a top debate topic whether you will join the Goldynlockes or challenge them for the crown. *And* Alice says she has seen more signs of rebel activity popping up—even in the Palace. You will have support."

"But I do not know how much. It will be impossible to gauge until we are in motion. This is still a gamble, Willa. This is your most daring scheme. They could simply shoot you on sight and order you to be detained. They do not have to play along with your games," she warns.

"They–"

The sound of dozens of boots pounding by causes us to freeze. We reach for weapons immediately. They must be doing searches of the Palace *again*. This is the first week they have begun to search our hall regularly. Too regularly to be a coincidence.

My breath gets caught in my throat, heart slamming into my ribcage. May stands frozen, staring at the door. Her magick the only thing keeping us hidden from the countless guards sent out on a singular mission—finding me.

A few moments pass, and the hall falls silent. We both sigh and return to our conversation.

"But they will not. You said yourself that the Goldynlockes' thirst for power will always be their weakness. It makes them too bold. Too arrogant. They need me. If they are caught publicly harming me, it will only inflame the rebels' cause. It will make me a martyr. When presented with such an opportunity, I believe Viktoryn will take it. Take me. He believes me mindless, easily manipulated. I am his blind spot," I reason.

"The Goldynlockes believe they have it all. They believe me powerless and alienated. They have no idea I am aware of the rebels. They believe I am hiding because I fear them. And if this was a couple of months ago, they would be right. But things have changed. I have changed. I refuse to cower any longer." I tip my chin up. "A daughter of flames is born to burn. Not hide."

"You are certain this is the best approach?" May questions, hands fiddling nervously.

"Yes."

"I cannot decide if you are brave or stupid," May muses, not unkindly. "It is a question I have pondered since the day I pulled you from Cyrissa Lake half-alive, dripping wet and clutching a dagger painted with Nixies blood," she flashes me a grin. "Either way, I stand by what I said then. I respect it. The Goldynlockes never expected you..."

She studies me. "They expected two fearful, cowering little mortal girls who would hand them the power they craved while begging for mercy. I sincerely doubt Viktoryn ever planned to stay in Mayfair as long as he did. But you were more than he had bargained for. You, my dear friend, have set fire to their best-laid plans as if you have never feared a flame. You have laughed when you ought to have cried. And even when the odds have been stacked against you, you never cowered. It is an honor to start fires with you. It is an honor to lie in the ashes with you. It is an honor to be a part of your blaze." May's words are laced with warmth—a warmth I did not deserve.

I wonder if she has ever suspected the truth—that every moment I have spent in Elphyne, I have spent afraid. Despite my fire and bravado,

I am always afraid. I have been afraid for so long that I do not know what it might be like to not be dripping with fear...

And though I may have fooled May, I know I have not fooled everyone.

But the Fae do not care if I am afraid. They do not care if I am scared—worse yet, I think they *prefer* it. Like they can sense the human weakness radiating from my body. It emboldens them. It is a sickening sweet wine they wish to be drunk upon.

That is why I decided, the day that Fabelle chose the Goldynlockes over me, that I could no longer afford to be afraid. I had to be brave. Bold, brash, *stupid* even. Every time I felt that telltale prickle of fear, I would shove it down, compressing it so deeply within myself, it would be forged anew.

So, if the inevitable comes, and I die at the Goldynlockes' hands, at least I will not die afraid. I will die bold, brave, *angry*. I will not allow them to feast on my fear as well as my blood. They will not take more from me than I allow.

I will not be afraid. Even when I am.

I am ready to bury it all within myself when I feel a sudden need to voice the thoughts I have been drowning in.

"I am going to tell you a secret," I begin quietly, taking a step towards May. "I *am* afraid. Almost always. And I often believe that the only difference between bravery and stupidity is the outcome of the story. Who is writing the tale and how they divulge the details. With the stroke of a pen, you are painted—hero or villain, triumph or tribulation, bravery or stupidity. So, I simply have to hope that whoever pens my story when I am but dust and ash sees my actions through a lens of bravery."

I take a deep breath. "These lands... they were not made for me. I think any mortal who is still clinging to their sanity would be afraid. But fear can be a tool—it can protect me if I let it. Or it can consume me. But I do not lie to myself. I am aware of all the areas where I am lacking. I am persistently and painfully aware of my mortality lurking around the corner, waiting for me to make a mistake—just one. One mistake is all it takes when you are but flesh and blood, not cocooned by immortality."

"I am afraid of the flames. But I will not hesitate to let them consume everything. I will burn and hope my fear burns with me. Maybe that makes me both brave and stupid. I guess we will have to wait and see which reigns victorious," I say.

May's smile softens and she takes my hands in hers. "I think admitting you are afraid is brave." She swallows hard, eyes damp. "Your mother once told me, '*There is something about being afraid to burn that means you were born to do it.*' And after meeting you, I can think of no truer words."

I feel a resounding truth in those words.

I feel my mother in those words.

"I once thought all Faeries were cruel, unkind, and tricky. You have proven that untrue. I am grateful to have you at my side. I am proud to be the one who will burn this court to ashes so that you can be free," I reply softly. "So that we can be free."

May pauses, a thoughtful, uncertain look on her face. "I am tricky. Do not be mistaken. But I am glad you think I am not cruel or unkind." May smiles but then sighs. "I know it does not negate the wickedness of our actions, but immortality often forges the sharpest blades. One can only spend so much time perfecting oneself into the finest blade before one wishes to cut—and cut deep. When time uses up all the goodness in your heart, yet you live on, boredom becomes a curse you wish to solve with chaos and debauchery and cruelty. Kindness does not bring with it much entertainment. Not all Fae turn to cruelty, but I often think immortality is more a curse than a blessing. We are not born cruel but created. Crafted by our own worst intentions over eternities."

I nod, not sure what to do with that particular truth. "Will I continue to age? Or will I be seventeen forever? I know I will not die of old age as long as I remain in Elphyne, but I do not know if forever is for me."

"I am not certain forever is for anyone. Though, as you came here so young, you will age until you reach adulthood and then your aging will slow and eventually halt. If you were to return to the mortal lands, the years would rush into you, all at once, compounding interest for a human life lived too long. A life-defying death. Mortals who come here older remain as they are."

"I am wildly glad to not be seventeen forever."

I am left alone for the evening in the spelled hideout. May triple-checks the wards, more unnerved by the guards' increasingly frequent searches than she cares to admit. Then she dresses and leaves, an unusual sadness hanging from her shoulders as she goes to attend one of her non-optional dinners with Prince Viktoryn.

I rise from the mattress on the floor, the one I am now sharing with May, who has a habit of blessedly ignoring the nightmares that shake me from sleep more often than I like to reflect on. I snatch a curved dagger from The Weapons Table, along with some strong liquor May snatched from the cellars earlier. The new ronan berry and iron-charmed bracelet Alice provided me with is a steady weight in my palm.

I take a swig from the clear liquor as I saunter into the small attached bathing chamber. The liquor burns my throat, causing me to sputter and cough.

"What is this stuff?" I mutter to myself, studying the bottle like it is a venomous snake as I catch my breath.

I begin to strip off my pants until I stand in only a loose white tunic. I close my eyes and prepare myself. Opening them, I pour liquor across the top of my thigh and over a small dagger. Sinking my rear onto the side of the tub, I hiss as the cool porcelain meets bare skin, bracing my legs in front of me. I line the dagger up with the meaty flesh of my thigh, gritting my teeth.

Then, I dig my dagger into my own flesh.

A pained grunt escapes my throat as I swallow my scream. My hands tremble. I push harder, deeper. The short slash floods with blood, immediately spilling over the wells of my thigh to pool on the stone floor.

My head spins and I pull a ragged breath in through my nose. The air is metallic—I did not expect this much blood. I drop the dagger to the ground with a clang as stars bloom in my vision. I snap the twine that links the bracelet, and dried berries scatter to the ground. I gather three, along with the iron charm, in my palm, disinfecting them quickly with the alcohol. Silently praying it will be enough.

My head swims, my thighs trembling against my weight as the pool of blood grows. An expanding carpet of crimson. I force myself to take deep, even breaths as I push the berries, one by one, into my parted flesh, groaning through my clenched teeth. My fingers sink into the wet warmth of my flesh, meeting raw muscle with a squelch until the berries sit close to the bone. I repeat the steps with the iron charm.

I pull my hand free, heaving as the edges of my vision blacken. My head grows heavy, dipping. I grip the sides of the tub with both my blood-slicked hands so tightly that one of my fingernails cracks.

Once my vision clears—which takes longer than I am comfortable with—I take another swig of alcohol. Then I grab the needle and white thread I stole from the seamstress workspace earlier in the week and douse them in the liquor.

I close my eyes tightly and mentally talk myself through the steps of stitches. Having had to give them to myself a few times throughout my childhood when my mortal mother beat me until my flesh split or when mistakes were made in Knights' training.

Never this many, though.

Never with a cut this deep.

It somehow never gets easier, convincing your mind to repeatedly force a needle through your flesh.

I allow myself one more moment before forcing the needle into one side of the parted flesh. I cry out, reaching for a nearby piece of cloth. I shove it in my mouth to silence myself.

I knit the first stitch, pulling the flesh until it closes.

And then I do it again.

And again.

And again.

I do it even when I do not think I can do it again.

I repeat until I am able to tie off the thread, sweat dripping from my brow and chills skating down my back.

Part of me wonders if this was all for nothing. If this will even work.

It is the last thought I have before my knees buckle, and I slide to the stone floor, sinking into the pool of blood as the room fades away.

I am shaken awake by a *furious* Spring Princess. I wonder if she knows that she is just as radiant, angry as joyful.

"What did you do?" she hisses.

I blink until my blurry eyes clear. The pain in my leg is a bolt of lightning. May's blue eyes are locked on mine and *livid*. Her beautiful light pink dress stained with my blood, lips turned down in a frown so foreign to her features.

"Sorry about the dress," I mutter, my heavy head dipping to the side.

"Willa!" May growls, slapping my cheek lightly. "I do not care for the dress!"

"I would have asked you to help but I thought you would say it was crazy," I mumble, my mouth dry. So dry. I try to wet my lips with my tongue but find it is dry, too.

"Say *what* was crazy? What have you done?" May demands, shaking me still.

Every shake hurts. But I do not respond. I am too tired to fight. Too weak to explain the insanity of my actions.

May steps back from me, scanning the bathing chamber floor, noting the items scattered across it. She leans down to pick up a rogue ronan berry, and her brows furrow.

I watch it click, and I almost giggle.

"You did not," she whispers in disbelief, her eyes flicking from the berry to my face.

"Use compulsion. It will give you the answer," I challenge.

"Ugh! You stupid, *stupid* girl. *This,*" she hisses, pointing around the room, "was not brave. Only stupid. So very stupid."

I manage a weak smile and a one shoulder shrug. I can feel sweat pooling on my forehead and dripping down my spine. The pain in my leg is now a sharp ache, and my head is fuzzy.

The shock wears off her features, and she bends down, gripping my wobbly head by the chin, forcing my eyes to hers.

Pretty blue. So blue.

"I am aware," she mutters. I did not know I said that bit out loud. May's eyes shift and her voice takes on a heady, warm quality. "*What did you put in your flesh?*"

I feel the compulsion slam against my skull, feel the pull of the magicks, but with the berries and charm in my flesh, I find it much easier to push back. The feeling lessens, loosens its grip, and eventually vanishes.

I grin, *triumphant.*

May's mouth falls open.

"You stupid, foolish, *brilliant* girl." May shakes her head, cupping my cheeks as she examines me. "How... you could die of iron poisoning, you fool!" May snaps, pushing my shoulder hard. My back bangs into the tub, and I moan in pain. "Just because your crazy, untested, *dangerous* plan worked does not mean it was a good plan!"

"You are incorrect. That is precisely what it means. It is much better than dying because Viktoryn forced me to take a blade to my own throat."

"You are borrowing luck. It is not endless," she warns.

"I am mortal. I am borrowing everything."

May bites down on her bottom lip, but I watch as her anger melts. She tries to tamp down her amusement, but it floods her eyes.

"You are insane," she snarks, but it does not have much bite.

I grin brighter, warmth expanding through my chest. Yes—yes, I am. Maybe I am not clinging to my sanity as well as I thought. But I find I do not care much anymore.

May wipes her bloody hands on her dress, streaks of crimson staining the pale pink fabric. She leans down to begin healing the gash, removing the poorly done stitches. I hiss at her in pain.

She only smiles a little cruelly. "You are insane," she repeats as my wound closes. She surveys the state of the room once more, then bursts out laughing. "Though a little insanity might serve you well in what is to come."

Lamansa arrives quickly. The gathering is held in an orchard of lush Fae Fruit trees. Each decorated with tiny sparkling lanterns that create a ceiling of stars against the sky. The effect is breathtaking, and I turn on my feet, staring up. The setting sun paints it in swaths of gold, pink, and orange. Its beauty is something out of a painting.

As we descend down the hill that leads to the main party, I take in the large circular cushioned seats, big enough to accommodate a small group. In them, Faeries lounge, kissing and chatting and drinking in various states of drunkenness and undress. Music filled with wild, vibrant energy ignites the dancing crowd.

The air is cooler here, closer to the border between The Seelie and Unseelie Kingdoms. I wish I had thought to bring a cloak.

We pause before the main entrance.

"Are you certain you wish to do this, Willa?" May asks for what feels like the hundredth time. "Once this is done, it cannot be undone."

I smile at her. "Yes," I say. When she shoots me a disbelieving look, I repeat the word with more conviction, "*Yes*. I am certain. I could be dead in a few months. No human has entered The Calling. We do not know if I shall exit mine." I turn and take her hands in mine, willing her to see the certainty in my eyes. "I wish to make the last of my life—if that is what it becomes—worth something. There is no risk I fear anymore. I am living on vanishing time. My wrath will not vanish with it."

If I die when I enter The Calling, I want to die knowing I have done all I can to avenge my family. I want to know I have done all I can to destabilize the Goldynlockes' rule. I want to give Elphyne a chance to be saved—even if I am not the one to save it.

May nods, eyes shiny with unshed tears. "You will not vanish. I promise you this. I will not forget you. I will not let them forget you."

My eyes burn. "Let us burn this court down."

May and I enter the crowd through the main entrance—two trees, branches twisted to form a grande archway decorated with white and orange flowers. There are hundreds of Fae in attendance, the crowd a large living wave of dancing bodies and smiling faces.

Many Fae dance barefoot, wearing scraps of fabric and buzzing with good cheer. They seem relaxed and sensual yet radiate a wildness that seems to bleed into everything they do—everything they are.

"This is very different from The Summer Solstice," I whisper to May.

She dips her head in acknowledgement. "Only the gentry were invited to the Solstice. At Lamansa, anyone can atten-"

I am faster on my feet now, more aware of my surroundings. So when a Faerie drunkenly wobbles into my path, I dash out of the way. May catches my eye and grins. Perhaps recalling the circumstances under which we first met. I find myself smiling back.

"Have you heard?" a passing Fae female whispers, arm linked with a Fae male. "Queen Valda's heir is said to be in the Palace. Prince Archer's soon-to-be wife is her younger sister."

May and I share a look, slowing our steps to listen.

"Perhaps a golden rule is in our grasp once more," the blue-haired Fae male mutters.

A third Fae shushes them. "Do you wish to lose your head? The Crown is trying such comments as *treason*. You fools!"

That spurs us both back into motion, leaving the gossiping Fae behind. We stalk confidently together into the heart of the party, my heart dropping to my toes when I lock eyes with a certain Prince.

Raven.

I stumble a step. For some reason, when I formulated this plan, I forgot to consider that he might be in attendance.

Even masked and in low light, I would know it was him. An undeniable magnetic force draws my eyes to his. His hair is disheveled, blue-black curls falling in his face. It is longer than when I last saw him. His black half-mask is crafted with raven feathers and lace and it lays askew, those storm-blue eyes wild, glinting with mischief. His legs are spread wide as he leans back in one of the circular chairs.

I am so caught up in his eyes that it takes a moment for my mind to catch on to what he is doing.

My surprise must show on my face.

Raven lets a slow, wicked smirk grow on his lips as he maintains hungry eye contact with me. I watch as a male Faerie with deep brown skin, long lashes, and two thick black braids kisses down the side of his neck. The Faerie's hand is buried beneath Raven's half-buttoned silver dress shirt, the material untucked from his pants. Raven's hand is in his hair, fist wrapped around his braids.

If that is not enough to make me halt, a gorgeous female Faerie is straddling his thigh. She has iridescent wings the colour of ripe plums, straight lavender hair, and long limbs that move with the grace of a dancer. Her dress is parted scandalously high as Raven's spare hand trails dangerous lines up her inner thigh.

The Faerie follows his gaze, her large alluring maple eyes finding mine as she kisses up his throat. She smiles at me before tracing her tongue along his jaw. Raven's head falls back, eyes shut with pleasure. I grit my teeth against the sinking feeling in my stomach and the fierce redness in my cheeks.

When his eyes re-open and find mine, Raven winks. I grit my teeth, hating how he toys with me. We are enemies now. We are nothing to each other. I do not care what he does—*who* he does. I do not care that he is looking at me like that. Like he can see right through me. Like he always has.

May sighs beside me, grabbing my arm and dragging me back into motion. The spell breaks, and I blink as my surroundings come back to me in a rush of motion and noise.

We pass tables full of fresh, still-steaming pastries that cause my mouth to water. Buckets full of bottled wine and crystal cups are set out as functional centerpieces. I remember what happened last time I drank Faerie wine and shudder.

"You should tell him," May remarks.

"Tell him what? There is nothing to tell," I say a little too sharply.

"If you insist." May smiles impishly as she turns her head to peer over her shoulder. "His eyes are still on you."

"Stop it!" I hiss under my breath, refusing to look but feeling the heat of his attention.

"Where is all of your foolish bravery now, mortal?" May teases, poking my side.

I scowl at her. "I left it at the Palace. It clashed with my gown."

May's expression shifts as she watches me, a sad smile on her lips. "You cannot stare into a mirror and force the reflection to show what you wish. You and he are a mirror. It will be your ruin."

"I know not what you mean. Nor do I care. And you can change a mirror quite easily if you are only willing to shatter the glass," I counter.

"And shatter the glass you will, for you are far too stubborn. You both clutch your pride as if it can shield you from your true feelings." She narrows her eyes on me. "Do not expect me to gather up the broken glass when you refuse to see what stands before you. When it is you, not the mirror, in pieces."

"I have been in pieces many times and have put myself together. I have had enough of The Winter Prince and his ever-changing mind. He wishes to be enemies. He wishes to hate me in peace. I wish to let him," I declare.

"But you do not wish to hate him, too?" May asks.

I hesitate a heartbeat too long. "I wish to hate him endlessly."

"If you say so."

"I say so."

"You lie to yourself so well. It is almost an art form." She chuckles. "I think you will find the line between love and hate much thinner than you wish."

"Shall we get on with what we came here for or not? I do not wish to speak of this anymore," I snap. "A line is still a line. And tonight, I shall cross it with someone else. What I feel or do not feel for Raven matters not."

"If you say so," May repeats.

I want to rip the knowing look from her face, but I school my expression and turn back to the crowd. My heart leaps as I spot my sister mingling near one of the many wine tables. I share a look with May.

"I have to–"

May waves me off with a lazy grin. "I know how to improvise."

I scurry off towards my sister, taking in her golden gown as she chats with an over-friendly Fae. I scan the nearby crowd for Prince Archer and my heart soars when I see he is nowhere nearby.

I do not give Fabelle a chance to run from me. I link my arm through hers, not slowing my steps. I mutter an 'excuse me' and drag her from the crowd.

"Hey!" she hisses. "Let me go!"

"It would do you well to shut your mouth unless you wish for both of us to end up in a situation far more precarious than this long overdo sisterly chat," I whisper harshly.

Elle tugs against my grip, frowning, but I do not let go. We continue into a thicket of trees, and I release her only to block her return route with my body.

And even though I already know it is likely hopeless, I decide to try.

"I am giving you but a moment to get to the point before I call the guards. You are missing! You are a fugitive!" Elle whisper-shouts furiously.

I roll my eyes, laughing. "You are a fugitive," I mock.

She scowls and moves to step around me, but I grip her arm tight. Fabelle's eyes are twin flames. The expression is so familiar, it is like staring at myself.

"Fine," I snap.

"I am counting," she snaps back.

The words I wish to say tumble out less eloquently than I wish.

"I know you have grown up reading Faerietales where the Prince always rescues the Princess. And there is nothing wrong with wanting a Prince to swoop in and save you, Fabelle. But never forget, the Princesses *always* have the power to save themselves. And you, sister… you are a far cry from a hopeless Princess lost in an epic tale. You forget I know you. Better than *him*." I gesture with my head back towards the party—towards Archer. "Better than *them*. You are doing yourself a disservice. That boy would not deserve your heart even if he ripped his out and handed it to you. Do not let Archer be the hero—that route leads only to despair and disappointment. Chart your own path, Elle."

She studies me with scrutiny so blazing it burns. "I *am* charting my own path. And right now, I am charting it far, far away from *you*," Fabelle hisses as she stalks back towards the crowd. "You will ruin this if you do not stay away."

"I know how he really treats you when no one is looking!" I shout.

She freezes.

Slowly, she peers over her shoulder at me, and she smirks.

"You have no clue what he is to me."

This time, when she storms away, I do not try to stop her.

It takes me a few heartbeats to stitch myself back together, my eyes glued to the spot where Fabelle disappeared back into the crowd. Once my heart stops pounding, I weave my way back to May, who looks at me expectantly.

"Well?" she asks, brow raised.

"It went about as well as you would expect," I mumble.

May grins. "Well, you are still here and not being carted off to the dungeons, so it could not have gone that badly."

"Excellent point. Though that may not matter in a moment's time," I say.

"Ready?" May asks.

I nod, but I am not ready—not in the slightest. I do not want to doubt my plan, but it seems doubt has taken root in my stomach nonetheless. Growing into a large, unwieldy tree whose leaves brush against my gut like a thousand wings taking flight.

I try to ignore the feeling as we find Prince Viktoryn and Prince Archer in the crowd. The second my gaze lands on them, I notice the King and Queen of Summer are notably absent. According to May, their hatred of The Unseelie bleeds so deep they wish to not linger in a celebration that joins the two kingdoms, even when they are hosting.

The sun is almost behind the horizon now, casting the world in the inkiness of dusk. The world is a web of elongating shadows, and I try to imagine I am one of the beings to fear in the dark.

May grabs my upper arm, turning me to face her. "You can do this. If anything goes wrong, I am only a few steps away," she whispers gently. "But also, get it together, or this shall never work."

I laugh at May's bluntness, grabbing a crystal glass off one of the food tables as her body blocks us from view. She fills the glass with a purple juice that will, to any outsider, mimic Fae Wine without leaving me prey to any of its effects.

I down half the glass and turn away from May. I grit my teeth and place a grin on my lips, taking my first of many stumbling steps towards Viktoryn.

I scan his face, concealed by a half-mask of gold and burgundy. His gold eyes striking beneath it. He wears a deep burgundy tunic that brings out a bit of red in the blond of his hair. A crown of spiked golden metal that resembles a sun sits at his brow.

I take another swig of my fake wine, and all too soon, I am standing directly in front of Viktoryn. I fall, crashing forward until my hands meet his chest, wine spilling down the front of his tunic. Warm hands wrap around my waist as I peer up at him with what I hope are dazed eyes and a drunken smile.

"Hello, Viktoryn," I purr, using his body to support my weight.

"Willa," Viktoryn replies evenly, but surprise is written on his raised brows and his panicked blinking.

He recovers quickly, eyes dipping to my mouth as I lick wine from my bottom lip.

A hundred emotions tumble through me. Viktoryn's arms close around me so tightly they are borderline painful, and for a moment, I worry he will call the guards. Or crush me with his bare hands. Or kiss me. All equally terrifying outcomes.

But I have the element of surprise, and I must keep it.

"I am tired of hiding. I am tired of fighting. I do not want power or to be a Princess. I miss my sister. I miss how things were. I do not forgive you, but I want to try to fix this," I mumble.

He chuckles. "Do you, now? Very interesting." One of his hands leaves my waist to trail a line across my throat. "Of course, your attempt at an apology for your outrageous behavior would be laced with an anti-apology."

"This is not an apology. If you wish for one, you will find my lips empty. But I do wish for a truce." I force my gaze to trail to his lips. An easy smirk finds his mouth, but it is gone quickly.

"A truce," he echoes.

"Yes, a truce. Must I repeat myself?"

"No," he says, searching my expression as if he can seek out the truth written in the freckles on my cheeks.

He pulls me back to my feet, and I let myself wobble as he turns me, pulling my back into his chest. Hot breath whispers over my ear, causing me to shiver. Viktoryn chuckles darkly.

His hand slides up my body, fingers assured. He has mapped this territory before, knowing it better than anyone. His other hand traces threatening circles over my hip.

My mind screams at me to lean in or run, but I ignore both. Even as his warm fingers wrap around my neck and squeeze tightly enough to restrict my breathing. I will myself not to fight, my eyes falling shut as I force my fear to bloom into boldness.

"I am finding it rather hard to believe that after disappearing and remaining in hiding for *weeks*, you now stumble up to me, drunken and vulnerable," his tongue traces the shell of my ear, and I whimper, "to throw yourself at my mercy and request, of all things, a *truce*. Though the insulting tone does make this act more plausible."

"I loved you," I whisper.

His hand loosens abruptly, but his body stiffens.

"I think I could love you once more..." I continue. "I never wanted any of this. I never wanted a crown or power. I only ever wanted a better life for my sister and safety for myself... but she has chosen your side, and now I am alone. I have no one. I have lost the very thing I was fighting for. And for once, I find I do not want to keep fighting. I do not want to keep hiding. I am so tired. I am so tired of it all, Viktoryn. Let us find a way to make this right."

He huffs a disbelieving laugh. "Am I to believe that a spiteful little thing such as yourself is willing to forget the indiscretions you believe I have committed against your family?"

I have the sudden need to drive my dagger through his heart as he so casually refers to the murder of my mother as an *indiscretion*. But I let that rage rise, I let it fuel me.

"Am I to believe you do not wish to avenge your mother? Your sister? Yourself? That you have no loyalty to her cause?" Viktoryn accuses.

"Forget? Never. But you have done what I never could. You have given my sister more. You have made her what she always wished to be. No matter the hurt I feel, I am *grateful* for that." I pause. "I did not know my mother, Viktoryn. She is dead. I owe no loyalty to the ghosts who have left me haunted. Why would I hand my loyalty to someone who built me a fragile life of lies in a den of lions?"

"What is it you propose then, darling?" he questions.

"I propose that one should not make bargains with tricky Faeries while wine-addled—or rather at all. I propose we dance until my head is clear of the stars swirling in my eyes. I propose a parley for the evening. Let me prove to you I will not run."

Viktoryn chuckles. I feel it vibrate from his chest into my back as he presses my body harder into the heat of his.

"Alright, little mouse. I accept your proposal, but need I remind you that this party is surrounded by guards. If I find anything amiss, one single misstep, I will have you detained. You will find my hospitality is not nearly as kind this time..." His hand flexes. "You will behave, or I will see to it that you suffer and suffer well."

I nod once, and he releases me, letting me stumble forward. I catch myself before I faceplant into the dirt. He smirks, gripping my wrist and pulling me off to dance.

I have stepped into the cage with him. I have handed him what he wants more than anything. Now, I must beat him at his own game—or die trying.

Viktoryn pulls me into a bustling crowd of rowdy, dancing Fae. I watch his eyes flick to the guards, but he makes no move to beckon them. We both know it is in his best interest to have no one aware of my presence. Especially with the rumors circling in support of a Caprimore rule.

We begin to dance. Unlike at The Summer Solstice, the dancing seems to follow no specific choreography. Instead, these movements are wild and reckless—scandalous, even. Fae wind their bodies into each other, brushing figures twisting to the erratic music flowing through the air.

Viktoryn places both his hands on my waist, pulling me close. I sway my hips in time with the beat. The lights sparkle above us, and if this was anything but what it is, I might be having fun. I might even say it is beautiful. I might just be a girl at a party with a boy.

But I am not just a girl at a party, and Viktoryn is not just a handsome boy who asked me to dance. I gaze into his eyes, thinking of all the ways I will enjoy seeing him plead for mercy when I ruin everything he is. The thought causes me to smile, and Viktoryn mistakes it as one for him, pulling me closer. I let him because, when focused on his ruin, one dance seems like so little to pay for vengeance.

The lovely high I felt the first time I danced to Fae music overcomes me, and I drown in bliss. The feeling makes it harder to keep my head but the ronan berries in my skin help dull the effect.

Viktoryn spins me so fast my head whirls, and a laugh slips from me, followed by a pang of longing—*grief.* Grief that belongs to a girl I no longer am. A girl who looked up at the man holding her now and thought the world began and ended in his eyes.

It is strange. To know I have outgrown him. Even if things had not changed between us, even if he was not wicked or cruel. I am not the same girl who fell in love with him. In this new world, with these new versions of ourselves, we no longer fit.

And though I thought I'd feel sadness, I am glad. To be more. To be larger than I once was. To have grown. I am glad that I have become something new. Something built from all the broken pieces of my previous selves—a suit of armor.

Still, it is odd to think how quickly my world has expanded. How fast lovers, sisters, and friends have become adversaries. Who knew one girl could collect so many enemies? Who knew this would make that same girl feel so alone?

How ridiculous it all is. How ridiculous it is to know all of Elphyne is in an uproar over a teenage girl. And yet, here I am, in the arms of my enemy. In a world so magnificently and terrifyingly large that I am drowning and swimming all at once.

Suddenly, I am ripped from Viktoryn's arms—and my thoughts. I am spun around, and my eyes meet Raven's.

"Get your hands off her, bird boy," Viktoryn snaps.

"Now, why would I do such a thing when she so seems to enjoy my hands on her?" Raven drawls, smirking.

My blush is *apocalyptic*—but so is my anger.

Viktoryn moves to step forward, but I hold up a hand to halt him.

To my surprise, he stops.

And I wonder if this just became a test.

"Let me," I say, turning back to Raven. "Is there something I can do for you, Prince Raven?

"Why are you here, Willa? What are you doing with him? After all he has done to you. He will *ruin* you," he hisses.

I shove him away, tilting my chin back.

"And you will not?" I question.

Raven pales. "I–"

"As I thought. Now, run along," I wave him off, "and return to your little trio to kiss the night away. I have business to attend to."

I do not have time to play Raven's games.

And I no longer have the desire to.

His lips split into a smile, "Jealousy suits you. It paints your eyes in fire and your cheeks in blood."

My eyes narrow on him as they run over his unbuttoned shirt, half-tucked into his pants. His black curls glisten in the light, thoroughly messed and falling in front of his eyes.

He looks well and proudly debauched.

And to my disdain, well and truly *extraordinary*.

I hate him for flaunting this in my face. Can he not leave anything untouched? Anything untainted?

He thrives on watching me, taunting me, toying with me.

An alley cat playing with a mouse. But I am no mouse.

I have found my teeth and claws. And I am prepared to use them.

"Oh, please, spare me. It was not I who stormed over here to tug me out of the arms of another. Whatever could I be jealous of?" I pause, meeting his eyes. "Your hands may have been on them, but your eyes—your eyes were on *me*." I smile wickedly.

Raven eyes narrow, but then he leans in, lips brushing my ear. I hear Viktoryn step closer.

But all I can *feel* is Raven—invading my oxygen and setting my skin aflame.

My breath catches, and my fists curl. I wish to punch him. I wish to pull him closer. I wish to punch him and then pull him closer. I wish to tell him how he vexes me. How his words are the sharpest of blades and sweetest of honey.

Instead, I do nothing but hold my breath and plead for my sanity to return.

"I wish to gift you a secret, pretty girl," Raven whispers, breath dancing along my skin. I fight a shiver. "Did you know your heart speeds, if only slightly, when you lie to me?" He places a kiss on the hollow behind my ear, and all the breath rushes out of my lungs. "Such sweet, pretty lies—they fall so gently from your lips. What fools we are. To trust them. I do not any longer," he whispers. "I trust your *heart…*"

Said heart is pounding so hard I can feel it in every part of my body. "You have had so much practice, one could miss it," he hums. "It is but a *flutter*, a single flap of a bird's wings—so slight."

I scoff again, but my heart kicks up impossibly higher. Raven leans back, studying my face with a tilt of his head. His eyes fill with that all-encompassing intensity. And again, I find myself wishing to punch him or kiss him, if only so he will stop looking at me like *that*.

"You think too highly of yourself," I scoff, holding his eyes.

He smirks, his thumb traveling the length of his bottom lip. "A truth."

I am surprised that Viktoryn does not move to rip us apart. This is most definitely a test. He wants me to prove my loyalty.

"I will not play games of truths or lies with you, Raven. I no longer wish to entertain your games and your ever-changing moods."

"A lie."

"*Raven*," I warn.

"Oh," Raven drawls, face laced with the sweetest surprise. "Your heart just skipped a single beat."

I feel my face and neck flush. I curse myself for the reaction, *mortified*. Viktoryn finally takes a step closer to me.

"Be gone, Raven. I do not want you here," I say, keeping my voice even despite the fire on my cheeks.

"A lie. You wish for me to stay." Raven grins sinfully.

My patience slips, and Viktoryn clears his throat behind me. But Raven does not even bother to meet Viktoryn's eyes. His gaze never wavering from mine. He stares at me like no one else exists, as if he sees the beginning and the end of everything in my eyes, like the world has narrowed to only him and me.

I am the air he breathes, the melody in his music—a fascination and obsession.

It hurts.

"She said be gone, bird boy," Viktoryn snaps, stepping forward to place a hand on my shoulder.

I fight my flinch but still react slightly. Blinking. My mind unwillingly flashes to Viktoryn's hands around my neck when he strangled me in The Crystal Palace.

Raven's expression turns icy as he trails his glowing eyes, slowly, from Viktoryn's hand to his face. His gaze pins him in place—twin frozen daggers. His playful demeanor vanishes.

"You know, Viktoryn, I think it is time you come up with a new nickname. This one has grown rather tired, do you not think?" Raven drawls, deadly calm. "You have had all of eternity to come up with something fresh, something *inspired*..." Raven tsks. "Yet you still lack creativity, wit. A shame. The crown is wasted on you."

"Oh, goody. This always goes well," I mutter under my breath.

Raven's gaze shoots back to mine, the warmth returning to his features for a flash. "Lie."

"Do not look at her," Viktoryn growls. "Look at me."

"Oh, but she is just so pleasant to look at."

"The night is young, Unseelie Prince. Join me for a fight—let us entertain our Folk. Show them who the real champion of The Courts is. What fun it would be to bathe in your blood."

Raven's smile is a chilling threat. "You are a pony of so few tricks. Why must everything degrade into violence, Viktoryn? Hmm?" he muses. "You should be a jester, not a King—all these *theatrics*. It leads one to believe you do not possess the mind for cunning debate. All brawn and no brains." Raven's unimpressed eyes drag across Viktoryn's frame.

"We were simply playing a little game, yet you take such offense. So quick to anger. So emotional. How do you plan to rule with such an absence of restraint? You lack the composure of a King... I could teach you if you wish?" Raven purrs, a challenge in his eyes, venom dripping from his lips.

Suddenly, Amira and May appear beside me, and the crowd that has been gathering grows to a mob. Viktoryn takes a swing at Raven's jaw, and a collective gasp sounds like a chorus. Raven easily sidesteps the blow, and Viktoryn loses his balance as his fist flies uselessly through the air.

Prince Archer appears, rushing forward to see what all the fuss is about, his brows shoot up in surprise. But he does not interfere. Instead, he smirks as he eyes the two Princes. My sister, two steps behind him, takes one look at the scene and laughs.

I am about to step between them when arms close around my middle, yanking me back.

I look over my shoulder to see Raith's grinning face, and I relax a little. Everyone's eyes are on the Princes as Raven swings and catches Viktoryn in the gut, making him double over with a groan. I see Amira pulling May away with a furious expression on her face. I am endlessly glad to not be a part of *that* particular conversation.

"Raven's got this," Raith assures. "We must speak."

"Not now," I growl.

"It is not a request."

A gasp followed by a cheer rises from the crowd as Raven lands another punch to Viktoryn's face. Viktoryn rises, his eyes aflame as blood runs in rushing rivulets down his face. He spits blood and lands a punch of his own. A crack sounds, and I flinch as Raven's jaw takes the brunt of the blow.

"Always so slow, Prince. And I am not speaking of your brains," Raven jeers, smiling with a split lip.

"I have to stop them before they kill each other," I hiss, but Raith only laughs.

I desperately try to scoot forward, but Raith lifts me clear off my feet, hauling me over his shoulder.

"Hey!" I cry out, beating my fists down on his back as he whisks me away.

Raith does not set me down until the party's noise is but a whisper on the wind. He drops me onto the grass behind a grand oak tree. I right myself, smoothing down my dress and crossing my arms to pin him with a glare.

"What was that about?" I snap.

"I will not play games with you. Raven is the diplomat, not me. You know what that was for. You know what you did. *I* know what you did," Raith states, his usual charismatic manner absent.

His disappointment ripples through me, and my confidence wavers. For the first time, I see him as his soldiers must. No nonsense, no excuses. Singularly focused on the battle to be won.

The cool night air starts to feel oppressive as it brushes against my skin, trying to locate cracks in my waning armor.

"Fine. That still does not explain why you carried me away like a sack of potatoes," I hiss.

"A very beautiful and light sack of potatoes." Raith softens for a heartbeat as if he cannot resist his own charm, but his solemness returns. "What happened with you and Raven? What happened with May? I have never seen our group so divided. I have never seen Raven so detached. I know that you would not betray us without good cause. Despite what the others think, I see your heart. So tell me, please. What has happened?"

He takes both my hands in his, gaze kind but serious—as if he is truly trying to understand. I sigh.

"If I tell you, we must make a bargain. You must swear not to tell the others," I concede.

"I do not wish to withhold information from them, Willa." Raith sighs. "That is not a fair ask."

"Then my secrets are to remain in the vault of my mind."

Raith drops my hands, gazing up to the sky. He lifts his arms behind his head, hands brushing the back of his scalp.

He blows out a long breath and nods. "Fine. For the next few moments, anything we say to each other is to remain between us. I will repeat nothing in word or in writing of which we speak from now until the end of time. It is a bargain."

I scrutinize his wording, not willing to be tricked by a Fae bargain. "Anything we say this *eve*. Not for a few moments."

Raith nods tightly. "Anything said between us this eve is to remain between us. I will repeat nothing in word or in writing of which we speak from now until the end of time. It is a bargain."

"It is a bargain," I echo, feeling the metallic snap of magick sealing the words. "What do you want to know? What is it you want me to say?"

"Why did Maylea leave our side for yours?" Raith questions. "I have wracked my mind, but I cannot figure out what would motivate her to leave the side with infinitely more resources and bodies."

"You sound like a strategist." I smile.

"I am an army commander, after all. Now, quit stalling and tell me." He levels me with that no-nonsense look.

I cross my arms. "She said she owed the late Summer Queen a *lifetime* of favors. I do not know more than that. And if I take the crown, she is free from her engagement with Viktoryn. Plus, working solely with me keeps Amira from danger. I have agreed that once I am in power, I will assist her in claiming The Spring Throne and in changing the marriage laws. In exchange, she will change the mortal servant laws. I would have changed the law regardless, but if I am expected to be a diplomat now, I must act as such. And I cannot watch another human be whisked away and forced into a life of ensorcelled slavery."

"I knew it! I knew you both would not leave simply because you could," Raith responds, relief coating his tone, and I realize how badly he *needed* that to be true. "*A lifetime of favors...* odd wording."

"I, too, thought it odd, but May has not been forthcoming about how she came to owe the Summer Queen such a dramatic sum of favors," I mutter with a shrug. "What else? Time is ticking, and if I am gone too long, I will end up in Viktoryn's dungeon. They cannot punch at each other all night."

"Oh, worry not, Princess. They can." Raith smirks. "This does not explain everything. What happened with you and Raven?"

"Other than the fact that he led Viktoryn to my sister and I in Mayfair?" I choke out a laugh as Raith grimaces. "If you figure out the answer, would you grace me with it? I do not know. He said something about owing a favor to a dead Fae?" I shake my head. "I believe that favor has somehow bound him to me, and because of it, he has grown to despise me. But again, your kind does not often offer up a plethora of information. Speaking with Faeries is like picking up dropped puzzle pieces, but they all belong to a different picture, and they never drop more than one at once."

"Dead Fae and favors," Raith murmurs, more to himself.

"Any other questions?"

"Yes, one," Raith says, eyes meeting mine. He takes my hands in his gently once more. "Are you alright?"

"*Oh.*" The question hits like a slap.

I do not have the luxury of not being alright—I have not for many years. I have been slapping the shattered pieces of myself back together each time they crack for as long as I can recall. Forging them into jagged, jaded armor and not stopping to apologize when others catch on the sharp pieces and bleed.

I open and close my mouth, staring up at him. His eyes are searching as he scans my face, then nods as if he understands, pulling me into a tight hug. I resist for a moment but then sink into him, filled with surprise when my eyes well with tears. He whispers comforting words as I cry in his arms. Releasing some of the weight I have been carrying as it flows from my eyes in streams of distress.

When my tears slow, I pull back, wiping my cheeks. I nod at him, hoping my gratitude shows. I turn to head back, but he grips my arm. "Willa, wait. Take this," he pleads, pressing a small green gem the size of a pea into my palm.

My brows knit as I squint to see the object in the dark. "What is it?"

"A messenger of sorts…" he hesitates. "When activated, it will send me a signal and your location. If you ever end up in a situation where you need backup, no matter what is happening with the others, use it. I will come to you," Raith says, eyes soft and honest.

But even with the sincerity of his words, a bolt of panic shreds my chest, and I pull back.

"No. I will not take another tracker. Never again," I vow, tossing it back at him.

He catches it effortlessly, eyes flashing with hurt.

"Willa, please. I will not tell the others I have given it to you. I swear it. It cannot track you without being activated first. Once activated, the signal only lasts for three days and nights. I swear that I am speaking the truth—it cannot be used unless you wish it." I know he is telling the truth as magick floods the air. "I only hope to provide you a way to contact me if you find yourself in danger," he states, placing the gem back in my palm and wrapping my fingers around it.

He takes my shoulders in his hands gently and presses his forehead to mine. His voice drops lower. "I know what it is like to lose your family. I know what it is like to have no one left. To be unable to trust a soul but your own. That burden is heavy to bear alone."

"Are you saying I can trust you?" I question, staring into his eyes.

"In this? Yes. In everything?" he sighs, looking troubled. "My court will always come first. It is my duty to protect The Folk of Winter. But I will always try to balance both. Even when the scales tip."

I take that answer for what it is, closing my eyes and wrapping my resolve in iron. When I am steady, I open my eyes.

"Alright. Tell me how to activate it if I must?"

Raith smirks, a small chuckle leaving his lips and confusion floods me. "You may find this odd. It is activated by your saliva. You can simply lick it, or, if you are being detained, open your mouth and swallow it."

"Pardon?" I choke, wrinkling my nose.

"If you swallow it, they cannot remove it from your person when they realize what you are attempting." He laughs at my shock, smiling, and I find myself smiling, too.

"Disgusting... but brilliant."

"I have my moments of genius," he drawls, and I pull him into a quick hug.

"Raith?" I mumble against his chest.

"Yes, Willa?"

"I am surprised you are not trying to talk me out of what I am about to do. I am surprised you are not telling me to get as far away from Viktoryn as possible."

His chest rumbles with soft laughter as he gently smooths my hair down. "Would it make a difference if I did?"

I smile against him. "No..." I pause. "Raith?"

"Yes, Willa?"

"You are a good friend."

"I know."

We rush back to the party to find two bloodied princes still throwing punches. I sigh loudly. I step forward and place myself between them, holding my arms out as two chests collide with my palms.

"*Enough.*"

They both look down at me as if drifting out of a haze of bloodlust, eyes slowly clearing as they blink at me. Both princes pant, dripping in blood and brimming with violence. They peer back up at each other, lips curling with disgust, and for a moment, I think one of them will swing again.

I sigh again loudly. "Are you quite finished? Or shall I send for a measuring stick so you can whip them out to compare and settle this once and for all?"

The crowd lets out an '*oooo.*' A few Folk shout out some rather lewd encouragements. They both shake their heads, and I revel in the flush that paints their cheeks pink.

Not so tough now.

The tension melts from their bodies, and they share a tight nod. The hatred in their eyes seems to say, 'This is not over,' but it is over, for *now* at least. The crowd starts to dissipate, returning to their party as the show abruptly ends.

"Well, that was fun," I deadpan. "You do not see Princess Maylea and The Autumn Court heirs brawling. They must leave all the dramatics to you two. You certainly excel at it."

Raven chuckles, and Viktoryn wipes the back of his hand across his lips, smearing his face with blood. My eyes slowly trail across the blooming purple bruise on Raven's sharp cheekbone. I have the urge to reach out and drag my finger across them but resist, clearing my throat.

It seems neither of them noticed my brief clandestine meeting. And for that, I am glad. Raith and I lock eyes and he discreetly nods as if he thinks the same.

"Well, I, for one, would like to call it a night. Watching you beat each other bloody was rather exhausting. Prince Viktoryn, do you mind finding me accommodations in your palace so we may continue our talks of peace in the morning?"

"Talks of peace?" Raven growls.

I cross my arms as the tension floods back into him.

"Indeed. Not that it is any of your business, Prince Raven," I state sharply.

Raven hesitates then nods, the disgust in his eyes so thick it coats me like oil. "When you are done making your bed and find you are lying in a grave, do not beg me for a shovel," he says icily and stalks away.

I grit my teeth against the sting of his words and struggle to keep my face plastered in a neutral expression. It feels as though he has ripped my still-beating heart from my chest and taken it with him. But I manage.

"It seems you both have a flare for the dramatics," I breathe, turning back towards Viktoryn, whose face is flooded with conflicting emotions that I find difficult to make any sense of.

"Your room shall be heavily guarded," Viktoryn warns. "I do not trust you one bit."

I smile sweetly at him. "Nor I, you."

I wake in my new lush bedchamber that functions as a gilded dungeon. The sun is cresting over the horizon, chasing away the darkness of night with extraordinary swatches of deep orange and pale pink. I watch the sunlight dance across the calm surface of Cyrissa Lake from my balcony.

My new room is high in the east tower, heavily guarded—isolated. One door in. One door out. Both lead to the one and only stairway down.

In this, at least, I feel an odd thrum of satisfaction.

It seems Viktoryn has finally located some wisdom in the deep, buried regions of his brain and stopped underestimating me.

But this also poses a new array of problems.

The room itself is lovely. Familiar, somehow. It differs in design from the rest of the Palace in a way that is refreshing. A welcome escape from the gaudy gold below.

It is hexagonal in shape, with a pointed roof that has been painted to resemble a cloudy sky. Large blue and purple stained glass windows are placed along the room. The walls are a delicate blue, lined with sea shells, and light wood crown molding, carved with images of Fae in boats riding wild waves. A large wingback chair with deep azure cushions, a small wardrobe, and a huge four-poster bed take up the remaining space.

I let the cool morning air kiss my cheeks as I wait for the sun to fully rise. I cannot risk meeting with May—or leaving this room, for that matter—until after Prince Viktoryn has visited.

And I am certain he will.

During my first search of this room, I found a sun emblem—the same emblem as the one on the key Alice gave me—hidden under a cream-coloured carpet in front of the hearth. I have yet to test it, somehow worried for the first time it will not work. Or that the floor will open up to a dark, endless fall into nothingness.

A knock at my door steals me from the spiral of my thoughts. I turn, grabbing a soft, lace-laden, red dressing gown off my bed and tie it around my waist as I rush to the door. I crack it open, allowing the wall scones from the hall to bask my face in the light.

"Hello, Willa."

"Hello, Viktoryn."

"May I enter?" he requests.

I laugh. "May you enter the room you have provided me that doubles as a cell?"

"Perhaps it is an odd request when you voice our circumstances."

"You may, though I did not expect you so early. I am afraid I am rather underdressed," I remark, glancing down at myself self-consciously.

In truth, I did expect him to come early. I have been up for hours, pacing, staring out at the landscape from my balcony. I assumed he would want to check that I had not somehow vanished in the night.

Viktoryn's eyes trail down my body, lingering on my exposed skin. He follows me into the room, and I perch myself on the bed. Instead of taking the wingback chair as I expected, he leans against the wall, studying me thoughtfully with a note of suspicion. I fiddle with my hands in my lap, my gaze falling to my fingers.

We are quiet for a few moments.

So many words remain unsaid.

Finally, he clears his throat, and when I meet his eyes, they are narrowed.

"Why are you here, Willa?"

"I told you last night."

"Why are you *truly* here, then?"

I sigh, raking a hand through my hair. "All I have ever wished for was a better life for my sister. It is all I have ever worked for. Without that purpose, I have found myself, well... *lost*."

"Go on."

I take a deep breath. "Fabelle was my true north, the driving force of all I was. I am not certain who I am if not her protector if not her keeper," I confess, and his eyes soften.

"You are correct that I do not trust or forgive you. But I am tired of floating aimlessly in a hurricane of court politics and power plays. I am tired of waiting until the holes that continue to appear in my boat finally drag me under. I fear without you at my side, I will drown in a world I do not understand," I continue.

Viktoryn breaks my gaze and looks at his boots as if considering the weight of my words. I push on, smoothing my robe over my legs as they dangle from the bed.

"I miss my sister dreadfully," my eyes well with tears, "and I miss my life. Even though it was broken and full of hardship, it was *mine.*"

I may hate her for what she's done to us, but I miss Elle.

I am not whole without her.

Where I am lacking, she is abundant.

Where I am empty, she is whole.

We are meant to be side by side.

"I have been stripped of my choices, my family, and my love. And yes, I have fought because that is all I have ever been good at." I laugh—a defeated sound. "All I have ever been taught to do is fight. Fight until my hands bleed and my lungs collapse. Fight smarter, harder. Fight and fight and fight until my rib cage explodes, and I inevitably find my heart on the sharp end of my enemy's sword. It was the last lesson my father left me," I confess, swallowing the hollow attack of grief that wells in my throat.

"Did I ever tell you..." I smile sadly. "He said he knew the day I was born that I was a fighter. A warrior. I wailed and flailed my little limbs like after only moments in this world—I was ready to conquer it. But it seems I am now fighting the inevitable. I do not know if I am willing to die fighting something that cannot be conquered. I am but one girl, and

I am in a land where I am not sure how to spot enemy from ally…" I find Viktoryn's eyes.

"But once, before all of this, *you* were my ally, my friend. You were… you were someone I loved and leaned on. I wish for that once more. I wish for a life with my sister again. I wish for the protection you once offered. I may have scoffed at it then, but… Viktoryn, I am tired."

He is silent for a long moment, and the quiet prickles my skin.

"Let me speak plainly. I believe what you say is true. But I fear it is not the whole truth…" He looks away and sighs before looking back, his eyes intense—almost desperate. "And as much as your presence is a sharp thorn in my side, the lack of your presence is like a world without flowers. Without colour. A world without the beauty that should accompany pain. You are the thorns and the petals…" Viktoryn laughs, but it sounds like it pains him. "I have not yet decided which you possess more of."

I look away, unable to hold his eyes. "The Calling is but months away, and without your help… I am not certain I will survive. I do not want to die," I choke on the words.

I am not finished yet.

"So it is true, then. He has told you everything. About who you are. What you contain," Viktoryn says.

"Yes."

"And yet you are here with me. Not him."

I swallow. "Yes."

Viktoryn's eyes flood with hope.

He clears his throat. "I do not know how we move forward so that we may be allies. But I want to be... You could simply be here to convince me of your loyalties so you can wait under my roof or in my bed," he gives me a heated look, "for the perfect moment to drive a blade through my heart."

I stiffen, my cheeks heating.

"I am not certain I would blame you..." Viktoryn sighs. "However, you now know the truth of your power and kin. You know what you possess. You know I can help you. Give you what you want. Think of all we could be together. All we could accomplish, Willa."

And I do.

I think about all we could be together.

We, who bring the worst of each other to the surface.

"We would be unstoppable. I see it now. I see it all so clearly now, Viktoryn. Let us work together. Let us conquer."

Viktoryn's grin is instant and sharp. I see a spark of victory in his eyes. "Your room will remain guarded. But as an act of good faith, you will be allowed to visit the library, walk the grounds, or visit the ladies' parlor when you wish. You are to take no fewer than five guards with you. They will be notified that—unless otherwise directed by *me*, and me alone—these terms are not to change. You will subject yourself to being searched each and every time you exit or enter this room."

I nod, and he continues, "Your sister will be permitted to visit your room if she pleases. You are not to contact her or attempt to visit her otherwise. All visits will be supervised. Your meals will be brought to you until you have proven that you are not a threat to have in the ballroom."

I smile. "You finally see me, it seems."

Viktoryn smiles darkly. "So it seems... Since you have taken a liking to Beatrice and Alice, they will be on call if you require assistance. I will personally meet with both of them to notify them about the change in your circumstances. Do you believe these terms to be fair? I will allow you to renegotiate when you have proven yourself trustworthy."

I scoff slightly. "Yes. I believe your terms to be reasonable. But I would like to add that if I send for you, you come to speak to me at your earliest convenience."

"Reasonable enough. If my guards find a single weapon in your room, you will be moved to the dungeon for questioning. Am I clear?"

I laugh. "Crystal."

Viktoryn nods, and I assume he will leave, but he remains against the wall. Watching me like he expects I will leap up, sprout wings, and fly off the balcony. Or pull out a hidden dagger and jump forth to stab him.

I sit still, watching him back.

"I am ever so curious about what you will do next, darling," Viktoryn says, turning to leave.

"So am I," I whisper as the door clicks shut.

Hours later, Beatrice and Alice enter my room, and I rush into their awaiting arms as they fold tightly around me. I melt into their touch, their support.

"Oh, my dear, I was worried sick about you," Beatrice mutters, cupping my cheek with one of her hands.

"I am alright," I reply.

"Are you?" Alice asks, bright blue eyes finding mine as she releases me. "Are you really?"

I laugh. I do not mean to. "As well as I can be, certainly. Better than I once was. I know what I must do now."

Beatrice studies me top to bottom as if searching for signs of harm. When she finds none, she nods.

"Your mother would be proud," she whispers.

Tears form in my eyes, trailing down my cheeks. "I wish I had the chance to get to know her. I wish I *remembered* her.

"I remember her well. Not that I say such these days. I miss her often. She was as strong as steel and as bold as an ox. And I am telling you, she would be *proud*, child," Beatrice says, taking my hands in hers.

My mouth falls open. "You knew my mother?"

Beatrice grins, her eyes wrinkling kindly, her dark brown hair and skin warm. "Very well. I was her lady-in-waiting... or at least, that is what we told the court. In truth, I was her spymaster. The Fae tend to speak too freely around their human counterparts."

I laugh, surprised and impressed.

"I had no idea! But I should not be shocked."

"If you had any idea, I would be no good at my duty. Or what once was my duty." Beatrice's eyes fill with grief. "Your mother was my dearest friend, and I hers. She is the one who tasked me with caring for Alice when she arrived here as an orphan." I look to Alice to see if this fact makes her uncomfortable, but she is grinning. "I hope in this, I have made her proud."

Alice beams at her, and in unison, we both say, "You have."

"That is my daily wish." Beatrice's eyes that well with tears. "You are a foolish girl. You should never have returned here. But I suppose I should have expected such. You are so very like your kin."

A question arises. "Why did my mother not task you with giving me the key? Why Alice?"

"She always feared someone might uncover who I once was. Alice, in the eyes of all who rule, is innocent," Beatrice explains. "Now, enough of all this. What can we do for you? How can we help?"

"Oh! I know!" Alice declares, bouncing on her toes. "You will require new gowns. I shall have to take new measurements," she mutters, pulling her lip between her teeth.

"Soon, Alice." I smile a bit wickedly. "First, I have a few ideas that require both of your expertise. Send for May and meet me in the library."

I am draped over a plush golden wingback chair, a blanket wrapped around me, with a book in my hand, when May traipses into the room like a spring breeze. She slows, her face twisting with mock surprise.

My five required guards line each of the doors and windows. They make no move to stop the Princess as she descends down the steps into the sunken reading space.

"You have returned, mortal," May says, looking me over as if she did not just see me a night ago. "How charming. I have heard tales about your lips meeting those of my betrothed. Is it true?"

I feign shock, biting down my smile while glancing around with panic at the guards. "Oh! I did not know him to be promised to another."

"Did you not? Hmm. And yet, knowing this now, you do not run. Brave."

"Or stupid," I counter, and she chuckles.

I close my book and slide my legs down the arm of the chair.

"Is there something I can assist you with, Princess Maylea?" I question.

"I find there is." May turns to the guards and meets each of their eyes individually. "Leave us. I wish to speak to the mortal alone."

Klein, the tallest and highest ranked of the group, shakes his head, tucking his hands behind his back. "I am afraid that cannot be arranged, Princess. Orders from above."

We assumed it would not be that easy.

But it was worth a shot.

"Pity." May smiles too innocently. "Do remember those orders come from a male soon to be my husband, not that it seems to matter to the mutt. I am soon to be your *Queen.* Do you wish to be cast in my displeasure?"

Klein does not flinch. "No, Your Highness. However, the order stands. You may take up the issue with your betrothed. I can do nothing for you."

May's smile turns sharp, and in a blink, vines crawl up from the floor, wrapping around each of the guards' arms and legs. They go to shout, but flowers bloom in their open mouths, choking them. I press a hand to my mouth as if shocked, but it is mostly to suppress the laugh that bursts from me.

I rise from my chair as if to run, but vines grip my ankles and tie them to the legs of my seat.

"Not so fast," she snaps at me before turning back on Klein. "I find I have grown tired of your voice and excuses. If you can do nothing for me, perhaps this shall be more amenable."

"Princess Maylea, please, I meant no harm," I profess. "They will tell Prince Viktoryn!"

May's sparkling eyes find mine as she tosses her hair over one shoulder, smirking.

"Let them."

"Princess, please. I did not know him to be yours. I swear it!"

"Fine. Very well. I do not care all that deeply for him, but it is the principle, you see," she waves me off, and the vines begin to crawl away, flowers wilting in the mouths of the guards. They spit to clear their mouths, cursing. "What foul words to use in the presence of a lady. Perhaps I will speak to Prince Viktoryn after all."

"You–"

"Do not finish whatever it is you wish to say, Sir Klein. Either run off to whine to Viktoryn like the spineless coward you are. Or be silent. If I wish to play with the mortal, I shall. It is only good fun. They do scare so easily."

"Very well. Speak to her, then. Harm her, you will not. We remain," Klein counters.

May rolls her eyes, turning back to me. "I could simply kill them all," she says almost wistfully.

"I would not recommend it," I say, gripping the arms of the chair tightly.

"No. It would be unwise," she agrees. "But I am feeling rather stupid…"

The guards tense, armor creaking, but May just sighs, her emerald gown flowing around her as she drops into a settee beside me.

A metallic crackle fills the air as she effortlessly weaves a spell to muddle our voices. Klein shouts at her to drop the spell, but May waves him off over her shoulder like a pesky bug.

"Is it wise to show them your magicks?" I wonder aloud to her, feigning fear. They may not be able to hear us, but certainly, they can see us.

"As I said, I am feeling rather stupid. Playing pretend has grown rather tiresome."

I almost grin but catch myself. "Well played."

"Yes, well, now they believe you will try to stop me if I decide they should meet their end. Let us hope your moment of loyalty makes it to the ears of Viktoryn," May says.

"Anything to report?" I ask, making a show of looking uncomfortable and pulling at my skirts.

"Nothing, it seems. No one is yet aware of your return, though that will seldom last. Alice will make sure of it. However, it will be difficult for us to meet. I cannot play the scorned bride forever. Viktoryn will not believe I care much at all what he does with his lips or with whom."

"I shall be able to use the tunnels soon. I have located one in the tower. But it is in our best interest that I play nice for a while. Until then, Alice and Beatrice can deliver messages between us." I adjust my skirts once more, gathering my thoughts. "What was that tower room? It is unlike the rest of the Palace."

May smiles gently. "It was your nursery, I believe. But it has been left unused until now. I figure Viktoryn had it furnished because it is easy to defend and difficult to escape."

"Oh." A pang of grief hits me, but I shake it off. "The guards are getting restless," I mutter. "Go, we will meet as planned."

Maylea rises, tossing a decorative pillow across the room. "Indeed. Everything is in place. Apologies for this," she says as she rises and pushes my chair backwards. I go flying with it, landing on the floor, pain shooting up my hip.

Guards rush us as she whispers, "In five days' time, meet me in our room. Let us hope we have primed this Kingdom to fall."

I bring books back to my room to study Elphyne's history and look for any clues as to how my mother summoned the Goddess and transferred the power of the lands into my body. But it seems the practice is never mentioned, and if it is, it seems it is deemed impossible. Clearly, my existence disproves that, but it is no use telling ancient books that.

I am combing through my fourth book of the day when a knock on my door startles me from the pages. I rise from where I am lying on the rug in front of the fire, placing the book on the shelf beside the hearth. I open the door wide, and Viktoryn hands me a tray of lush pastries. I glare at him with suspicion.

"Hello, Willa," Viktoryn chimes in, dressed more like a warrior today than a Prince—more like the man I once called Toryn.

"Hello, Viktoryn," I echo.

"You have not scurried off yet, I see. I must say, I am surprised. Especially after what you learned from the lips of Maylea that you should have learned from me... I heard of your actions in the library yesterday.

I do wish to apologize for my betrothed's... *hysterics*," he says, and I grit my teeth, trying not to roll my eyes. "She can be a bit excitable at times."

"You failed to mention you had a betrothed at all," I hiss, stomping back to the hearth.

Viktoryn takes that as permission to enter and follows. I commit to the act, crossing my arms across my chest.

"Yes, it seems I did. I hoped her presence would not become an issue. We are not yet wed. Our arrangement is political, that is all. I feel nothing for her, nothing like what I have felt for you," he explains, leaning against the opposite wall. "I must say, I did not expect you to care, after all of your... *adventures*," he grimaces, "with bird-boy."

"*My* adventures did not cross the lines of adultery!" I snap.

Viktoryn holds up his hands. "We have both made errors in judgment in the past. Let us forgive those transgressions and move forward. Stay furious if you wish. I do not mind—I missed your fire. This Palace is rather dull without it."

"You wish me to pretend away your betrothed?" I give him an incredulous look.

"Believe me, she is rather hard to pretend away," Viktoryn grumbles, running a hand through his hair. "But no, I wish for you to *become* my betrothed."

I stumble back a step.

I did not expect him to say such a thing.

This was not part of the plan.

My heart beats rapidly until I can hear a faint roaring in my ears.

Viktoryn tilts his head. "How else did you expect us to work together, Willa?" He pauses. "No matter. I see it is too soon for me to ask such of you. But time is not a luxury I can afford much longer. I am certain there are things I can offer you to make this arrangement lucrative. If I am King, I can forbid Archer from marrying your sister. I can change the laws in which we govern over humans. I can give you riches and wonder and rest. Tell me what it is you want, what it is I can offer you to become my Queen, and I will find a way to make it so."

I think my mouth is still agape, but the shock has immobilized me as Viktoryn continues, "I did not tell you this for I feared you would refuse me, but my mother has promised me the crown if only I can..." he seems to search for the proper word, "contain you."

"Contain me?!"

"Yes, contain you. Willingly or not, my dear, you have become a figurehead of sorts. Symbols are powerful. Yours has become too powerful. I know you do not wish to rule. I know you, Willa... Our court will fall into madness if we cannot contain the spark that your arrival has lit. The Folk are dying, starving, suffering. Help me make it stop. Help me free your sister. Help me save the soul of this Kingdom. All you must do is say *yes.*"

"What do you mean?"

He sighs. "Some... weaker minds have begun to rally around the idea that a mortal Princess of the Sun Goddesses line would be a preferred alternative to our current... circumstances. But you must know that is nonsensical," he says, looking to me for agreement.

So, I nod.

"A soon-to-be powerless human would not be able to keep the throne. Your mortal body is too weak—too extinguishable. The Winter Prince has filled you with false hope and fantasy. Your only hope at survival is at the side of someone powerful... a *conqueror*."

"Oh, and that someone is you?" I almost laugh.

"I see we will not be coming to an agreement today... Very well, I prepared myself for such. You are too stubborn to see how this could be for the greater good. I shall let you think on it for a few days. I do not want to force your hand. Think and tell me what it is you want for your hand. For Fabelle's freedom," Viktoryn says. "For now, I am feeling rather nostalgic. Let us go train in the yards, for old times' sake."

I agree because I must be agreeable and because swinging a sword at Viktoryn's head sounds like a luxury.

☀ ✦ ☾ ✦ ☀ ✦ ☾

I should not have agreed.

It is too easy when we play pretend to slide back into a reality that no longer exists, into the role of a girl long dead at my own hands. It is too easy to look at the Prince and see Toryn.

My Toryn.

I duck under the swing of his blade, the armor on my body a slick second skin. I do not use the new movements I have learned. I force myself to glide into the steps Viktoryn taught me. Adrenaline surges through my veins, leaving me feeling heady and high.

I feel so alive. Vibrant. As we enter our third fight of the evening, I realize I *missed* this. Training had been my sanctuary once. Somewhere I did not have to make myself smaller or quieter to avoid my mother's wrath. It had given me a goal, a purpose, a place where I could be seen.

I am happy to find it still makes me feel that way.

Viktoryn grins at me, warm and wide, and advances with sure steps. Our swords meet with a clash, and he reaches forward, gripping the front of my armor and forcing our swords tightly between us.

I blink, and his lips are on mine.

It takes me a moment too long to pull away, or maybe I do not even try.

I slip into the land of pretend and let him kiss me.

Maybe because it feels a bit like revenge.

Maybe because it feels a bit like punishment.

My stomach churns with nerves and butterflies, but my body does not light up like it does when Rav–

I push away, panting and horrified. "We cannot. I cannot. Viktoryn... it is too soon."

And I hate you.

"I apologize," he huffs, cheeks red. But he does not look the slightest bit sorry. "I got carried away—old memories."

I wince. "I know what you mean."

We share a long, painful look—raw and vulnerable.

He steps forward, and I take a small step back. He holds up his hands in defeat.

"I did love you, in my own understanding of the word. I do love you still, Willa," he confesses.

I shake my head. "Your understanding was not enough. You told me once that Fae do not love as humans do. But I am a human girl with a human heart. You know nothing of how to love me."

I need to meet with May today—and I have not tried to sneak through the passages since I arrived in my new bedchamber. And after my time with Viktoryn but days ago, I find myself needing to flee.

I cannot wait any longer.

I roll back the carpet, revealing the sun emblem on the floor. I grab the key from around my neck, biting down on my tongue until it wells with blood. I let the blood pool in my mouth before spitting it onto the medallion.

I press it into the emblem, wincing as the stones rumble and slide away to reveal a long, spiral stone staircase—a staircase completely enveloped in darkness. I pause, waiting to see if the guards will burst down my door. But after a few moments pass, I realize they likely did not hear.

I do not give myself another second of hesitation, descending into the darkness. Without a faelight, I am completely blind.

I close the passageway door but have no way of covering it with the carpet again. I try not to think about what will happen if someone comes for me while I am gone.

May said this should lead to the base of the tower, where I can switch passageways until I reach our hideout. But if someone comes to search my room and finds me gone, the ruse will be up.

But this is a risk we must take. May cannot use the passageways without the key—and the key needs my *fresh* blood to work.

Each step I take echoes—a taunting laugh. My chest tightens as I descend, but I try to wrestle the feeling into submission.

Eventually, I bump into the door at the bottom. I press my ear to the stone, listening for sound on the other side, but the wall is too thick. All I can hear is the slamming of my own heart against my ribcage.

Without another option, I activate the door, and after a *click*, it swings open, light flooding in. Slowly, I push it further open, stepping into the empty hall at the base of the tower.

To my luck, no guards are at the dead end to my right. So, I shut the door quietly and sneak down the hallway toward the other passage. I round the corner—thinking of how close I am—when I slam into a wall of muscle.

My heart rips through my throat as I swallow a shriek.

"Hello, Willa."

Viktoryn.

"You are not nearly as good of a liar as you think you are. I was wondering how you were moving through the halls of my Palace like a wraith. Clever, really," Viktoryn purrs, hands moving to grip my arms firmly. "However did you discover such paths?"

I move to free myself, but a cacophony of armor creaks around me. I peer over my shoulder to find myself surrounded by two dozen Knights, weapons raised. I close my eyes and shake my head at myself, my arrogance.

"You thought you had me fooled? So naive." He laughs, cold and cruel, as he caresses my jaw. "As much as you wish to erase history, it is already written. You may have thickened your skin, but you are still the same scared little girl I met in Mayfair. You were nothing before me. I have made you *something*—something coveted and desirable. You should be thanking me, pet. Not fighting me. You should have said yes."

He releases me—but I cannot run.

I am desperately outnumbered and weaponless.

"Viktory–" I start.

"No, no, do not speak. I do not want to hear your lies. You forget yourself. I know you. I know your tells, how you hold your breath when you are uncertain. How you fidget with your fingers when you panic... I do have to give the dreadful bird prince some credit, though. He handed me the key..." I suck in a breath. "Your heart does speed, if only in the *slightest* when you lie. I will be certain to thank him when I see him next. It is funny." He laughs without humor. "Who would have thought that *he,* of all beings, would be the one who would lead you to your doom?"

"No," I breathe.

"Oh, *yes.*" His lips form a serpentine smile. "And your little escapades with my so-called betrothed end here. She is being dealt with as we speak. Worry not, I made them promise not to ruin her pretty little face." He taps my cheek.

"Harm her, and I will *kill* you," I snarl, eyes blazing.

I go to swing but am met by the sharp tip of a blade placed gently against my spine. My breath catches, and I glance behind me to find a golden Knight, stone-faced and waiting for orders. I drop my fist.

"I forgot how entertaining you are when you are angry—*truly* angry. Not whatever you pretended to be nights ago," he muses.

I do not cower, sword at my spine or not. I raise my chin defiantly until I am staring into Viktoryn's eyes.

May can handle herself—she does not require my rescue.

But something in me crumples. I really thought I had fooled him. I really thought that, for once, I was five steps ahead.

"Why?" I ask, voice hollow. "Why, Viktoryn?"

"Why? *Why*?" He snaps. "Ask yourself. This was supposed to be easy. If you had come to Elphyne and behaved, all would be well. I want you to remember that. When you suffer—when those you love suffer—I want you to remember this was all avoidable if only you had been a good little pet." He gently tucks a piece of my hair behind my ear.

"*You* are the reason you lost your sister. *You* are the reason Maylea will suffer. You have protected nothing. Only wasted time—delayed the inevitable." Viktoryn bends down until his lips ghost the shell of my ear. His voice a midnight caress, a lover's whisper. "Try as you might, you will never beat me, Willa."

"I will if it is the last thing I do," I vow. "I will en–"

Viktoryn's palm meets my cheek with a *crack*. My cheek explodes with pain. He grabs me by the hair and slams me into the wall. My skull rings with the impact, and I cry out.

"The sooner you bow, the sooner the senseless suffering stops," Viktoryn continues, his eyes locked on mine. "I have been so gentle with you. But you have left me no choice but to break you by *force*." He punctuates his point by slamming my head back again, so I am forced to look at him as he smiles down at me. "Oh, how I will enjoy seeing you shatter. How beautiful you will be broken. Mine for an eternity."

My head throbs and my thoughts run circles around each other. Something wet trails down the back of my neck, and I raise my hand to touch it. My fingers come away red.

Viktoryn trails his hand down my jaw, slowly folding his fingers, one by one, around my throat. I suck in a breath, preparing for him to squeeze.

But he does not.

A bit of relief fills me as I breathe out. But I realize too late my mistake as his hand squeezes until I cannot draw a breath. My hands fly to his wrist as I scratch him. He slams my head back again, and I see stars. I whimper.

"Promise me one thing, dear?" he coos as I fight wildly. "Break slowly. I want to watch each piece of your foolish hope shatter. Let me savour this. The harder you fight, the more I get to make this hurt."

He lifts me by the throat onto my toes. I try to rip his wrist away, swaying in the air, the tips of my boots dragging across the stone. My eyes blink, slower each time. I feel myself go limp as tears spill from my eyes. My body stops, conceding to the oncoming blackness dancing in my vision.

The pressure vanishes, and my eyes fly open. I gasp in desperate breaths, hauling oxygen into my burning lungs.

"*Uh uh*. Not yet. You must stay awake. This is only the beginning."

I sag, and his arms are my only support. I do not fight. My singular focus is breathing.

"Good girl," he whispers as I wheeze. He leans in to kiss the tears from my cheeks. "You see, if you do not fight, I will not hurt you. Do you understand?"

My head breaks through the fog of dizziness ensnaring me, and I attempt to pull away from him. The feeling of his skin on mine is sickening. Unbearable. He sighs, dragging me forward by my throat so hard I stumble into his chest.

"You never did learn your lesson the first time, did you?" he tells me. "This is a lesson you must learn."

I scratch at him like a wild animal, cornered. My vision fixed on his golden eyes, overflowing with pleasure and malice. My lungs burn, the world blurring as I begin to slip from consciousness.

Finally, blissfully, my body goes limp. His hand continues to hold me up as my limbs buckle. Wheezing, pained breaths pull me back from the blackness beckoning for me.

I grit my teeth as my chest rises and falls quickly, my head slowly spinning to a stop. My panic and terror turn to fury as I stare up at this pathetic coward of a male.

"Do you want the truth, Viktoryn?" I pant, my eyes full of the living fire burning in my soul.

"Enlighten me."

I pull the hair out of my mouth with my fingers, tucking it behind my ear. I push my hand into my pocket as I steel my spine and speak.

"You are a *coward,*" I spit, and his fingers tighten, but not enough to stop my words. "You use fear and pain to rule because you know if anyone saw the *real* you—the truth that lingers just beneath your cruelty—they would not see a leader or a King. They would see hollowness.

Emptiness. Nothing and no one... Everyone seems to know it but you. You have not what it takes to be a King."

I smile up at him. "So you can hurt me. You can make me suffer. But I will die knowing that you are not half the ruler I could be. That you killed me because you *feared* me—feared what I could become, what I could *take* from you. I will die knowing that if it had come down to who we were, who could lead, The Folk would never *choose* you. Tell me, do I lie, Viktoryn?"

He cannot.

He cannot, so instead, he proves that I speak the truth.

A truth he cannot face.

A truth he does not want to hear but cannot stop from slithering up his spine, staking a claim in his mind.

His fingers close tightly, and this time, I do not fight.

I do not fight—but he does not stop.

I do not fight, and this *enrages* him.

He slams me into the wall so hard that my ribs shatter. My head rings from where my skull impacts with the wall, and stars twinkle in my vision. Viktoryn's eyes glaze over with bloodlust, his focus so entirely on my suffering that he misses the way his own Knights glance at one another with uncertainty, weapons sagging in their arms.

I wheeze as I smile at him wildly. Letting him see what he truly is reflected in my eyes. I keep my defiant gaze glued on him as I slip into the blissful embrace of nothingness.

Right before it claims me, something like horror appears in his eyes.

The horror of the truth.

I wake in a badly-lit stone chamber—windowless and thick with an oppressive stench. At first, my head cannot understand why my limbs ache, why my head feels as if it has been trampled by horses.

Viktoryn.

I am tied up, standing with my arms stretched above me, attached to loops on the ceiling by a rough rope. My ribs scream in agony, my head pounds, and I struggle to stay conscious. I am blinking in and out of reality, trying to study the room in the seconds my eyes remain open for an edge—an understanding.

It reminds me of a blacksmith's forge. A roaring fire in the center causes sweat to drip from my body. Tools are laid out on large wooden tables, and the smell of metal and smoke hangs heavy in the air.

I realize I have no idea how long I have been out. If it's been more than a—no, I cannot think that.

I pull at my restraints but cry out as the sharp pain in my body intensifies, and white spots plague my vision. I take in painful, heaving breaths, waiting for the sensation to dull so that I can think. I need to think. I am wading through a thick fog of confusion when a voice jolts me into a waking nightmare.

"You are awake. Good," Viktoryn says from behind me.

I crane my neck over my shoulder, the movement strained, and find him entering through a thick wooden door. It creaks.

"What do you want?" I hiss, my voice coming out *wrong*. Rough, ruined.

"You know what I want."

I do. But he cannot have it.

He can take my life, but not my fear, I remind myself. *I will not be afraid, even when I am.*

I say nothing. He takes this as answer enough.

"Very well, let us begin."

"Begin what?"

"Reminding you of your place. Your purpose. Reminding you who you belong to. In such a way that you may never forget."

The sinister look in his eyes makes my stomach crawl. He looks at me like he can see the power he will possess if he can control me—break me. The power I have *always* possessed, even when I did not know it.

He claims he knows me, sees me.

But he does not see *me*.

He sees the weapon I could be caged.

But I was never meant to be caged or controlled.

I am the daughter of a Queen, both ruthless and kind, a Princess by birth and blood, the offspring of one of the greatest Unseelie warriors to ever walk these lands. My very blood, since my first breath, has been pumping with the need to *rule*, not be ruled.

I was built to fight, conquer, *lead*.

Born to burn.

I now see why my father worked so hard to ensure I was ready for whatever life decided to throw in my path. He knew the day would come when I would have to fight with all I possess to rise to the throne—and rise alone. The very throne my mother left for *me*—not Viktoryn or Archer or Daviana—not even for Fabelle.

For me.

Viktoryn walks to one of the tables in the room and dutifully pulls on a pair of thick black gloves.

The scene is hauntingly familiar.

I do not have to wonder where he learned to be cruel.

Where he learned to hurt the people he claims to love.

Where he was taught that love is suffering.

He turns to the fire, wrapping his hand around an iron pole protruding from the flames.

"I normally do not do such work, but I felt it critical to your lesson that you see me, and only me, when you suffer. That you look into my eyes and see your future, your fate, smiling down at you. Are you ready? This may hurt," he warns.

I bite down, gritting my teeth. My eyes are wide, locked on the pole that Viktoryn lifts from the flames. The brand—which is the size of my palm—glows red hot and, to my absolute horror, holds Viktoryn's royal crest. Swords crossed over a flaming sun.

I fight my restraints, ignoring the pain assaulting my senses. The ropes burn, biting into my wrists.

"Willa, my darling." Viktoryn sighs as he watches me uselessly wrestle the restraints. "This is for your own good. One day you will understand. One day you will thank me for making these difficult decisions."

It is like an echo.

An echo of what his mother has said to him for years.

His eyes burn as deeply as the glowing metal as he steps forward, gently pulling the collar of my shirt aside. The soft material slips down my shoulder, leaving part of my chest exposed. It is nothing he has not seen before, but I feel exposed, vulnerable.

A lamb in the mouth of a lion.

His fingers brush below my collarbone, a feather of a touch. Before he steps back, pressing the scorching metal to my flesh. A hiss sounds as the brand sears into my skin.

I cannot stop myself.

I scream.

I scream as the smell of burning flesh floods my nose. I buck viciously, screaming as seething, angry pain eviscerates me.

He pulls the metal away, and my head falls forward, body sagging. I try to lift my head to meet his eyes, but it feels as though someone has tied lead weights to each of my eyelashes.

I want to plead with him to stop, but I force my voice to remain locked in my throat until I can manage a scathing reply.

"You will not break me," I vow.

"Of course I will."

When I meet his eyes, my body floods with hatred. He *smiles* at me as he runs his fingers across the brand, causing me to hiss. I scream as he pushes two fingers into the fresh burn.

"Beautiful," he breathes to himself reverently. "Forever mine."

I hold his gaze, willing fire into mine. "You can burn me and brand me and beat me, but I will *never* be yours. I will never stop fighting you."

"You already are," he whispers, his face so close to mine that his lips almost brush mine. "You already are, and you do not even know it."

I spit in his face.

He flinches, backhanding me across the jaw. Leather meets flesh, and I cry out. He steps back to the fire, returning the brand before grabbing a new one. I blink away my tears.

I was born to burn, but not like this. Fire is supposed to be mine. The thing I will one day harness. The thing that will protect me… but now…

I wrestle the panic rising in my chest. My eyes track the bright red brand as he nears me again.

I want to beg him to stop.

I want to plead him for mercy.

But I cannot—I do not.

I refuse.

I will not give him the satisfaction.

I will not allow him to feed on another drop of my fear.

"You are a coward. I could never be yours. Control is not love. You know nothing of love," I spit. "You will never have my heart."

"Control—is everything," Viktoryn whispers, taking my chin between two fingers in a bruising grip. He turns my head until my cheek is bared to him. Understanding comes too late as he presses the brand into the soft flesh of my cheek.

A scream of agony is ripped from my throat as the pain overcomes me.

I wake to someone slapping my cheek gently, over and over. The rancid, sickly sweet smell of burnt flesh assaults my nose. My eyes open, meeting golden ones that glimmer with amusement.

"There she is. Welcome back," Viktoryn coos. "It is no fun if you are not awake."

"I will kill you," I rasp.

Viktoryn smiles. "Will you?"

"I will."

"I wish you luck."

Viktoryn reaches for another brand, and I struggle weakly against my restraints, each movement agony. He turns back to me, lifting my tunic to reveal my soft stomach and ribs.

"While you were out, I had a healer look at your body. Not heal it—just *look*. Mortal bodies are so delicate. I did not want the fun to end too soon. Two of your ribs are broken right *here*," he says, pressing the brand into the shattered bone.

My scream rips from my throat until my vocal cords fray, the sound echoing back to me. He presses harder, but my voice is gone, only a soundless scream leaves me. I start to faint, but he pulls the brand away, lightly tapping my cheek to keep my fluttering lashes open.

"*Uh uh uh.* Remember what I said. I want you awake, so you will stay awake. You listen to my commands now—only mine. My voice is your guiding light. You do only as I please."

I find myself nodding gently and hating myself for it. But my body is a wasteland of pain, and my mind is clinging to my sanity—grains of sand slipping through open fingers.

I shut my eyes and think of all the pain I have endured before.

I can endure this. I can survive this. I think it like a chant, a promise, a curse.

Drawing in deep breaths, I wade through my own consciousness, seeking a place of solitude within the sea of pain—but I am drowning.

Viktoryn does not wait for me to recover this time. He presses a brand above my left hip and then another on my back—right where my broken ribs are.

The searing pain intensifies.

And despite his demands, I lose my hold on my consciousness, once and for all.

I wake with a hammer in my skull and a noose around my throat.

It hurts to breathe.

It hurts to move.

It hurts.

I *hurt*.

I choke in a gasping breath and wince when I am met with a sharp stabbing in my lungs.

The ground beneath me is hard, and I groan as I attempt to sit up, but my head bumps into a solid surface. I cup my forehead, the movement costing me. I groan again.

Confusion and panic wash over me like a waterfall of scalding water. Parts of my body burn with agonizing pain. My eyes rip open, and my heart stalls as I find myself in complete darkness. I reach out my hands and feel anxiously around the space, hitting solid wood on each side of me.

Trapped.

I am in a coffin.

Or a small box.

I am *trapped.*

Broken and buried alive.

Forgotten.

A hoarse scream parts my lips as my fists pound on the solid surface above my head. My mind whirls around, slamming into the sides of my skull as wild, unwavering panic becomes a singular thought.

I am trapped.

I am trapped.

I am trapped.

My chest feels tight as if someone is sitting atop it. My breaths are short, rough, and painful as I sob. I continue to pound and pound until my fists come away bloody and broken.

I try to claw my way out like a feral animal backed into a corner. My nails split, one ripping from my hand, and splinters imbed in my fingertips. I try to kick my feet up, but I do not have enough space to force them into the lid.

I am trapped.

I am trapped.

I am trapped.

Hours or minutes or days pass—I am unsure.

All I know is panic, pain, *fear*.

I am drowning in distress.

I am choking on despair.

I never knew I could be so all-consumingly afraid.

Help. Help me. Please.

I am suddenly a child.

A terrified little girl locked in a closet.

Unwanted, forgotten, helpless, beaten, slowly starving to death. Waiting for someone to whisk her away to safety.

My mortal mother's voice haunts me, images appear in flashes. Yelling. Lips that reek of whiskey. Her mouth inches from my face as her spit sprays my cheeks.

You are nothing. Useless, wretched girl. You will stay in there until you learn some respect or starve. I should throw you to the streets. Do you know what happens to girls like you on the streets?

The voice taunts me until it becomes *voices.*

Fabelle.

Mother.

Viktoryn.

My father—my father who would be so disappointed in me.

A chorus of venom, pain.

"Please, please stop. Make it stop. Let me out," I rasp, not recognizing my voice—so small, so *broken*. "I will do whatever you want, *please.*"

My cheeks are wet with tears and blood. I pull at my hair, strands ripping free. I am trembling, clawing, but even in all my panic, bone-deep exhaustion wraps me in its embrace.

I am so tired.

Please, I think.

Pleading with anyone, anything.

Please make it stop.

I will do *anything.*

Please.

Viktoryn's voice enters my mind, unbidden and taunting.

If you do not fight, I will not hurt you.

Understanding comes at me like a brick wall and I battle against all my instincts to calm myself. But I cannot get my breathing to settle.

I pull my hands away from the lid and squeeze them into fists so tight my nails pierce my skin. It hurts, but the fresh wave of pain brings with it clarity.

My head swims with dizziness, and I know that if I cannot find a way to control my breath, I will faint. Only to wake confused and trapped and terrified again.

I know that if I faint, Viktoryn will not count my silence as obedience.

I must be awake—awake and obedient.

Or this will not stop. *He* will not stop.

He chose this for a reason.

The perfect test—the perfect punishment.

Obey or drown in your worst nightmares. Choose to stop fighting. Choose to fight your own instincts. Your own panic.

Please him.

Even though it is already dark, I close my eyes. I try to picture all of the most breathtaking landscapes I have seen in Elphyne. The Winter Court mountains. Stunning, vast, and powerful. I picture Cyrissa Lake's dazzling teal surface and angelic white beaches. The gardens of Ember Palace with glowing gold trees and peaceful fountains. I picture glowing pixies dancing and laughing as they play in the trees.

Slowly, my breathing settles, and my heart rate follows.

I force myself to remain perfectly still. I keep my eyes closed, refusing to acknowledge where I am. I only think of all the beautiful places within Elphyne. All the beautiful things that combat the terrors living amongst them.

Unbidden, Raven's face, half masked and extraordinary, appears in my mind. His lips swollen from kisses, his neck marked, but this time, I imagine it was *me* he was kissing.

I wonder what it would be like to feel his soft, full lips on mine. I do not want to die without knowing the wonder of his kisses. I do not want to die without knowing what it is like to drown in his affection. And I find in this moment, I do not hate him. I only wish he was here with his cunning mind and clever plans.

I do not know how long I drift in my fantasies—barely able to keep the panic at bay. But the creaking of a lid followed by brutal light rips me from them.

I am in a nightmare once more.

Viktoryn peers over the lid of the coffin, a lock dangling between his fingers.

He grins at me. "Very, very good. I thought you would fight much longer. You are learning."

I nod. I nod because it is all I have left.

I want to curse at him.

I want to fight.

But I have no fight left.

And I wish that did not make me feel so disappointed in myself.

A wicked numbness floods me like freezing rain until I feel nothing. Nothing but a deep well of hopelessness and fatigue.

"Nothing to say?" he questions as if he does not quite believe my compliance.

My head floods with images of him slamming the lid, locking me in the darkness, leaving me to drown in my own despair, to live in a nigh–

I shake my head, hugging my arms around my body. I am trembling, and I wish nothing more than for him to pull me into his arms and out of this place. The thought makes me shudder in disgust at myself. I do not want his skin near mine. But I want nothing more than to leave this coffin and never return.

Viktoryn reaches down, and I let him scoop me up, hating myself as I lean my head into his chest. Hating the silent tears that trail down my cheeks. Hating myself for not fighting. Hating him for terrorizing me until his arms feel like comfort.

I wish I could sink into my numbness and disappear.

I wish to be anyone but myself.

And for the first time in my life, I wish what people said about me was true.

I wish I was nothing.

I wish I could cease to exist and never have to fight another day.

My thoughts must read on my face because Viktoryn studies me, a terrible, victorious smile growing on his lips.

I know he thinks he has won, and I worry he is right.

"Are you going to fight me?" he asks, almost gently.

I want to scream, *Yes, always, forever.* But I glance down at the dark wooden coffin sitting below me like open jaws ready to swallow me whole...

Yes, I think. *I will.*

But not today. *Not right now.*

"No," I croak.

I watch his face as he reads my heart rate and am filled with dread and disappointment when he finds only the truth in my damning confession.

My hand brushes over the gemstone in my pocket, and a small, minuscule bloom of hope bursts in my chest. Viktoryn takes me to his room and places me on his bed.

We are alone.

I am bleeding.

I am covered in bruises, cuts, and burns.

And he lets me bleed.

He does not send for a healer.

I know I am in his room because weeks ago, I broke in. Watched him while he slept. Considered ending his life. In this moment, I wish I had. I curse myself for my mercy. For my hesitation to take a life. I curse myself for proving May right.

This cannot continue. Viktoryn cannot continue.

I never wanted to rule. I never wanted power or a crown. I pretended to wish for it with May, but I never planned to keep the throne for long.

But perhaps this is exactly why I *should* rule. Greed and power have corrupted Viktoryn. He does not rule with The Folk in mind. He rules to become all-powerful using fear and oppression. I have seen that first hand. He rules with a thirst for more. A thirst he will chase to his ruin or the Kingdom's.

He will not stop because he *cannot.* To him, everything and everyone are pawns to be manipulated. I know without a single doubt that Elphyne will fall if the Goldynlockes continue to rule.

And perhaps—after everything, after *everyone*—I do not want it to. Perhaps, for my friends, for Maylea and Raith and even Amira, I do not want it to.

Viktoryn will never know what it is like to be human, but I do. I know what it is like to suffer and struggle and starve. I know what it is like to feel as if you have no power at all.

In Mayfair, I stood back and questioned the choices of the crown. Raged against the injustices committed and wished I could change them. But here, I *can* make a change. If I am only brave enough to reach out and seize this chance in my hands, even when they tremble.

Mortal or Fae, suffering is suffering.

And if I claim the throne, I will have the power to fight for what I believe is right. I will have the ability to help those who have spent their lifetimes suffering.

I will make mistakes—no Queen is born overnight. And I know I have much to learn about Elphyne and The Folk. But until my last breath, I will *try*. The Folk deserve someone who will try for them—who will fight for them. Because surely, if we tried, we could do better—be better.

If we want it enough, and fight for it fiercely enough, with all that we are and everything we possess, maybe it does not have to be like this.

Perhaps, I do not know how to stop fighting because I am born to fight. I do not know who I am if not a protector because I am built to protect. Maybe, at the core of who I am, this is what I am meant to be—what I've always been. Now I only need to learn how to direct it. To *ignite* it. To burn away every injustice and wrongdoing, so I can try to rebuild something greater from the ashes.

I will stand before Viktoryn and do and say what I have to. I will beg, plead, and bow. Lie, cheat, steal, and charm to ensure that, when the moment presents itself, I can fight.

So I will bide my time. Even though I want to leap off the bed and rush over and end him. Instead, I listen to Viktoryn wash and dress. Frozen, unmoving. My eyes glued to the canopy, unblinking. He ignores me, going about his evening as if it is any other day. As if he had not just brought my greatest fear to fruition and basked in the glory of my brokenness. I am so lost in my thoughts I do not hear him approach.

"You will sleep in here with me. Cuffed. From this moment forward, I will be with you always. You will not walk a step without my permission. You will never leave my sight. You will never be freed from my company. You are mine. You will do as I please and nothing more. Your power, your heart, your mind—everything you are and will be is *mine*," Viktoryn explains.

He talks and talks until his words become a wash of noise with no meaning.

"How long was I in there?" I rasp.

"The coffin?" Viktoryn studies me thoughtfully. "I think it best not to tell you. Let your mind war with itself."

"Alright."

"Alright?" he questions, confused, peering down at my face from beside the bed.

"Alright," I repeat numbly.

"I must say, you are rather dull without any fight," he mutters, scowling slightly. "I should have considered that. No worry, you will reignite, and I will live to snuff out your flames over and over."

He lowers himself into the bed beside me, surveying my body with a slight frown. Taking in the damage he's done. My hands are torn and bloody. My clothes are disheveled and coated with sweat, tears, and blood. The brands still burn and shoot agony through me any time they brush the fabric of my shirt. Viktoryn scans it all—expression shifting. He rises from the bed, moving to my side before running his fingers lightly over the damage.

"I should clean you up. The maids shall throw a fit if I let you bleed all over everything all night," he muses.

I nod.

He moves to carry me, and I let him.

I let him wash and dress me as if in a haze. Too tired to fight him. Despite all his threats, his touch remains respectful and gentle. As if he can smell my relief, read my thoughts, a shy smile paints his features.

"When I touch you like that again, it will be because you wish it. Because you beg me for it. I have no interest in forcing myself on you. It will be much sweeter when you come to me willingly."

"Alright."

He places me back in bed in a small white nightgown, already stained red. My hands continue to bleed, embedded with splinters, knuckles split and gory.

I startle when his fingers brush my cheek lovingly. He stares down at me, his eyes landing on the brand that is still blazing on my cheek as he pulls the covers over me. He places a chaste kiss on my forehead, making my skin crawl, but I do not move or curse or cry.

I will kill you, I vow silently as sleep drags me into her gentle arms. *I will be your end.*

I wake with a start, and it takes me a few breaths to remember where I am. I test my grip and find I am still cuffed, in Viktoryn's bed, my hands damp and crusty with blood. I scan the darkness as the sound of bustling and grunting fills the room.

My eyes start to adjust, and I see figures wrapped in shadows, fighting. I pull my knees to my chest and press myself into the headboard. My shackles clang softly. A soft moan falls from my lips as the brands on my back connect with the headboard. I try not to cry out, fearful of drawing the attackers' attention.

I glance down to find Viktoryn no longer beside me, and my mind whirls, trying to make sense of the chaos. My heart beats wildly, and I suck in quiet, soft breaths, willing myself not to scream. Silent tears gather in my eyes, falling onto my cheeks in fat drops. A hard clank followed by a body thumping to the floor has my heart leaping into my ribs.

"Willa?" a voice whispers gently as one of the figures approaches.

I flinch away from their outstretched hands.

Back in the coffin, *trapped*.

Touch means branding, burning, *pain*.

"Get back!" I whimper, kicking at them, my nightgown pooling on my thighs.

"Willa, it is me. It is Raith, sweetheart. I am not gonna hurt you. You activated the stone. I am here to help," he explains softly.

My eyes squeeze shut as my head spins, and my hands push into my hair, tugging the strands. My chest is tight, my breathing too quick.

"Are you certain we can trust her, Raith? She went back to him willingly. She is in his bed," Amira asks, not unkindly—it takes a moment to place her voice.

"Look at her. Does she look *willing* to you?" May snaps with more bite than I have ever heard her direct at Amira. "What did he do to you?"

"May," I gasp. "You are alright. He said he would hurt you."

"*Ha!* He tried," she laughs, bright and proud. "It went about as well for him as one would assume."

The sound is like a blanket of warmth. I feel a little less lost in the fear and confusion.

My head aches as I try to make sense of why Raith, Amira, and May are here. *How* they are here.

I realize with a slap of surprise that it *worked*. When I pulled my saliva-slicked hair back from my face as Viktoryn's hands wrung my neck, I slipped my fingers into my pocket—brushing the green tracker gem Raith had given me.

And it worked.

I worried that I gave it too little spit, but I could not risk Viktoryn discovering what I was attempting.

"Can you walk?" Raith asks, reaching out his hand for me. Instinctively, I flinch, my arms wrapping around my knees protectively as I start to shake. "Whoa. Alright. Alright. I am not going to touch you, okay? Not until you are ready. No one here is going to hurt you, sweetheart."

I nod but cannot bring myself to move. Too terrified this is not real—that I am still trapped. What if this is all a dream, and I awake back in the darkness of the coffin?

"Something is wrong. I can smell her blood and burnt flesh. She is covered in wounds and bruising," Raven says, a thick darkness in his tone.

Raven.

His voice feels like a dream.

Soft clouds of comfort.

Like a manifestation of my fantasies.

That is when I know with a dreadful sinking in my stomach that I am dreaming.

"No, no, no, no," I sob. "Please, no. This is a dream. Oh no. He is going to kill me," I murmur, pressing my face into my knees as tears flow from my eyes.

"Careful, Raven," Amira says.

"Willa," Raven breathes, closer now. So gentle, as if not to spook a terrified child. "You are not dreaming. We are here to help. *I* am here to help. I need to get you out of here, so you must let one of us take you. I know you are scared, Princess. But I need you to let me pick you up. I need you to let me touch you. I do not know what he did to you, but I will kill him for it," he vows with so much certainty I believe him. "I will not hurt you."

"*Liar*," I hiss. "You always do—you *did*," I whisper. "You have hurt me before. You can hurt me again." I look up slowly, finding the room lit with a faelight, only to meet Raven's haunted eyes.

My heart stalls in my chest at how broken he looks. His normal mask shattered. His features pained, eyes swimming with devastation, and a regret so bone-deep that I feel it as my own.

You cannot stare into a mirror and force the reflection to show what you wish. You and he are a mirror. It will be your ruin.

He holds his hands in front of him, palms up and shaking. He looks so young, so lost and scared. I imagine I look the same. Raven closes his eyes so tightly that lines draw around them. He sucks in a deep breath through his nose.

When he opens his eyes again, he looks at me like I am the reason he breathes.

Like the world begins and ends in my eyes.

He looks desperate, like he is drowning.

"You are right," he says firmly.

"Alright. Yes. This has to be a dream," I whisper. "Definitely a dream." Despite everything, a small smile tugs at my lips.

Raven's returning smile is sad, and it falls away quickly. "I did hurt you. I have hurt you. But I swear to you, here and now, before my friends—I will not hurt you again. I will never lay my hands on you in anger or malice. I will not use my magicks in an attempt to cause you harm. And if I do, I give my court the right to hurt me as I have hurt you. Today, tomorrow, and always let this be my truth. My promise, my *oath* to you."

Someone gasps.

I look away from Raven and find May, Amira, and Raith sharing a look that holds such emotion that a part of me breaks. The metallic taste of magicks swirls across my tongue, filling the room as Raven's words bind him and his friends. I can tell by the way they peer at Raven like he has lost his mind that what he has done is no small feat.

I do not have time to consider the enormity of his promise—the depth of his oath. What it might mean for him or his friends if I try to attack him.

I am still shaking so badly that I feel like a leaf weathering a torna-do—clinging to a tree branch, about to rip free.

But maybe, I wonder as I meet his eyes, *maybe Raven would catch me.*

Maybe, I *need* him to catch me.

And maybe, today, that is alright.

Maybe, today, I believe his vow.

"Alright," I say shakily, still crying. I swallow and try again. "Alright," I repeat. "Please get these off," I cry, lifting my shackled wrists. "Please, I need them off! Get them off!"

Raven nods, his relief visible as his shoulders drop. He gently approaches me, his eyes never straying from mine. I cling to them like a lifeline. In the darkness, the grey-blue looks even more stormy.

I flinch as the sound of a groan comes from the other side of the bed. Amira scoffs. Raven fiddles with the shackles until they fall to a heap on the floor. Relief floods me as my wrists are freed.

"Viktoryn always did know how to ruin the moment," Amira quips. Moving toward the opposite side of the bed, she brings her heel up and slams it down on Viktoryn's skull.

Despite everything, despite myself, a laugh flies from my lips. A wild, broken noise. But instead of looking at me like I have lost it, the room bursts into laughter with me. May's bright giggles are a salve on my soul.

Olden snorts, and I only now notice he is here, too, standing in the shadows. Amira graces us with a dark chuckle, an utterly wicked smile on her lips. Raith chuckles, his smile as charming as ever. My gaze meets his, those grey-green eyes shimmering in the low light.

I hope he can see my gratitude.

"You came," I whisper.

"Of course I did," he states as if it was nothing. As if breaking into a palace and rendering a Prince unconscious is nothing. And I find I cannot even be upset that he had brought the others when he said he would not because he came—*they* came.

Even more surprisingly, after everything, *Raven* came—Raven, who declared me his enemy.

He came.

Instead of heading towards The Crystal Palace as I expected, Amira leads us deep into The Summer Court woods. I am too tired to question where we are going.

Greyish light is slipping through the opening of the canopy, casting the forest floor in a symphony of slow-moving shadows. Every rustling branch and flickering shadow causes me to flinch in Raven's arms.

No one comments on the brands on my body, though Raven keeps eyeing them. I am wrapped in his cloak, being held in his arms.

Part of me knows I should shove him away, but I am plagued with exhaustion. Even with the fatigue, the pain is untenable, each of Raven's steps causing it to assault my senses.

"Willa?" Raven whispers, sounding unsure.

"Yes," I breathe through a wince.

"Would you allow me to spell you to sleep? Only until we reach the tree house. May shall be able to help heal you soon," he says softly.

I tense, hesitating. "You cannot."

"Cannot? Whatever do you mean?" Raven asks, brows knitting together.

A sinking feeling starts in my stomach as I study his face, trying to marry this version of him with the one who has caused me so much pain. He looks radiant in the moonlight. His cheekbones sharpened by the shadows. When my gaze brushes his lips, I am met with the image of them on mine. I quickly look away.

"You just.. cannot," I whisper.

"Of course I can... I know you do not wish for me to use compulsion, but... the pain must be..." he trails off.

"I am fine. It does not matter." I press my lips together tightly.

"It matters. Tell me," he demands.

May clears her throat and slows her pace, appearing beside us. "You cannot because s–"

"May," I object, shooting her a glare. She eyes Raven wearily and then me. "Do not dare."

My words are met with a pitying glance, and Raven's arms tighten around me.

"Why can she not be glamoured or compulsed, Maylea?" Raven asks, voice low and deadly. "Viktoryn would not have allowed her to keep a charm while in his presence. He may be stupid, but he does not have a death wish. Tell me what it is."

May opens and closes her mouth, her eyes burning with violence at Raven. She hesitates and then shakes her head. But I can see her itching to tell him. To watch him piece together exactly what I did and *why*.

Amira peers over her shoulder from where she leads, watching both Raven and May carefully. Olden moves closer as if he might separate them while Raith hovers close by. But they all pretend as if they are not listening to what feels like a private conversation.

"Tell. Me." Raven growls. "*Now.* That is an order, Maylea."

"I do not take orders from you, Prince. Or have you forgotten who I am?" May asks, too sweetly. "What I can do? What I *will* do to those who hurt the ones I love?"

Raven levels her with a look that would have most cowering, but May simply smiles.

"It is the least you owe me, Maylea. Do not think I have forgiven you for getting us into this mess," Raven growls.

"It was my plan, Raven," I counter.

"She let you—she helped you—walk right back into his arms, his Palace!" Raven hisses. "She let him do *this* to you!"

May laughs suddenly, her eyes filled with wrath. "*I* let him do this to her? Do you so easily forget what *you* have done to her?" she bites, her eyes finding me. "Forgive me," she says before her eyes harden on Raven. "She cut the flesh of her thigh—made an incision down to the *bone*—and inserted an iron charm and rowan berries inside of her body. Then, she stitched it shut," May explains. "So far, it has worked to deter glamours, resist compulsion... but it was quite a bloody process."

Raven's angry gaze leaves May's to find mine.

"Wha–why would you do that? The risk... Willa... the iron could poison your body! What were you thinking?" he demands, looking at me for an answer, but I close my eyes, shaking my head. "Why would she do such a thing? You could have *died*," he croaks.

"I did not," I whisper, but his eyes are on May.

"You are the genius schemer, Raven. Are you not? Why did she do it? Why *would* she do it?" May challenges.

Raven's arms go slightly slack as the realization strikes him. I groan in pain as the movement jolts me.

"Oh," he breathes, face shuttering, instantly emotionless. "*Me.*"

Everyone in the forest halts, turning to Raven. A silence descends on the trees, the sound of nearby crickets becoming uncomfortably loud. The group watches us, done pretending they are not eavesdropping. I squeeze my eyes shut hard, unwilling to see their pity and anger at my stupidity. Shame assaults my chest, threatening to swallow me.

"Raven, I swear to the Goddesses," Raith, as always, breaks the silence.

My eyes snap open, and what I find is disorienting. Raith is before me, looking unsure if he wants to rip me from Raven's arms and hold me protectively or hand me off to someone while he pummels Raven into the ground. His chest heaves, eyes wild and overflowing with fury. I realize I have never seen Raith angry. He is terrifying. Even Raven seems shaken.

Amira watches us from her point at the head of the group, warily eyeing Raven with a narrowed gaze. She tosses a deadly-looking curved dagger in the air in a slow, controlled, threatening movement.

Olden's face is pale, paler than normal. May has sunken away into the trees, clearly not interested in being a part of whatever is about to happen. She has done her part. *Traitor.*

I see no pity in their eyes for me. But I do see *anger* directed at Raven. But Raven only tilts his chin up, ready to take whatever is about to be thrown his way.

"You made her one of *us*... and at her first misstep..." Raith shakes his head, reaching for me. He scoops me from Raven's arms, and, to my surprise, Raven *lets* him.

Raith gently hands me to Olden. I tense, but the Troll gives me a sad smile, his embrace gentle. I have the urge to trace his horns with my fingertip but resist.

"How many times have I failed you, Raven? How many times has each one of us misstepped?" He looks at each member of the group but avoids my eyes. "Made the wrong call in an impossible situation? *Huh*?" Raith shouts, pushing Raven by the shoulders.

Raven stumbles, his jaw ticking, but he does not fight back.

"Answer me!" Raith barks.

He does not, his eyes an ice-cold fortress. But his chin drops slightly.

"We are supposed to be a family, Raven," Raith's voice cracks. "How could you? She has no one left. No one to protect her." Raith pushes Raven again harder, expression pained. "Like me," he whispers so softly, my heart shatters. "Like all of us."

"I know," Raven says finally. His head lifts as he meets Raith's eyes. I am surprised to find them brimming with tears. "I know," he repeats softly.

"It does not seem like it." Raith shakes his head, eyes flooded with disgust. "What happened to you? I do not know you anymore. I cannot even look at you," Raith mumbles, turning away and looking at Amira. "Let's go."

"Rait–" I try.

"Do not. He is the big tough Prince. Most powerful, *blah, blah, blah.* He can handle it. Do not defend him. Not in this," Raith hisses. "Let's go."

Raven swallows twice, shoving his hands into his pockets as his eyes grow distant.

Amira nods once and continues her path through the woods. I am appalled to see her take an order from Raith without complaint or comment. Raith rolls his shoulders and follows.

Everyone else trails behind, but Raven hangs back, and when I glance back at him, he is gone. I open my mouth to alert the others, but Olden holds a finger to his lips.

"He will return. He needs time. Worry not, little mortal. He can care for himself. Some burdens must be felt alone if one is to learn from them," Olden murmurs. "Now, get some rest. I will protect you with my life until you wake."

When I wake, it is in darkness, and I scream.

Back in the coffin.

I am trapped.

Panic slams into my body, bubbling up my throat, and tears plummet from my eyes. I claw at the air, my heart pounding.

"Whoa, hey, it is alright," Raith's voice is gentle, a cool stream. He cups my cheeks in his hands, wiping away my tears with his rough thumbs. "Someone light a fire. *Now*," he commands, and seconds later, a hearth ignites to life, basking the room in a warm orange glow. "Look at me. Good girl. Right here. I have got you." His eyes are gentle. "Good. You are alright. You are safe. You made it out."

"I made it out," I choke.

"You made it out."

My breathing starts to slow, and I nod. Raith continues to watch my face, searching my expression with such a soft worry that my heart aches.

"Raith," I whisper.

"Yes, sweetheart?"

"You are one of my best friends. I do not think I ever told you that," I mumble—it hurts to talk. "I should have. I should have told you."

Raith smiles—that brilliant, full-teeth grin—and *blushes*. The great Unseelie war commander—*blushing*. He looks away, eyes filled with quiet emotion.

"You are telling me now." He swallows. "You are one of my best friends, too..." Raith hesitates. "For what it is worth, I am sorry. For what happened... Raven can be..." Raith shakes his head and rubs the back of his skull, words failing him. He blows out a breath.

"I am alright," I say, but my voice comes out small, uncertain. "Where are we? Do I even want to ask where Raven is?"

Raith's face falls, but he covers it quickly with a wide, charming smile that is much too stiff. "He is outside. We are at the treehouse. It is Amira's base of operations for her Summer Court spies. It is safe. Heavily warded and spelled. No one can hurt you here."

I nod, looking around as my panic melts away. The room is carved from dark brown wood. Simple, plain, small. It has a large bed, smaller bunk beds, a few chairs, a hearth, and a small kitchen.

Earthy and cozy.

Not a coffin.

"What were you thinking?" Amira snaps, stalking over to us.

I am slumped in the bed beside Raith, who keeps smoothing down my hair. Amira stands at the end of the bed, sharpening the blade of her dagger on a stone. A vision and nightmare in black.

"I–"

"Not now, Amira," Raith snaps protectively, positioning himself in between us.

"Yes, *now*. I do not take orders from you, Raith. If you take a moment to recall, you take orders from *me*," Amira spits, her attention shifting back to me. "You could have died, Willa. Viktoryn can be unpredictable. His temper is volatile at best. Why did you not come to me first? I could have gathered information. You acted without thought. Without a purpose, I can understand. So I need to know what you were thinking," Amira growls, the clang of her knife against stone increasing in intensity. "Convince me why I should not stab you to save myself the headache?"

My stomach flips. Under her frustration, I feel the truth of her words. She would have helped me. If May and I had not turned our backs on her. She would have. I know that now. But I did not include her. Include any of them. I made a mistake.

"Amira," Raith warns.

"Raith, it is fine. I can fight my own battles."

"Apparently not," Amira snarks.

"I know. I know, alright? I thought I could earn his trust. May and I had begun to destabilize the court. I just needed more time. If I want to overthrow the throne, I cannot do it without support. I cannot do it without weakening the Goldynlockes. Learning what they know. Which of their allies will flip with the right motivation. It may not bother either of *you* that I am mortal—but asking a court of immortal beings who think themselves superior to me to throw those long-held beliefs aside and let me lead... I thought the best way to do that was beside them. I was wrong."

Amira looks surprised. "Overthrow the throne?" Her eyes narrow. "You have become mighty ambitious, mortal. What happened to not wanting the throne? What happened to the little girl who wanted to grab her sister and flee? How did we go from running away to starting a war?" Amira hisses, her cat-like, topaz eyes flashing with irritation. She steps forward, towering over me.

I do not cower. I do not sink back.

"If not me, then who?" I argue. "Do you think we should stand back and allow the Goldynlockes to rule? To ruin Elphyne in their thirst for power? To torture mortals and neglect The Folk?" I run a hand through my hair. "I was short-sighted. Naive. I still am, but I see now what I did not before. It does not matter what *I* want. This is about more than just me," I state firmly.

I am shocked to find Amira looks pleased, something akin to respect overtaking her features. I feel a pleasant hum in my chest. Out of all of them, Amira's respect has been the hardest to earn. She does not hand it out freely. And I wronged her deeply. But I do not wish to let her down. I do not wish to disappoint her again.

"I underestimated you," Amira says, eyes assessing me with new scrutiny. "I thought you would run away with your tail between your legs. I must question, though, why would you ever wish to rule the Fae after how they have treated you?"

"Fair question," I say, sitting up straighter, even when my ribs tinge with pain. "I am under no illusion that the Fae will ever see me as an equal. Though, according to Alice, the rebels may have begun to shift the tides of those beliefs. Nonetheless, suffering is suffering. And if the Goldynlockes continue to rule... Elphyne will suffer. The Fae will suffer. The Folk will die. The humans here will continue to be mistreated and abused. I think..."

I take a breath, organizing my thoughts. "I think I can make a difference. I think I can try to do some good. And even if I cannot, at least if I sit on the throne, I can prevent the ruin of thousands of lives for the sake of power. I can prevent Elphyne from destruction. My mother sacrificed her life for the chance that I might survive. That I might live to claim the throne and legacy she left me. I will not allow her sacrifices to be in vain. Or worse, be the cause of more undue suffering," I explain, meeting her eyes. "I cannot."

"Alright," Amira says, and it is my turn to bury my shock. "Do not believe this is me saying we are fine. We are not. I will not forget what you have done with May. But for now, for more than me, how can I help?"

I awake with the metallic taste of magicks on my tongue. My eyes flutter open and daylight streams through a small circular window. May smiles down at me, bright as sunshine as her hands brush my skin. I feel the pain begin to recede.

"You once told me you were no good at healing," I croak, and she laughs, beaming.

"Well, one of my friends nearly drowned and is *extremely* prone to injury. So I decided it was time to learn," she remarks with a friendly wink. "I am still no good. But I am no longer all bad."

My heart flutters, cheeks heating as I glance up at her. "You learned for me?"

She blushes slightly and nods. Her blue eyes gentle. "Yes. Do not give me too much credit. Royals tend to be born with more power than common Fae. I have always been able to summon water, earth, and healing magicks. I am gifted with a hint of air as well. It is rare for any Fae to have four magicks—I cannot do much more than sound-cloaking spells with it. As for healing... I simply never thought of refining my the skill—until you, that is. I much prefer my other elements."

"Well, I am both grateful and just the tiniest bit insulted," I remark, and she chuckles. Quieter, I whisper, "I am so glad you are alright. I was so worried he would hurt you."

May's smile drops as she scans my body, the brands still visible—I try not to look at them.

"You almost died, and yet you worry for me." She shakes her head, biting her lip, disbelief and something else I cannot make sense of warring in her gaze. "Look at yourself." She gestures to my body. "You need not worry about me." May takes a slow breath. "I am loathe to admit it but Raven was right. We should have been more careful. *I* should have been more careful."

"We could not have known, May. I knew it was a risk—but it was one I was willing to take. We both did. What matters is that I am fine now."

She nods but does not look convinced as she studies my injuries. "This may take me a while. Your ribs are in pieces, shards have pierced your organs. By some miracle, they missed your lungs." She shuts her eyes for a moment. "The brands are resisting my magicks... I worry he used some type of spelled metal..."

May sighs heavily, rubbing her forehead as sweat beads on her brow. I notice for the first time how tired she looks. Her blonde hair is a mess of disheveled, tangled strands, and deep purple crescents have settled below her eyes. Her body sags with exhaustion.

"Your hands…" My face flushes with shame. "Will you tell me what happened?" May asks.

Panic tears into my body as flashes of my hands beating against the wooden coffin in complete darkness assault my mind. I blink rapidly, trying to wipe the memories away.

Viktoryn's hands wrap around my throat.

A brand searing my flesh.

Echoing screams.

Sobs.

Golden eyes watching in fascination.

Beautiful.

Forever mine.

I cannot breathe.

"Willa. *Shh*. It is alright. I am right here," May soothes, holding my hands gently in hers, careful to avoid the damaged skin.

I meet her eyes, and the memories flash away. I am panting. I squeeze my eyes shut, dropping her hand and pressing my hands to my face.

"I cannot," I croak, shaking my head. "I–I."

"Alright. That is alright. I understand," May says gently. "Let us speak of something else." I swallow, nodding. "Ask me anything and hold still while I work."

I nod, letting my mind drift, seeking questions in the dark shadows that have descended on my mind.

"Where are the others?" I ask as I look around the empty room.

"Giving us some much-needed space," May replies. "Now, ask something *interesting*."

I smile weakly. "Right. If the Goldynlockes have no magicks, how do they have healers? How did Viktoryn's Folk heal me after the Nixies?"

"They did not," May says, and I raise a brow. "They borrow ours. Spring Court healers. But they keep such a fact quiet so as not to look weak."

"*Hmm*. And what are Raven's powers? *All* of them. If you can control three elements as well as heal, what can he do? What about Amira? Or Raith? Or even Olden?"

"Well, as you know, he can shift into bird form. Aside from that, Raven controls water, mostly in the form of ice or snow—a preference. He can also manipulate air and shadows—another oddity of four magicks," May explains, hands moving over my skin.

"Shadows?" I ask, surprised.

"Yes. He can manipulate shadows. Cloak himself in them and use his air magicks to silence his movements and scent until he is nearly invisible. He is also remarkably quick. It is what makes him an equally good thief and spy as a Prince," May tells me.

"But... if Fae can see in the dark... how do his shadows conceal him?"

"I do not know the exact of it. You would have to ask him. I know his shadows are different from natural darkness. They obscure, bending light in a way that renders him almost invisible. Similar to a glamour, I presume," May explains, biting her lip.

It makes a lot of sense—a puzzle piece sliding into place in the never-ending picture of The Winter Prince. It explains how he moves quickly and quietly between rooms as if he can walk through walls. How he made it into Viktoryn's room the night, I placed the marigolds without being discovered.

I wonder how many times he has watched me from the shadows or spied on me in the form of a bird. The thought makes me uneasy. Like I will forever be glancing at the walls as if they have grown eyes and ears.

"Huh... and the others?"

"Amira can control air. She is especially talented at cloaking sound—she is the one who taught me how to do the spell I used in the library. She can move without any sound, manipulating the air around her to render her movements undetectable to even the most sensitive of Fae ears. She can also adjust the acoustic blanket of a room to listen in on someone's conversation from afar. It is what makes her the perfect spymaster," May says, radiating pride.

I smile. "And Raith? Olden?"

"Raith can shift into a fox. He does not have particularly strong elemental magicks. A tiny bit of water magicks but not enough to use in battle. Though what he lacks in element he makes up for in strength and speed. He is a true warrior. He need not for anything but a sword and an axe to fell even the strongest of enemies. And Olden... Trolls are not known for possessing elemental magicks... the Goldynlockes believe this is because they are cursed by the Sun Goddess. It is a ridiculous old pixie tale." May rolls her eyes. "They say she cursed them for being unworthy of such magicks. It is nothing but nonsense. Olden can memorize any text or map in a single glance. He is a walking library. We are lucky to have him," she says earnestly.

I am grateful for her voice, a distraction from the slowly dimming pain.

"And Viktoryn? Before he lost his magicks?" I whisper as if asking is somehow shameful—my curiosity about such a thing... unworthy.

May's hands falter. "Viktoryn could manipulate fire, air, and weaker healing magicks. His strength did not parallel the true royal line, but he was strong."

I look away. "And now, because of me, he can conjure nothing."

May nods, gnawing at her bottom lip.

I wonder how it would feel to be a being of such incredible power—only to have it ripped away. By a mortal. Forever living with a phantom limb. A piece of yourself—out of reach, disconnected. I wonder if I would hate me, too. I wonder what I would do to get that power back.

I wonder if I will find out.

"Ladies," Raven drawls too formally. "Maylea, an update?"

I flinch.

I did not hear or see him approach.

I guess I should get used to that.

My eyes snap to his face and then immediately drop. I stare at my lap as my heart pounds.

"As good as can be expected. I am not a natural healer, but I will manage. *We* will manage," she says, giving me a reassuring smile.

"Very good," Raven says, hands folded stiffly behind his back, shoulders squared, chin raised as if to support a crown.

I watch him from beneath my lashes. He looks as if he wishes to say more, but he does not.

He seems nothing like the male I have come to know. He looks like a stranger. A boy popped into the mould of a perfect Prince and set in clay, preternaturally still. Cold and unreachable. So unlike the wine thief I first met in the depths of The Ember Palace. All charisma and charm.

His eyes flick from my downturned eyes to the brand on my cheek, and shame coils in my gut. I cover it with my hand, unable to bear the pity and disgust in his eyes.

He clears his throat. "Are you alright, Princess?"

The nickname has none of its normal playful lit. No, he is *addressing* me. Formally. By my rightful title. I hate it. I hate the distant way it rolls off his tongue.

"Terrific," I lie.

Raven looks unconvinced, irritated even, as if I am somehow inconveniencing him. His gaze shifts back to May.

"Princess Maylea, would you be so kind as to give us the room? You have been working all night. It is only right that you go rest, replenish your energy," Raven commands gently but firmly.

For once, she does not snap back at him for the command—I do not blame her. I, too, would want to flee the tension dripping from the walls.

"Of course, Prince Raven," May defers, her eyes finding mine as she gives me an awkward grin and heads for the door.

Raven stands beside the bed silently. I peer at him from the corner of my vision. He shifts from foot to foot, pushing his hands into his pockets—his clay cast cracking.

"Nothing I say to you will fix what has been done. I will not offer you an apology, for words will not undo my actions. I have wronged you. I have mistreated you. I have not acted with the respect you deserve as my equal. I stand by what I did to protect my court. I, however, wish that I had acted with more tact while performing my duty," he remarks woodenly.

My eyes fly to his, my shyness dissipating to make room for my all-consuming anger. At his tone. His formality. His distance. His actions. I want to shake him until I shake free some sense inside his head.

"Tact?" I laugh, and the sound is cold.

Raven swallows and looks away.

"You are a skeleton of contradictions and hypocrisy. A head made only for a crown. When you torture me, it is your *duty*. When Viktoryn tortures me, you threaten to take his life. What a precarious line you walk. How blurred your vision must be," I say, shaking my head and trembling with anger. "I bet Viktoryn uses the same logic to justify his mistreatment of me. The same cowardice. But at least he is consistent. You hide within absence and avoidance."

"I–"

"Do you want to be King?"

His shock is palatable. He blinks. "What?" He pauses. "No one has ever asked me that."

"No?"

He shakes his head. "I–I am the heir."

I do not think I have ever heard Raven stutter before. I do not think I have ever heard him speak without full confidence in himself and his words.

He pulls his hands from his pockets and rubs the knuckles of his fist. "I was born to rule, Willa. I was born with a duty—built in. A duty as deeply ingrained in me as my bones. I have never had the luxury of wanting or not wanting. Wishing or not wishing. I was bred and groomed to be a King. The singular purpose for my existence. No one has stopped to ask me if I wanted it—if I wanted anything." His chuckle is a bitter thing. "Do you want to be Queen?"

"Of course not," I state firmly. "But I think that is why I should be. Harder to be poisoned by power when you do not want it. The Goldynlockes cannot remain in power. Not only for their crimes but for the future and betterment of Elphyne." I take a breath, gathering my racing thoughts. "I stopped feeling as though I had a choice the moment I was told I was the heir..." I pause, studying him. "I cannot imagine growing up that way. I think I am lucky I got to live seventeen years, not knowing the weight of an impending crown."

"It is heavy," he mutters.

"It is," I agree, and his shoulders slump. "You have let the weight shape you, Raven. *Define* you. You have let it chain your hands and turn your eyes. You cannot see past the confines of your crown. And if you do not learn how... this family you have built," I gesture to the room, "will buckle under the weight."

"It is not that simple."

"It is. You have always had a choice. You still have a choice—in everything you do—with every breath you take. Life is a series of hard choices—one after another. A series of mistakes and corrections," I say, finding his eyes.

"I kno-"

"Do you? You do not behave as such. It is far past time you reclaim your choices—your fate. *You* rule the throne—it does not rule you."

"You do not understand what it is to have the duties and responsibilities I do," he explains.

"I am so tired of you using your *duty*," I spit the words like a curse, "as a justification to hurt the people you love. It is cowardly and beneath you. Your actions are your own—crown or not, weight or none. You do not get to separate them to keep your conscience clear. Do you wish your legacy to be one of a male who let duty blind him? Or do you wish for your legacy to be one of a bold, brave male who dared to defy the rules set before him? Who dared to be greater than a kingdom, a crown?"

Raven blinks, lifting his hand before him as if he can ward off my words. He opens and closes his mouth, stepping back as if to defend himself from the sharp knife of my words.

But I am not done.

"You want me to believe you are better than him? Different from him? *Be* better. *Be* different," I demand.

He steps back again as if I have struck him. His jaw slams shut as his lips thin.

He nods once, turns, and leaves.

It takes May three days to fully heal my wounds. I do not complain when she removes all my scars—even the ones I once wished to keep. Those scars feel like they belong to a different girl—a girl I do not recognize anymore. One who had died—drowned in the lake with the Nixies—suffocated beneath the hands of The Fire Prince. A girl who had suffered and was reborn. *Reforged.*

May apologizes for how long it takes to heal me—but I do not mention that the worst of the wounding will not be so easily fixed. Golden eyes twisted with sick pleasure haunt my nights, and sometimes the eyes shift, becoming my mortal mother. Sometimes Fabelle.

Despite being out of danger for days, my body is strung tight. Ready to snap. Prepared for enemies to leap from the shadows and drag me back to the golden eyes and endless dark.

May is still off—I wish to ask why, but assume it is because I got hurt. I try to pretend for May and her weary looks.

I try to pretend for Raven and his damning distance.

I try to pretend for Amira, who does not know—or does not care—that I can hear her outside consoling and arguing with May as they try to rebuild what I broke.

I try to pretend for Raith as he fusses over me while tension continues to build between him and Raven. I feel horrific guilt for the fissures I have caused within Raven's Inner Circle.

But I can do nothing to fix it.

The damage is done.

I do not bother to pretend for Olden, who watches me as if he can see what is playing through my mind. But he never pushes, for which I am grateful.

Mostly, I try to pretend for myself—pretend that I can be whole again. Pretend I am not in pieces that, for once, I am worried I cannot put back together.

But I am tired of pretending—I am not fine. But I *must* be. For the sake of everything and everyone. So I pretend and pretend and pretend until I do not know what is real and what is imaginary.

I am play acting in my own life.

I dance at the end of my own puppet strings, I smile, and I laugh. I put my friends at ease. I do what I need to do, say what I need to say to convince them I will prevail.

Even though I am hollow, empty. I feel nothing but the occasional piercing slam of fear. I start to wonder if I will ever feel like a person again. Or if I am doomed to dance for a part I do not want forever—pretending until I am nothing but pretend.

I am surprised to learn that Raith is a *marvelous* cook. He creates a mouth-watering stew with rich vegetables and meat so tender it melts on my tongue. All with fresh loaves of steaming bread, filling the treehouse with the smell of baked goods.

Olden returns to The Crystal Palace to oversee Raven's duties in his absence. Raven remains at the treehouse, only visiting once a day. He asks May for updates before nodding at me and leaving—choosing to sleep outside in the branches as a bird.

I try not to think about what this means and how much it hurts.

I try and try and try not to think of the berries and iron under my flesh.

A permanent reminder of how ruthlessly he slew my trust.

But mostly, I fail.

Amira stops by a few times a day to deliver information on The Summer Court's movements. To no one's shock, Prince Viktoryn is *enraged*.

Since my escape, he has spent endless hours trying to gather enough evidence to prove that The Winter Court launched an attack on him. But Raven cloaked them all in his shadows, so his evidence is thin.

Still, Amira explains this is bad.

Very bad.

If he can prove it was them, a war could begin. And the three other courts would be required, by law, to ally with Summer—as set by the terms of The Great Treaty.

If The Winter Court loses, Raven would be made to forfeit his crown while the remaining three courts would be free to rage a war on his territories.

Amira reassures me this will not happen. They did not leave behind any evidence and Viktoryn's word alone will not be enough.

In a sense, Viktoryn has already doomed himself. By regularly and vocally making his disdain for The Winter Court known, he has watered down his own words' worth.

But I still worry—doubt my decision.

Should I have simply waited? Suffered? Endured?

52

I wake with a start on the seventh night, chased from my sleep by nightmares with talons, teeth, and golden eyes.

The treehouse is quiet. I am alone.

It takes countless minutes for my heart and breathing to slow. A damp sweat drenches my entire body, leaving my nightgown slick and sticky on my flesh. A restlessness rattles my bones as I try to shake off the lingering memories.

Pulling a dressing gown from the back of a chair, I secure it around my waist, shoving my feet into borrowed boots as I head for the door.

The night air kisses my skin as the door swings open to a small raised platform, a ladder to my left. Leaning against the doorframe, I peer up through the intertwined sea of branches to the stars. They twinkle in the midnight sky, bright and untouchable.

I feel a pull towards them and slowly shuffle off the main platform and into the branches. The cool wood is rough under my palms.

I pull myself up further into the tree, finding hand and foot holds as I climb higher. Leaves brush my exposed skin, and I deeply inhale the wonderfully clear air.

Some of the ceaseless tension in my chest eases.

The higher I climb, the freer I feel.

I find a thick branch that intersects with another, an opening in the leaves above it. When I reach it, I wedge myself into a seated position with my feet braced on a strong branch. My eyes return to the stars—the view unobstructed.

Here, I do not have to pretend.

There are no witnesses, no stage.

My thoughts wander as I stare into that open, endless sky. I have never been one for religion, but I wonder if there is an afterlife. If my mother is looking down, watching me. Maybe she twinkles above with the stars. Maybe she burns aside the sun. The thought brings me comfort. I wonder if my father is proud. If he knows how hard I have fought.

When the tears come, I do not fight them.

I let myself break as the stars wink down at me.

I am shaken from my thoughts and tears by a rustling beside me. I startle, almost losing my footing, but I catch myself on a branch before I fall, my heart kicks into a run.

I find a large black raven peering over at me. With the back of my hand, I wipe away my tears as the bird watches with too-keen eyes.

"I am not certain I will ever get used to you being a bird."

Raven squawks. My lips tip up unbidden as my mind tries to make sense of the fact that such a powerful, wicked Prince is also a really adorable little bird.

Raven cocks his head, studying me. I reach up, hesitating, fingers an inch from his feathers, unsure. He leans into my hand, pressing his soft head into my palm. I cautiously stroke a finger down his neck. Raven ruffles his feathers and coos a happy little noise.

"I am still mad at you, you know. Being adorable does not change such," I say firmly, but the grin splitting my features is not entirely convincing. "Sweet little birdy Prince," I tease.

Raven snips at my finger with his sharp beak, and I huff an exasperated sound, swatting him gently. He leaps, flapping his wings furiously. He squawks again, leaping into the sky and taking flight. My heart sinks, my mouth falling open to ask him to stay.

But before I can speak, he lands on the platform, transforming into his Fae form. Raven shakes his head, black curls scattering across his forehead. His hand ruffles his hair in a way that seems a bit too bird-like as if he is trying to shake the last of his avian brain. To my surprise, Raven begins to scale the tree, settling on a branch beside me.

"I am not *adorable*. I am a feared and powerful Prince," Raven says incredulously.

"I think I like you better as a bird. Less yappy," I snip, miming zipping my lips.

Raven does not reply, shaking his head, but I watch as he fights a smirk, gaze turning skyward. I take the opportunity to study him. It is not often

I get to watch him just *be*. It strikes me that this way, he looks like a boy, younger than me. Something hangs heavy in his eyes.

"You are staring," he states.

"And?"

"I understand. I would, too. I am so irresistibly and devastatingly handsome," Raven drawls dryly, still gazing at the stars.

I roll my eyes and do not answer.

My attention returns to the sky as we sit in silence. I am hyper aware of how close our bodies are. Of how, if he shifted his hand over an inch, it would meet my thigh. My cheeks heat and I shake off the thoughts as my heart aches.

"What did you promise your father, Raven?" I whisper.

I need to know. I need to know what happened that has left him with such disdain for me. I need to know what keeps us stuck in this never-ending cycle of push and pull. Close but not connected. Wanting but not reaching. I need to know if everything he does, everything he has done, everything he feels for me is driven by some long-dead Fae's dying wish.

Or if some of it, any of it, is *real*—ours.

Raven goes deathly still, eyes never leaving the stars. My eyes track across his face, down his body—he seems frozen in time. Part of me believes he will not answer, that he will do what he always does when I broach the subject—freeze me out and run.

But then he swallows and says, "He made me promise I would do what I could to protect you. That I would help you find your way onto your mother's throne..." Raven closes his eyes for a second. "My father used his last words to bind me as your protector. And I have hated you for it ever since."

His next words seem to take a physical toll on him as he reaches somewhere deep inside himself to rip them free.

"I worked hard. I took his every direction. I spent hours outside my studies perfecting my knowledge of politics and law. I looked up to him, *admired* him. My sole goal was to become a King he would be proud of... and he never, not even once, acknowledged my efforts. He never gave me any form of reassurance or praise. And I admired him nonetheless. Craved his approval like oxygen..." Raven shakes his head.

"And then, in his final moments..." Raven chuckles bitterly, eyes wet. "He could have told me he loved me, or that he believed I would make a good King, or that he was proud of me. But no, he used his final words to chain me to the very girl that caused him to lay bleeding in my arms. Gasping his final breath."

A single tear tracks down Raven's cheek, and his throat works. I blink once, twice. I do not have the right words. I do not know what to say. But I try.

"I am sorry. I am sorry that you lost him," I whisper gently. "I am sorry he did not recognize what is obvious and true to everyone who exists in your orbit. You are great. You will make a great King."

Raven nods once bitterly, and his eyes narrow on the stars.

We are quiet for quite some time.

"It was my fault," he whispers so quietly it is hardly a breath.

Raven drops his head into his hands. "He was helping your father flee with you and Fabelle. He had told me to stay in my room. Commanded me to not, under any circumstance, leave the Palace. But I could tell something was wrong... And my pride and curiosity compelled me to find the cause. I followed him deep into the forest, and then I saw you. Your father had Fabelle tucked under his arm, your hand in his, and the *entire* forest was ablaze. I have never seen anything like it."

Raven's eyes meet mine, a bolt of ice striking my heart. "But you were not afraid. And I remember thinking that your father looked at you as if you were the key to everything. He did not hide his love for you. His adoration. William looked at you as if he could not be more proud of this little slip of a girl."

Silent tears track down his cheeks. "And I thought about how many times I had wished, internally begged my father to look at me like that... I had worked day and night to be the very best. The perfect Prince, the almighty heir. And never once did I see my father gaze at me with an ounce of what I saw yours do that night. I envied you." Raven swallows, gaze returning to the sky. "You were fleeing for your life... and I *envied* you." His face twists in disgust.

"And then... it all happened so fast. Even though the Goldynlockes had lost their power, they brought the most powerful Knights they had. Any who could wield fire—they did not care if they died doing so. And died, they did. As they wielded, they slowly turned to ash but still, they did not stop. I watched as they herded you towards a cliff's edge, deep in the forest. I remember thinking that you looked so small, and yet you ran as fast as your little feet could carry you. No shoes. Feet bloodied. But you did not cry or plead. Every time you stumbled, you got right back up..."

Raven smiles a small, sad thing, gone as soon as it appears. "My father was trying to hold them off, but there were so many... and then Prince Viktoryn found me... hiding in the trees."

Raven looks down at his lap. His eyes squeeze shut as he sucks in a deep breath. "He laughed with delight as he dragged me into the center of the fight, blade to my neck. I should have fought, but I was still learning how to control my powers and in my fear... I *froze*... and when my father caught sight of me... he *faltered*..." Raven's voice cracks, "for a fraction of a second. But it was enough. Queen Florence leaped from the treeline and drove her sword straight through his heart. Then through each of his lungs."

Raven is shaking, looking at his hands as if they might offer some kind of explanation as to why they failed him when he needed them most.

"There was so much blood. I remember the look on his face... the shock, the disbelief, and worst of all, the *acceptance*," Raven spits the word. "I learned that day that you never turn your eyes from your enemy. Not for anyone. Not for anything. You do not freeze. You do not falter."

"Viktoryn shoved me to the ground, towards my father..." Raven runs both hands through his curls, body sagging. "And I could hear William trying to fight his way back to me, and I knew that I should get up and fight. But I could not... I pulled my father into my arms, blade still protruding from his chest as he wheezed in labored breaths. There was so much blood, Willa. I had never seen so much blood. I remember thinking that it was too much. Too much blood. Even for an immortal."

Raven is looking right at me, but his eyes are far away, trapped in a memory that has haunted him for a decade. "And I could not help... I could not heal him. It was the first time I hated my magicks. What was the point of all this power if it could not save the people who mattered the most?"

"Rave–"

"They left me alive. Alone with his body. I watched as his breathing turned ragged and his heart slowed. And he watched me back with this satisfied smile on his lips as if he were exactly where he needed to be. But I *needed* him," Raven's voice breaks. "And then he opens his mouth to speak, and I think, 'These are his last words. I have to listen. I have to remember whatever wisdom he chooses to impart to me...' But there was no wisdom, no pride, no love... just duty, another command, a new responsibility, the very same one that killed him."

"It was not your fault, Raven. The only blame should be on the one who held the sword," I say softly.

Raven watches me like he just might believe me.

Like he *wants* to believe me.

Like he wants to close the space between us.

Instead, he scoffs, shaking his head and returning his gaze skyward. "If only life were that simple. You will learn that our mistakes will always cost more."

"What did you mean... when you said you led the Goldynlockes to me?"

"You heard that?"

"I did."

Raven sighs. "As my father wished, I tried to keep an eye on you. I would enter the mortal realm periodically in raven form and check on you and Fabelle. I thought I was careful... I *was*... but after all those years, I must have gotten compliant, sloppy. Viktoryn must have realized what I was doing... And I did not notice he was following me until it was too late. I was already in Mayfair at your front stoop. I hoped he did not know it was your home, so I flew an erratic route—stopping at random houses to try and throw him off your trail, but... I should have done more... stopped him. But all I could think about was my father... and the blood."

"You... Raven, you could have warned me."

"You did not even know who you were. Who I was... I did not know how to tell you. I did not know how to navigate seeing my father every time you were around. I kept checking on you. I saw you getting closer to him, and I felt so powerless. I could not legally attack him. Not without voiding the treaty. And I did not know what to do. For once, I did not know what to do, Willa. I never know what to do when it comes to you. I am sorry."

"I guess our mistakes always *do* cost more." My eyes burn.

"They do—they always will. Sometimes that haunts me." Something in him changes, shifts. He clears his throat, and his eyes soften. "But, despite it all, despite myself, since that day in the forest, I have admired how you kept getting up. How you kept pushing, fighting, even when your entire world burst into flames. You were so little, and yet you placed one foot in front of the other, pulling along your sister, who was half your size..." He shakes his head, but his lips tip up. "I knew then you would survive whatever the world, mortal or Fae, threw at you. I knew whoever pushed you down would regret it—pay for it tenfold. I knew the world should fear the unstoppable force inside you that made you rise when everything was burning."

Raven chuckles. "And I envied you for it because I did not. I stayed in the forest, painted in my father's blood, tied to you eternally while his body went cold. My head rested on his unbeating heart until a hunting party found us."

Raven clears his throat. "And when they did... I wished they had not. I wanted to stay there on the ground, I wanted to die with my father. But I thought of the determination in your eyes and knew I had to get up, too. That I had a promise to keep, one last duty to make my father proud. I may have been cursed that day, but I was also saved... I got up so I could ensure that when you fell and thought you could not get up, I would be there to offer you a hand and pull you back to your feet." Raven slowly shifts closer to me, climbing onto the branch that is supporting my weight until we share breath.

My chest feels tight, anticipation seizing my lungs, as his lips almost brush mine.

"And you did," I whisper.

"And I did," he whispers back, lips brushing mine.

"This is a bad idea," I mutter breathlessly.

"My favourite kind."

Then his lips are on mine.

53

His kiss is gentle, tender, *transformative.* I melt into him, my body clay for his hands to mold as he pulls me into his chest. I kiss him back. Hard. My hands clinging to the fabric of his tunic, spurring him on. His hand slides up my neck to cup my cheek, his palms gentle and warm. His other slips into my hair, tugging gently. I whimper.

It is better than anything I ever could have imagined. Better than any of the fantasies my mind created.

Raven kisses back the darkness, the nightmares, the fear. He kisses back the memories that haunt him, the memories that haunt me. The resentment he harbors. He kisses back the uncertainty until all I know is *him.*

He kisses me like I am everything and he hates it. Like he cannot stand wanting me this feverishly.

I am caught in his storm clouds, the air around us crackling with energy.

Raven pulls back only an inch. My eyes open to find his troubled.

"I am dangerous," he says, lips brushing mine in the barest of a touch.

"I know," I murmur, my chest rising and falling roughly—in time with his. "So am I."

"I know. Do you?" he questions, as his hands slide down to grip my hips, slipping under my dressing gown. My stomach is flying.

I do not have an answer.

I do not have words.

So I lean forward, capturing his lips.

His hands trail a dangerous path up my thigh, and a pathetic noise slips from my lips.

"I wish I could swallow that sound, bottle it, and get so drunk I drown in it," he mutters.

My hands slip under his tunic, my fingertips memorizing his skin.

I bite his lip, and he groans, retreating. "You are right. This is a bad idea. This is a mistake," he says.

But his eyes say something different entirely.

They are hungry. Desperate.

Hands eager. Wanting.

"You will always be my favourite mistake," I echo the words he once spoke to me.

I close the space between us, and this time, he does not retreat.

He stays—he does not run.

A low, needy sound escapes his throat, and I swallow it with my lips—I am on fire.

My body is *alive*.

Everything dissolves into nothingness as his lips anchor me. His hands explore, needy and rough. He is a storm. And I surrender to it.

Raven pulls back, panting, eyes wild and filled with wonder. But his expression shifts, turning angry, distant. He moves to put as much space between us as possible.

I feel him freezing me out, his fortress of ice blockading me from his heart. And a desperate, insistent panic floods my lungs.

"This is a mistake," he repeats bitterly.

"Rave–"

"No. Do not. My father died so that yours could escape. His last words were a plea that I protect you and your sister. That I ensure his sacrifice was not in vain. He bound my life as his ended. Took more of the little freedom I had left. My mother turned into a living ghost. And I was alone. I had no one left, Willa. But I formed my Inner Circle and finally stitched myself back together. Created a family."

He shakes his head, laughing bitterly. "And then you return. You return, and I do as I have been asked. I try to perform my duty. Even as you rush off into danger like you cannot be touched. I put my family at risk for yours once again. And what do you do? You *ruin* it. You ruin them. You earn their trust, their respect. My trust... And you betray us. You break apart my family all over again. You divide us. Whisking Maylea away. You get hurt. And when I ask you to *own* it. Own what you have done—you refuse me. You spit on my pain and deny my sacrifices."

He turns to me, his eyes cold and haunted. "And yet here I stand," his voice a plea, but for what I do not know, "protecting you still. Hating you and wanting you and hating myself for it. Driving myself mad. Risking the one good thing left in my life for a girl who has only ever brought me chaos and misery. Ruin and shame. But I cannot stop," he says roughly.

He takes my cheek in his palm, holding me as if I am something precious.

"I stay up at night and think of what I can do, what I must say, to get you to smile for me. You argue with me with your venomous tongue, and I can think of no sweeter poison. I would die a thousand deaths and come back for more. I hate you for invading my life, my family, my mind like a greedy weed. Sprouting wherever it touches, tainting all it grows on. But I cannot find it in me to cut you out, Willa."

He pauses before continuing, placing my hand on his hammering heart, "This is what you do to me. And you do not even know it. You do not even try. All I think of is *you*. When you are away, I wish for your nearness. When you are near, I cannot decide if I want to undress you or frustrate you until you yell at me. I live for your fire. For your anger. No matter how cold it seems or dark it becomes, you keep burning. My hands are singed, and my heart is ashes, and yet I would let you incinerate me again and again if only you would let me. This is madness. *You* are madness. And I hate you. I hate you. I hate you. But I want you."

I am shocked.

I am mortified.

I am guilty.

I am all he claims and worse.

And worst of all, I am selfish because his words make me want to kiss him again.

"I hate you," I whisper. "You have betrayed me, lied to me, hurt me. You have shattered me beyond repair, but I find, even in pieces, I still want you. With all of my jagged edges—sharp and unloveable—I long for you. And I am sorry. I am sorry for causing you pain. But I am not sorry that all of this catastrophe led you to me. I will not be sorry for *this*," I say breathlessly, leaning in and capturing his lips with mine.

He melts into me, his free hand tugging my body into his. We kiss like we are angry, like we are furious for wanting each other but we cannot stop.

I cannot stop.

I do not want to stop.

We part, panting, twin bewildered expressions on our faces as silence descends. I am flustered, a mess of half-formed thoughts and treacherous heat.

But I find I am so glad to not be running. I am so glad to be standing here with him. Even if I worry he will turn and run. That *I* will turn and run.

"Am I still adorable?" He smirks, watching the rapid rise and fall of my chest.

I roll my eyes. "You had to go and ruin it by opening your mouth, did you not?" I scoff, but a smile slips onto my lips.

"Always."

"Does this mean we are even?"

"Yes," he murmurs, lips swollen.

"Good."

His grin is wondrous. I wish I could reach out and keep it in my pocket.

But it falls, and his eyes fill with worry.

"Willa..."

"What?" I ask, shaken by how unsure he suddenly appears.

"Your eyes. They are *glowing*."

54

I stumble into the kitchen, stubbing my toe into the wooden counter. I curse as I swipe a shiny pan off the kitchen countertop, holding it in front of my face. My body stills as I peer at my reflection, my green eyes gently pulsing with *light*.

"What the–" Raith mumbles from behind me and I jump.

"When did you get here?" I squeak. "You scared me!" I hold the pan out in his direction like a weapon and narrow my eyes. "What did you see?"

Raith chuckles but sounds hesitant as he studies my eyes, scrubbing a hand across his chin. He shakes it off quickly. "I snuck past you and Raven... You were preoccupied and I did not want to interrupt what seemed to be an... *invigorating* conversation," he teases, grinning.

My cheeks flush maroon and I toss the pan at Raith. He dodges, grinning harder.

I cover my face with my hands. "How much did you see?" I mumble through my fingers.

"Enough."

I drop my hands to find Raith and Raven staring at each other, faces grave. Raven nods and Raith shrugs.

"What is happening?"

"It is starting," Raven mutters.

"What is starting?" I ask, glancing between them as they shift uncomfortably. "Nothing good ever happens when you two finally shut your mout–"

My hands burst into flames.

I yelp, leaping in the air. The fire catches the side of my dressing gown, and the fabric ignites, eaten away by a hungry fit of deep golden flames. The medallion glows around my neck, pulsing eagerly. My dressing gown and nightgown turn to a snowfall of ashes at my feet. Panic assaults my senses, but to my disbelief, I do not burn.

Amira and May burst through the door with Amira clutching a glowing rock. Their faces are matching expressions of surprise, wonder, and worry. I am suddenly and overtly too aware of my nakedness as my audience grows.

"Will someone please tell me what is happening?" I shriek, waving my hands around like I am trying to ward off a swarm of angry bees.

May looks at Raven. "Is it starting?"

Raven nods.

"Startin–oh! The Calling!"

"Yes," Amira confirms.

"Great! Does anyone want to help me or are you all going to stand there while I burn the treehouse down?" I gasp incredulously.

"Right," Raith mutters.

Raven lifts his hands as he uses his power to rip the oxygen from the flames. The breeze is marvelously cool, goosebumps rising on my skin.

May steps forward, moving her hands, and water douses the burning fabric at my feet, leaving behind a swath of smoke and hissing steam.

"What now?" I ask, glancing down at my hands distrustfully. I stand frozen, afraid if I move a single inch, they will reignite.

No one says anything for a minute and I cross my arms over my chest, trying to cling to some semblance of modesty.

"Great question," Raith mutters, rubbing his hand over his forehead, looking to Raven.

Raven, to my horror, *shrugs.*

"This is an Olden question." He stares a second longer, blinks, and rolls his shoulders back. "Raith, find her some clothes. Amira, send for Olden *immediately.* May, stay with Willa. One of us has to be with her at all times."

"On it, boss man," Raith calls, stalking off with Amira in tow.

May takes a few tentative steps towards me, hands raised as if she is also concerned that I might start burning again. She worries her bottom lip with her teeth.

"I feel... strange. How do I know if it is about to happen again? How do we know if it is going to hurt me?" I question, my heart causing a racket in my chest. "Is it not too soon?"

"It is not too soon. The Calling can happen at any time in the months leading up to your birthday," Raven says.

"And magicks tends to be tied to emotion, environment and connection," May explains and I wince, blushing. Raven gives me a wicked, unapologetic grin and I scowl at him. "As long as you remain calm you should be able to hold the flames at bay... for now," May finishes, coming to stand at my side.

"What do you mean *for now*?"

"This is only the beginning. Your power will continue to grow until you reach the peak of The Calling. As it grows, it will become harder to control... and if you cannot..." Raven trails off.

"You could die!" Raith calls out, *so* helpfully, from across the room as he roots through the wardrobe for spare clothes, fabrics flying through the air.

Panic floods back in and my hands reignite. May squeaks, leaping away startled, and throws a *humongous* wave of water at me. It slaps down over my head. My skin stings from the impact.

"*May!*" I shriek, soaked and gasping. The flames vanish. "Was that much water entirely necessary?" I hiss, wringing out my hair.

"I panicked," May squeaks, holding her hands up in surrender.

I shake my head, sending a spray of water across the room, aiming for May. She starts giggling, and I cannot help but join in. I look up to find Raven hiding a smile behind his hand.

The laughter falls away and fear eagerly slides into its place. Everything suddenly feels too real. I may die—it no longer seems like such a distant problem. A Faeiretale. A falsehood. This could be the last few days of my life. The power inside me could burn me alive before I get a chance to harness it.

A human has never entered The Calling—nor harnessed magicks—according to Olden. I am drowning in unknowns. I am drowning in fear.

My body begins to reheat, but Raven steps forward, taking my hands in his. Something in the way he touches me feels different now. Like something has shifted between us—slid into place.

"Look at me." I do. "Nothing else matters. Only this. Only *us*. I know what you are thinking. I will not allow it to happen. So look at me and breathe. I have got you. I have got you, and this time, I am not letting go," Raven murmurs, lips brushing mine in a whisper of a kiss, the resolve in his eyes reassuring me.

I push up on my toes as our lips meet. Raven tugs me into his body, uncaring of our audience. Someone clears their throat and we break apart but not before Raven places a gentle kiss on my forehead. We turn to find Raith smirking, a light blue tunic and some leather breeches gripped in his fist.

May does not bother to hide her shock. Or her joy. She squeals, leaping on her toes. "Finally!"

"That is what I was thinking. About time, right?" Raith agrees, passing me the clothes in his fist.

I snatch them away, face blooming a bright red. I toss the shirt over my head and dress hastily.

"Have I ever told you that you have wonderful timing, Raith?" Raven drawls.

"No," Raith says.

"*Precisely.*"

I laugh, startling Raven, but he eventually breaks into a beaming grin. I cannot believe he just did that in front of his friends. That *we* just did that in front of his friends.

Our eyes meet and I see the sentiment reflected in his gaze. I do not know how to make sense of what our kiss in the tree meant. What our kiss *now* means. If our talk changed anything.

Viktoryn's voice rises in my mind and I feel sick.

I do have to give the dreadful bird prince some credit, though. He handed me the key... Your heart does speed, if only in the slightest, when you lie.

I squeeze my eyes shut. Images of Raven's icy cuffs pinning me to the wall as he stripped me of my free will repeats in my mind. I take deep breaths as I feel my skin heat.

I force myself to remember that we are not friends—we are hardly allies. I am here because of Raith's promise. Not Raven's desire.

Raven only hurts me. He pulls me close just to shove me away. He uses his clever tongue to say all of the right things only to turn his words to venom with his next breath. His wanting comes with pain and distance and confusion. All we do is hurt each other and hate each other. And want each other so badly that we burn ourselves trying to chase what we should not.

Whatever the kiss meant, the talk, it still does not change that a part of him hates me—blames me for ruining his life and taking his father from him. Nothing has changed. I deceived him. He tortured me. And I can never trust him again because of it.

A few kisses does not undo all that has been done. Even if I wish it could. We cannot rewrite history, even if we burn the books.

My hands heat again, but no flame follows. My body is filled with a sudden, heavy exhaustion.

"I think I am tapped out," I say, keeping my eyes downcast.

"Good. You should stay that way for a while," Raven says, his voice strange.

A few hours later, once we are certain I am settled enough not to burn the treehouse down, Amira returns in a huff after sending notice to Olden. A new glowing stone in her palm. She bursts through the door, pinning Raith with a glare.

Raith grins at her from where he lounges on the chair beside me, arms stretched behind his head, ankles crossed. The picture of relaxation. I jump up, ready for trouble. May, who was reclining on the bed, stands, looking between them. Raven rolls his eyes, fiddling with something in the kitchen.

"Raith. Why am I here? Why did you activate the stone? I do not see an emergency," Amira snaps, gesturing to the calm, domestic scene in the treehouse.

"Test protocol," Raith drawls, mischief filling his eyes. "Wanted to ensure all was working as it should. Keep you on your toes." He shrugs. "Plus, you were taking too long. I was getting impatient."

"Says the one who is never on time," Raven points out, and I have to stifle a laugh.

"You mean to tell me I ran across the entire forest for *nothing?*" Amira hisses, pulling a dagger from her belt.

"Are you meaning to tell me that The Unseelie's best spymaster is all worn out after a brisk little jog?" Raith coos, putting the back of his hand to his forehead and closing his eyes as if faint. "Perhaps I shall perform this little test more often. Help you better yourself, Amira."

Amira throws a dagger at him, and Raith opens his eyes just in time to leap out of the way. The dagger embeds itself in the wall where his head was with a *thunk*.

"Foul play," Raith drawls, pointing at her, eyes narrowed. "I thought we could use some entertainment after all the *madness*," he gestures to the room, "earlier. Come on, 'Mira, lighten up. You should have seen your face."

"Call me that one more time, *Raithy*, and I will use your entrails as solstice decorations," Amira vows sweetly.

Raith has the good sense to appear a bit nervous. "Why does May get to call you 'Mira then? Huh?"

"Because I am beautiful and perfect and pretty," May chirps.

Amira takes a threatening step forward like she plans to strangle Raith, teeth bared, but May steps in her way.

"Amira," May whines, jutting out her bottom lip. "We talked about throwing daggers at Raith's head. What did I say?"

"No aiming for vital organs," Amira grits out.

"So why did you aim for his head?" May questions, running her hand down Amira's arm.

"You cannot truly believe that I must count his brain as vital? It is not as if he uses it." Amira rolls her eyes. "The brute is fine."

"Amira," May says more firmly.

"Fine. No daggers at his head or heart. His other body parts are fair game," Amira purrs as May wraps an arm around her waist.

Amira's attention shifts to May, a satisfied smirk on her lips as she pulls a second dagger from the back of her belt. May shakes her head, stepping back and gripping Amira's wrist before she can take aim.

"You are insufferable when it comes to your knives," May mutters.

Amira smiles smugly as she pivots with inhuman speed, tugging May by the waist into her body. May squeaks in surprise.

"You love it," Amira challenges, eyes dancing.

May blushes but holds her ground. "I love when you do not throw knives at our friends."

"Is that so?" Amira drawls, raising an eyebrow as she runs the tip of her dagger across May's jaw.

May swallows, face blooming a poppy red. "Yes."

"Even when they are abominably annoying?" Amira asks, running her dagger across May's shoulder.

May narrows her eyes. "Even then."

Raith clears his throat, but May and Amira do not break eye contact—lost in a trance of flirtation. I turn away, feeling like I am intruding on a private moment.

"As adorable as this is. Now that you have returned, we need to start formulating a plan," Raven states evenly, face an impenetrable wall of indifference. "When is Olden set to arrive, Amira?"

"He–"

The room around us explodes into a burst of heat and flame.

I stumble as the room shakes violently, shifting with an angry groan. The front wall of the treehouse ignites into a frenzied wall of flames. I lose my footing as a second explosion blows the door from its hinges.

"I thought you said we were safe here!" I shout to no one in particular, bracing a hand on the back of a chair as I rise.

Smoke and heat billow from the walls. The wood cracks, and flames roar. My heart is pounding.

Amira turns to me and my stomach sinks as I see the fury etched in her features. It is gone as quickly as it appears.

"We should have been. This location has been a secret for centuries," Amira says, brows furrowed in concentration, demeanor calm even as the flames spread to the floor and ceiling.

Amira allows her declaration to dangle in the air.

The accusation.

A deafening crack sounds, and the treehouse begins to tip. Amira sprints to a wardrobe by the bed, sliding a false back away to reveal a wall of weapons. She passes May a bow, Raven a sword, and Raith double axes, before she hands me a sword, a sheath, and a bow.

We make eye contact. And her eyes seem to scream, *'Do not die. It will be terribly inconvenient.'*

The heat of the room increases every passing second, an onslaught of blistering flame. Smoke continues flooding the space like an oppressive fog, rolling through the room like a storm off the ocean. I cough as it forces itself into my lungs.

"We need to get out of here!" May shrieks, diving for the door, but Raith yanks her back.

"I know," Amira says, eyes shut in concentration. "I know. But this is a trap."

Raven moves forward, using his power to wrench the air from the flames. They sputter and die. "I can hold this for a while, but they will keep throwing explosives until we come out," he says.

Raith nods in agreement. His face impassive, foreboding. "They are trying to draw us out. They cannot pass the wards. We need a plan. No one leaves. Not yet," Raith commands as he peers out what is left of the window. "Thirty visible warriors, likely more in the trees. Armor un-marked, but I would reckon they have been hired by that fire-breathing bastard." His eyes assess the scene and then us.

"How did they find us?" I call out.

Raven moves to my side, body shielding mine from the group, eyes filled with suspicion. He glances over his shoulder and shares a look with his spymaster. She nods. He returns the nod.

"Someone betrayed us," Raven says, lethally calm.

"Someone in this room," Amira clarifies with that same calm. "My spies are sworn by blood to not disclose this location. That vow would not allow them to share... but you all..."

Tension brackets the space, descending in a smog even thicker than the smoke. Five sets of suspicious eyes turn on each other. Despite the urgency of our situation, the room—time—seems to pause at the accusation.

I am suddenly overly aware of the fact that we are all heavily armed and trapped in a burning room with one another—with the *enemy*.

Raven shifts his body further in front of mine as if he is thinking the same.

"We do not have time to figure out who. We need to fight our way out of here. Deal with the traitor later," Amira snaps, dagger in each hand, countless more strapped to her body.

Raith looks uneasy but he nods. His expression battle ready, nothing kind or warm remaining on his face.

Another explosion rockets the treehouse, and the flames burst back into existence.

"May, blast the door with water—give us an opening. We have one shot to get out. Hang back with Willa. Take as many out as possible with your bow first, and only approach when you run out of arrows. Amira left, Raven right. I take center," Raith commands, meeting each of our eyes individually and waiting for confirmation that we understand his orders. We all nod.

"There are thirty of them, Raith, probably more, and five of us. The odds are not exactly in our favour," I reason.

"We make the odds," Raith states with a wild grin. "On my count, May."

I suck in a breath. Even as the fear floods me, a sense of wrongness gripping me in both hands, I feel a sense of pure exhilaration. I need this. I need to do *something*. After being trapped and helpless at Viktoryn's hand, I need an enemy I can slay. I need a reminder that I am a fighter.

I am not helpless.

I am my father's daughter.

I am a *warrior*.

May moves forward, her bow and quiver slung over her back, palms raised and beginning to pool with icy blue water.

"*Now.*"

May pushes her palms forward, and a torrent of water flies from her outstretched hands, dousing the opening as the flames flicker out. Raith rushes to the door, skipping the ladder and *leaping* from the platform. He lands gracefully even as arrows fly towards him, using the momentum of his fall to roll to the side.

Before he is even on his feet, his sword meets bone and flesh, a warrior falls, head now noticeably absent from his shoulders. His body does not even hit the ground before Raith is moving again.

A song of death.

A Warrior of Bloodshed.

I almost feel bad for his enemies as I watch him cut across the battle-field with years of practiced ease.

The light of early dawn seeps through the trees, swaying in the soft Summer Court winds. Warriors spill from the trees—too many warriors, far more than we predicted, rushing towards what remains of the tree-house. Arrows fly across the sky, dark blotches on a blue canvas.

It is chaos.

Raith cuts down a red-headed female Fae warrior with a battle cry, blood splatters across his chest. Amira and Raven hit the ground seconds later, a trail of bodies in their wake.

The treehouse makes a haunting crack, wood groaning. The floor tilts wildly, and I stumble to the ground. My knees smash into the wooden floor, splinters embedded in my flesh.

May calls out to me, grabbing my hand and lifting me to my feet. We rush for the opening, and I hesitate at the jump but May tugs me down with her. I swallow my scream as I fall.

We land in a heap on the grass as the treehouse collapses in on itself, folding like a house of cards in the wind. It slams the ground with such force the surrounding trees tremble.

I push myself to my feet in time to see Amira cut down three warriors in a single movement. Amira pivots, ducking beneath the blade of an attacker's sword as she tosses three knives in rapid succession. Each finds a home in a warrior's skull, faces still twisted with shock as they crumple to the ground. Amira moves like a ghost, a wraith of wind and ruin, through the trees and over fallen bodies as if she floats on a breeze of death.

My eyes find Raven, who has foregone his sword. His hands are held before him as he freezes a small group of warriors where they stand, sucking the air from the lungs of others. They scream—the ones who still can—before collapsing to the ground.

The enemies' numbers fall, and hope fills my chest as the tide of the battle turns in our favour. Raith continues to cut down warriors as if they are nothing but wheat stalks. So focused on the battle ahead he misses the warrior sneaking up behind him.

I am about to cry out to him, bow raised. But the warrior groans, falling forward to reveal a smug-looking Amira. She steps over the body—the back of his skull embedded with a dagger. She rips it free, wiping it once on her leather pants, and calls out a snarky 'Watch your back, muscles,' to Raith, who shrugs.

I am starting to wonder if they even need my assistance as Fae after Fae fall—when a second rush of warriors spills from the trees, honed in on May and me. I hesitate to shoot, the faces of the first lives I took flashing in my mind. May studies me, a strange expression overcoming her face, and she fires off a few shots to buy us time.

"It is us or them. Your life or theirs. Death will never be gentle nor kind when it comes at your hand, but let it be worth *something*. You have a Kingdom to save. You have people to love. Do not let this be the day you fall because you chose to value your life less than those who wish to strike you down. I have seen how you can fight when you do not hold yourself back. Do not trip on a leash of your own making," May commands, expression hard. "Fight. Fight to live, Willa. If you remember anything I tell you—let it be this. Fight because you deserve to live."

"Who am I to decide who lives and who dies?" I shout.

"You are you. That is enough. You are enough. You do not have to earn your existence. But you will be nothing if you let them slay you. They have decided for you—they say you die. Will you lie down and let them take your life? You do not have to enjoy death to win a battle, but if you plan to rule, I suggest you make peace with it," she says, eyes firm. "So tell me, mighty mortal, have you made your choice?"

"Yes."

"Good. Will it be the one that makes me proud?"

"Always," I say with a cruel, wicked grin.

I turn back to the onslaught of approaching warriors. They take me in, bow in my hand, and *chuckle.* Dismissing me. Dismissing May. Assuming that May and I are at the back of the group because we cannot fight—an assumption that proves to be deadly.

I take aim at a mossy-skinned warrior who slips past the wall of death that is Raven, Amira, and Raith. I let my arrow fly and it finds home in the warrior's skull. I aim and shoot. Over and over. Leaning into the familiar, comforting snap of my bowstring. One after another—warriors fall prey to my aim. One after another until they do not look smug any longer.

The next group is smarter, hesitating, learning from the mistakes of the dead. But exhilaration and adrenaline have me ready—waiting. My body beats to the rhythm of battle, everything fading until all I feel is the rough wood of my bow in my hand, my arrows singing as they fly, bodies dropping like the beat of a drum.

I am a chorus of death.

I should be horrified.

But I find that, with each body that falls, I feel the mark of their death less.

I know that should scare me. But I have never been one who listens to '*should.*'

I watch my friends fight beside me. Without hesitation. To protect the family they have built and The Folk who rely on them—on *me*.

I let arrow after arrow fly. And as the bodies pile up, realization strikes me.

I am and always have been a fighter, a protector.

I will not shy away from that integral part of myself any longer.

The part of myself that allowed me to survive.

Raven is right. For them, for those I love, there is no rule I will not break. No line I will not cross to ensure it is *my* friends who walked away from this fight. My *family*.

I refuse to let Viktoryn take one more person I love away from me. Not today. Not tomorrow. Not ever.

I will not back down—I will not break.

I am not afraid—of myself, my abilities, or the enemies I face.

I am not afraid—I am powerful.

I reload my bow, taking aim at a bear-sized warrior with grizzly black hair who slips Raith's guard. I let an arrow fly. The warrior ducks, sliding across the dewy grass, my arrow uselessly brushing the top of his head but leaving him otherwise unharmed.

I curse, pulling an arrow from my quiver. May beats me to it, her arrow lodging in the warrior's skull as he pushes to his feet, only to fall again.

I meet her gaze and she gives me a small nod. But her eyes are haunted, wrong somehow, her hands trembling.

I am about to ask what's wrong when she mouths '*Sorry*' and a hand closes over my mouth. Two arms band around me, knocking the bow from my hands and locking my arms to my body.

I do not even get a chance to scream.

The attacker drags me behind the still-smoking treehouse remains and out of view of the fight. I slam my heel down into the top of their foot. They cry out and release me. I whirl around, sword in hand, but balk at who stands before me.

He is cloaked, masked, but I would know those golden eyes anywhere. They have visited me each night in the horrors of my dreams. *Viktoryn.* Flanked by a large group of Knights.

But that is not what makes me falter.

Maylea—my friend, my ally—is now aiming her arrow directly at my head.

I hesitate, lowering my sword slightly. My eyes flit between Viktoryn and May. I feel sick. Words she once spoke swirl around my skull, taunting.

Do not trust anyone, even me. Do not think me selfless, or you may find yourself drowning in disappointment.

And drowning, I am.

I shake my head. Over and over and over.

"Why?" I whisper.

I only have eyes for her, even though I know it is unwise to let my gaze shift from Viktoryn even for a heartbeat.

I need to know.

Need to see it.

Need to hear it.

"Why?" I demand when she does not speak.

My heart pounds so viciously that I fear I may faint. May's eyes well with tears and her arms shake, bow wavering.

"I am sorry. I did not want to. I did not want this. Please. I am so sorry, Willa. You have to believe me," she pleads, voice cracking.

But she does not lower her bow.

And yet I do.

I do believe her.

I believe her as my heart breaks.

I believe her as tears trail down my cheeks.

I believe her as my chest aches, and it becomes difficult to breathe.

I believe her as I am paid for my trust with pain.

Again.

I nod once, hoping she sees the words I cannot bear to speak.

I gaze over my shoulder, hoping to meet Amira, Raven, or Raith's eyes. And yet, I feel a strange rush of relief even as my eyes overflow with tears, and her betrayal, somehow, impossibly breaks me further than I am already broken. I am unbelievably *glad* that Raven, Raith, and Amira do not turn. I do not think I could bear to know if they are in on this, too. And if they are not, I cannot bear for them to feel the weight of Maylea's betrayal. I do not wish for them to make this impossible choice.

"Well played, Viktoryn," I state, and mean it, nodding at the fresh wave of warriors.

Vikoryn grins, and my eyes find May's once more.

I study her. I should have been a better friend. I should have paid more attention. I knew she was off the past few days, but I thought... I do not know what I thought. But she was in trouble, *real* trouble, and I did not help. I thought her to be invincible. I let my perception of her blind me.

And now, here I stand, finding that, even as May's bow remains aimed at my head, I do not wish her harm. I will not let it be me or her. I will not make that choice. I cannot.

I look away from May and nod.

Understanding my fate and, for the first time, understanding hers.

I swallow as the puzzle pieces in my mind fall into place.

"Whoever you have on her, let them go. And I will come with you without a fight," I state evenly, meeting Viktoryn's gaze without an ounce of fear. "Disregard my request and suffer the consequences."

I hold my hands steady, even as they wish to shake, sword raised. I will the trembling in my legs to settle, raising my chin and channeling all of the confidence I have painstakingly built up as I keep my gaze even.

I want nothing less than to run.

I think of the coffin.

Viktoryn's hands around my neck.

A brand burning into my flesh.

But as I meet my friend's eyes and see the thousands of pleas within them, I stand steady, unwavering. I know that look. I know that desperation, that hopelessness.

I have seen it once before—in the mirror.

So I stand tall, wrapping my spine in iron.

Prince Viktoryn blinks, surprised, and I know I am onto something. "What a clever girl you have become. You did learn from the best." He smiles, but it does not meet his eyes. "Drop your weapon. You are not in a place to negotiate."

I chance another look back and find no one has yet to notice us.

I make a decision—a wild, reckless, *stupid* decision.

I drop my sword, slipping my other hand behind me to grasp my dagger. I bring the blade to my throat, feeling the cool press of metal on my skin.

"Very well. Your choice. Do not say I did not warn you," I state. Viktoryn's eyes narrow, and I hold his gaze with pure defiance. "Let May and her daughter go, or I will slit my throat," I command, expecting my hands or voice to shake, but both remain steady.

Viktoryn blanches. I smile slowly, *sweetly*. Feeling the stretch on my cheeks as I bare my teeth in a dooming promise. I will him, *dare* him, to see the grim determination in my eyes—the truth in my words.

I think of a young girl with blonde hair and blue eyes. A face so similar to May's that I wonder how I did not place it sooner. *Alice.* Alice, who May trusted with the key. Alice, a mortal, who, out of all the servants in

The Ember Palace, is somehow not glamoured or compulsed or drugged. Alice, who is treated with respect and cared for by *Beatrice*. Beatrice, who knew my mother, who was one of her closest friends. Someone she would trust with this secret—a child.

And May, who owed my mother a *lifetime* of favours. May, who felt the need to protect the late Queen's daughter, as the Queen once did for her. May, who handed me the answer in a riddle, months ago, so very Faerie of her. I almost laugh.

"Look who has taken up the dramatics," Viktoryn drawls, his voice a wall of indifference, but I see the uncertainty in his eyes.

"I learned from the best," I chime, sketching an elaborate mock bow, holding the dagger tight against my flesh. I rise, turning to my friend. Her eyes are filled with unspoken apologies. "Does she know?"

"No," May sobs, bow still trained on me.

"Tell her. Promise me you will tell her. I never got to know my mother. She should. Promise me you will keep her safe. Make this worth it," I say as tears trail down my cheeks.

I want to be furious with her. But I feel a heavy understanding. I, too, betrayed people that I loved for my family. For Fabelle. I would have done anything to keep her safe. As much as I pretend differently, I would still. All of this has been as much for her as for me.

"I promise," May vows.

I nod, pressing the dagger into my throat harder. My eyes meet Viktoryn's as the sharp bite of the blade causes me to suck in a breath, hot blood trickling down my neck, staining my tunic.

"*Stop*," Viktoryn commands, lurching forward desperately. "Enough. You would not."

"Would I not?" I ask, tilting my head. My eyes flood with promise and fire. "Are you so certain? You have underestimated me before, Viktoryn. Is this a gamble you can afford to lose? Would you bet your precious power on it? Would you bet your *throne*? Maybe you will get lucky, and, with my corpse, the power will be free." I press the dagger in harder, gritting my teeth. "But... maybe, maybe not."

Viktoryn's face falls, and he falters, eyes flicking back and forth between the fighting, May, and finally me. His distraction will not last forever—he knows it. I know it. All it takes is Raven, Raith, or Amira turning for this game to be over. I do not let myself think about what Raven told me in the treehouse about losing his father.

I learned that day that you never turn your eyes from your enemy.

Not for anyone.

Not for anything.

I do not let myself linger on it. Eventually, someone will turn. Notice my absence. I watch Viktoryn recalculate, his ticking jaw betraying his frustration.

"State your terms and do it quickly, you wretched girl," he growls, hands fisting at his sides.

He looks ready to throw a tantrum. And if I was not in such a dire situation, that might fill me with pleasure.

I shut my eyes, and let the plan I have started forming come to life. I meet Viktoryn's gaze—unyielding.

"You will, *immediately*, on returning to The Ember Palace, free Alice of her services on the terms that she will never be harmed or harassed by you or *anyone* you employ—Summer Court or otherwise. She will be whole and hale until old age befalls her. If she wishes to remain and work in the Palace, you will grant her space and a shop to work as a *paid* seamstress. You will keep her parentage a secret unto death, ordering your warriors and anyone with this knowledge to do the same, speaking it to no soul—aloud or in writing. You will publicly announce that you and Princess Maylea have decided it is in the best interest of The Summer Court to end your betrothal indefinitely by the end of this week. You will ensure Maylea and her daughter remain forever free from you. You will take full responsibility for the decision to spare her from any blame. And you will *never* harm Maylea or command anyone to do so. If you do this, I will come with you willingly and, more importantly—alive," I state.

"Oh, how you have grown, my darling." Viktoryn's eyes rage with hatred. "Very well. I want to add a term. But then I will accept."

"What term?" My stomach dips.

"You wish to rid me of my bride. It is only fair you give me one in return. Replace Maylea as my betrothed. The court will not believe that, on a whim, we decided to part ways. I require a *reason*. A replacement. A bride for a bride," Viktoryn says.

I swallow, looking back to my friends. I meet May's eyes and see such a deep well of hopelessness as her arrow remains aimed at my head.

Pieces of my soul shatter.

I want to scream. I do not.

"I will accept—with one amendment—as soon as I am out of sight, you call off your warriors. The moment you no longer require the distraction. No more than a quarter day from now. No delays," I say, forcing my eyes away from Raven.

"I accept."

Viktoryn repeats the terms back to me in full, adding our amendments. The tang of magicks thickens the air, wrapping around us, bounding us. I hold my breath.

"It is a bargain." Viktoryn smiles triumphantly.

"It is a bargain."

As an indie author, my readers are *everything*. You determine the success of my stories, and I am grateful to each and every one of you who has made it to this page. Again! Thank you. Thank you. Thank *you!*

If you enjoyed this book, please take a few moments to write a review or share your thoughts on social media.

Your hype ensures I can continue doing what I love and bringing you more delicious and devious stories. Plus, who doesn't want to be the one who gets to say, "I read it first!" "I read it before she was big!" ;)

The adventure continues in *The Queen of Ruin & Rebirth*...

And this time, nothing will stop Willa from overthrowing the throne.

For more details, check out oliviamgeib.com.

Acknowledgements

I honestly do not know if anyone bothers to read these, but if you do, hello there. Welcome back! I sincerely hope you enjoyed this story, and I am sorry—not sorry— for the cliffhanger again.

This story is so special to me, and I really feel like I have grown as a writer between The Daughter of Fire & Fury and The Princess of Shadows & Secrets. And I am *so* proud of these pages. Thank you for allowing me the absolute honour of sharing them with you. If you hadn't shown book one, so much love and support, book two would not exist. So thank you, thank you, thank you. I will never be able to say it enough.

And now a thank you to everyone who helped make this story possible:

To Sierra, the *Slay*-Osaurus Rex, The Goddess of Grammar: What would I do without you? You are so much more than just my editor. You've become one of my dearest friends, my biggest cheerleader, and the person most likely to humble me. My stories wouldn't be what they are without you. There is no person I'd rather argue capital letters with.

To George, thank you for taking a chance on my story and showing me unwavering support. Thanks for giving me a platform. I appreciate all you do.

To Lauren, thank you for being one of the first sets of eyes on this story. Thank you for always having my back.

To the Thursday Writers' Club, thanks for being a sounding board and a safe place to share and craft stories. Also, thanks for showing up. I worried when I started it weekly that no one would come. I wish I was kidding.

To Miranda and The Medicine Hat Library, thank you for all the support you have shown me. Thanks for being my favourite place to write. Thanks for having a writers' group—the friendships I have fostered there are invaluable to me.

To Shar, for being my ride or die. Your support and loyalty show no bounds. Thanks for always wanting to talk about Taylor Swift with me. Thanks for telling everyone about your "author bestie." Your pride in me helps me be proud of my accomplishments, too—something I really struggle with.

To Grayson, for all the real-life banter that inspires so much of my fictional banter. To your wit, second only to mine. Thank you for always encouraging me to be myself. To embrace all the good and bad as it comes. Thanks for pushing me and never asking me to show up as anyone but myself. I wouldn't have been able to craft this story the way I have without our hours-long conversations. I could write an entire essay on all the things I am grateful for when it comes to you. But that would get awfully wax-poetic. And potentially a little mortifying.

To my dear ol' dad, for always being a supportive force for not only me but also other authors at any and all events I attend.

To my Opa, for everything.

To so many more friends and family, blood and found, who helped me become the person I am today so that I could pen this tale.

And a big thank you to the entire Medicine Hat community! You welcomed my story with open and enthusiastic arms in a way I never could've expected. The local support I have and continue to receive is unimaginable. Being an indie author comes with a lot of obstacles, but you all took a chance on me. I will not forget that.

And, of course, most importantly, to my readers. I want to personally thank each and every one of you. You are the reason I can do what I love. Every single person who takes a chance on my books propels me closer to my dreams. I will forever be eternally grateful to you for loving this story and these characters as I have. And sorry, not sorry again for the cliffhanger. I'd say I'd stop, but I am indeed the villain when it comes to book endings, and I cannot be stopped.

Lastly, a huge thank you to the readers who left reviews online for book one: Lauren, Laura, Lyric, Adriana, Maury, Sierra, Amanda, Sharon, Griffin, Daleena, Jayne, Jkay, VMK, Kamryn, Tamari, Fatima, Josie, Mickayla, Miranda, Vienna, Nathalie, Kerry, Serena, Deborah, Sarah, Rob, MB, Carla, and so many more.

Until next time, folks...